I0604046

**Evorath: The Battle for Erathal**

ISBN 978-0-9978838-4-8


Free Dragon Press, LLC

www.freedragonpress.com

www.evorath.com

Book III of the Evorath trilogy. Immerse yourself in a world of
fantasy adventure with the Legacy of Evorath family of books.

Read free stories online and keep up with future releases.

# www.evorath.com

Please see the end of this novel for an appendices section, which
provides a reference for Evorath, a map, and presents additional
information within the world.

# PART 1

*Death's Demise*

# Chapter 1

A crisp, cool wind blew through the settlement. The overcast sky and the smell of freshly spilt blood set the perfect ambiance for what would undoubtedly be a day of historical significance. Yezurkstal looked out across his settlement, a curious sensation overcoming him as he did. Perhaps this was what elves would refer to as sentiment. Or perhaps he was allowing fear to damper his mood.

It was inconsequential.

For seven months he had been a prisoner in his own settlement. The first few months were agonizing. He had tried brute force, cunning magic, and even attempted to absorb the Avatar's energy field into himself. No matter how he tried to breach the barrier established by Evorath's Avatar, he simply couldn't make it through. It seemed none of his kind could escape.

Then followed the withdrawal. Yezurkstal wished to forget about this time, but as his freedom was so near, he felt it fitting to reflect on it one last time. Yes, he had given up hope. If not for the determination of Valkyrie, his wives may not have survived that time.

He grimaced as he thought through that time, remembering Valkyrie's suggestion that they start eating demon flesh to ensure they wouldn't run out of food. It was an abomination that they had to resort to eating such unclean meat.

But, the survival of the hájje outweighed any personal discomfort. This was about building the world where his kind were free from all these inferior species.

In fact, Yezurkstal found he had been reconsidering the power structure of his people as of late. Verandas was a competent military leader, but his blind loyalty to Yezurkstal left him without any initiative of his own. While he had tried to squelch the independence of his subordinates, he now realized it was essential to leadership. Valkyrie had already established herself as the de facto leader of his wives. It made sense that she would have a more fitting title: the queen of the hájje.

With each of his wives once again pregnant, he needed to take measures to ensure his people would continue. The hájje were the future of Evorath, but that future couldn't take form if they were stuck inside this damned barrier. And though he wished there was another means of escape, he was convinced his latest plan was the only path forward.

When his plan to escape worked, he would officially announce the coronation of his wife. And he would continue teaching her how to tap into the magic of Evorath. But now, it was time to take the plunge and put his plan into action.

Yes, his original plan to father all the future generations of this world was flawed. He'd need some leadership, but his children already born would be more than sufficient to ensure he could bring the world under his control. More important, this spell would ensure he could reign for eternity on Evorath.

He would be more than just a King to his people. Yezurkstal, the new God of Evorath would reign supreme. With queen Valkyrie and his many princes and princesses, the entire world of Evorath would follow his example. All the elves would be reborn as his hájje while the other races would be exterminated.

Looking outside from his view in the watchtower, he extended his hand, palm forward. As usual, the barrier did its job. He pushed as hard as he could, the invisible cage preventing him from even reaching outside the gate. Holding his hand in place, he felt the green magic repelling him. How had the Avatar attuned this field in such a way?

Whatever the case might be, now was the moment of truth. Surveying the watchtower, it looked like everything for the ritual was in place. He had drawn a ritual circle using the blood of a slain demon. Within the circle, he had traced out a central symbol for the goddess Frogatha. Around this, he had evenly placed symbols for blood, death, and darkness. The remaining demon's blood was stored in a bowl, which he'd left within the ritual circle -this would be the final catalyst.

Situated north, south, east, and west of this ritual circle, he had placed four candles. Ready to begin, he extended his right hand and released some magic, igniting them. With the candles lit, the circle drawn, and the blood ready, the ritual could begin.

Stepping into the circle, he looked down and ensured he was perfectly centered. Keeping his mind focused on the outcome, he closed his eyes and began chanting.

"Frogatha, grant me your blessing. Take my life and grant me life anew. My death is just the beginning of service to you. Spirit of night, soul undying. Spirit of night, strength unyielding. Spirit of night, death undying."

As he chanted, he focused on drawing in all the dark energy from within his settlement. He could feel heat coming from the moonstone on the pummel of his sword, the massive amount of stored dark magic being funneled out from the sword and into this spell. Channeling this dark magic throughout his body, he could feel his blood boiling. With a shout, he directed the energy down and into the demon's blood.

"Grant me eternity. I, your faithful and undying servant."

With these words, he opened his eyes and dropped to his knees. Reaching forward, he lifted the demon's blood and drank.

His insides felt as if they were on fire. Overwhelmed with a pain beyond anything he could have imagined, his vision faded. Every part of his body was on fire. The pain consumed him in that moment, overwhelming his senses and robbing him of all bodily control, his dropped flat like a corpse.

His heart stopped.

And then, the pain was gone. All feeling and sensation left his body and his eyes shot open wide. With a gasp, he rose to a seated position. Holding his hands out in front of himself, he examined his palms.

It had worked. He had changed the rules of the game. Without hesitation, he stood and leapt through the watchtower window, passing through the barrier without resistance.

4

Using his magic to slow the descent, he landed gently on his two feet. The free air was a welcome feeling on his undead skin.

With a smirk, he turned back around and faced the gates to his settlement. As he had commanded before starting the ritual, the gates were left open, and the portcullis raised. Stepping forward, he stood just outside the gates.

He could feel the Avatar's barrier from here. It pressed down on him, the oppressive green energy keeping the rest of his kind locked inside. The rest of his people had to live on, so blessing them with undeath was not an option. Fortunately, as he stood within the barrier, he confirmed his suspicion -there was another way.

Before the ritual, he had learned to tap into immense amounts of dark energy. But now that he had been transformed, it felt like a mere drop in the bucket. Standing within the containment barrier, he could see all around the outskirts of his settlement and along the kilometers of the wall.

Embracing the magic of this barrier, he focused on bringing it within. His vision blurred and a shockwave extended out from his body. The entire barrier was illuminated, a green glow running along just outside the walls. With a deep inhale, he pulled this energy in, the barrier imploding into him.

It was indescribable. With such massive stores of magic, he could do anything. The time for the dark elves had arrived.

## Chapter 2

Erathal City
22 Aethra, 1087 MT

Artimus lifted his axe overhead, exhaling a large plume of vapor as he let it fall. It split the wood clean through, the two pieces dropping to either side of the stump. Leaning the axe against the stump, he rubbed his hands together and bent over. Tossing the split wood into his working pile, he grabbed another log and placed it on the stump.

Lifting the axe again, letting it fall, retrieving more wood; Artimus continued at a steady pace. Despite his heavy coat and winter hat, he couldn't help but shiver as he continued chopping away.

Winter was Artimus's least favorite time of year. Sure, work was always slower. But, at what cost?

Aside from the need for so much firewood, this time of year came with a plethora of other struggles. Fresh vegetables would be in short supply, any amount of physical exertion would make his lungs feel like they were freezing over, and the shorter days meant less opportunities outdoors.

Continuing to chop away at the firewood, he wondered when the snow would start to fall. So far, it had been a relatively mild winter, but it was just a matter of time. The air today was heavy, a brisk cold. He needed to get this firewood finished to ensure they'd be ready for the inevitable snowfall.

As he lined up another piece to chop, he heard crunching leaves from behind.

"Back already?" he asked without breaking stride.

"Seems everyone else is expecting snow to start today," his wife replied, her sweet voice provoking some warmth in his bones.

"Were you able to get everything we need?" He split another log, bending over to retrieve the pieces, and adding them to the pile.

"For the most part. I got all the essentials at least. But would you mind helping your wife get everything inside?"

Artimus stood up and turned around, smiling as he looked Savannah over.

She was absolutely glowing, her thick green cloak covering her from head to toe. He could barely see the bump of her belly, her winter tunic and gloved hands concealing how far along she was in the pregnancy. The cart behind her was filled with provisions, hopefully enough to get them through the rest of the winter.

"I don't know," he started while regarding his pile of wood. He would need at least twice as much to shore up their winter stockpile. But he welcomed a bit of a breather.

"You don't know if you can help your wife?" Savannah asked, placing her hands on her hips, and smiling.

Artimus chuckled, grabbing a couple pieces of wood, and walking over to the cart.

"I suppose it won't kill me to help, but only this one time," he joked.

Cradling the firewood under his left arm, he grabbed the cart with his right.

"After you my dear," he motioned towards the front door.

She curtsied and extended her hands, motioning to the firewood. "I'll take those."

Artimus nodded and allowed her to take the wood.

He followed her as she proceeded to the front door, opening it, and stepping inside. The cart was so full that he had to lift it up over the final stone leading to the entry. But, with a bit of maneuvering he was able to bring it up and inside.

Savannah opened the stove, tossing the two pieces of wood into the fire. Artimus stepped around the cart and pulled the cabin door closed. It was at least ten degrees warmer here, so he wasn't going to let that heat escape.

While Artimus rolled the cart into the kitchen, he glanced over to his wife, who was removing her cloak. With her cloak draped over a chair, her belly was much more pronounced. Artimus couldn't help but smile as she walked over to join him.

"Have I told you today how beautiful you look?"

Savannah slapped him on the shoulder and shook her head.

"Remember to tell me that when I'm delivering this child of ours. I swear, I feel twice as big as I was yesterday."

"I don't know about that. But I do know you look twice as beautiful."

"Just stop," Savannah glared at Artimus.

With a nervous chuckle, Artimus turned his attention to the cart and started pulling out the goods.

A few heads of lettuce, some potatoes, leeks…after unloading the layer of produce, he saw Savannah had also bought something extra for herself.

Picking up the stack of parchment and ink, he turned back towards his wife and smiled.

"I see you've opted to start back at it."

Keeping her gaze downcast, Artimus noticed her lip quiver. She bobbed her head side to side slightly before replying.

"I know you've been encouraging me. Things have just been so crazy, but I do feel Evorath is calling me to share my thoughts. Maybe I won't be the next Artur Aurelius, but it would be unfair for me not to share my musing with the rest of the world."

"Sounds like something a wise man once said," started Artimus as he reached in a retrieved a couple loaves of bread.

"Do you mind bringing those into the other room while I get the kitchen situated?" Savannah asked, her voice wavering.

"Of course. Will you need me back here, or should I get back to chopping when I'm done?"

"Judging by the air outside, I'd say you need to get back to chopping. I don't recall us ever being this far into winter without snow, but I'm sure today will be the day."

Artimus nodded.

"I was thinking the same thing. Wish me luck my love!"

"May Evorath bless you," she replied, her voice rising in pitch to suggest a hint of sarcasm.

Grabbing the ink and parchment, Artimus made a swift departure to the left. Opening the door to the work room, he regarded his own workbench before walking towards the bookshelf and the small desk Savannah had set up before it. He noticed a copy of Erathal's Constitution laid out on her desk as well as a Xyvor. It appeared she had also laid out some quills and a simple cylindrical inkwell.

Laying the parchment and ink on the table, he paused for just a moment, a smirk coming over his face. He couldn't wait to read whatever she had in the works.

Without further delay, he exited the room, shutting the door behind him. With a glance at Savannah, he stepped outside, immediately wishing he could join his wife back in the kitchen. While he noted before that it had to be ten degrees warmer inside, he now felt it was at least fifteen degrees colder outside.

Shaking his head and rubbing his hands together, he strode towards his chopping stump. Not wanting to waste a moment, he setup a new log and started splitting. Focused on getting through this wood, he decided it best not to waste even a moment. So, as he split each log, he kept hold of the axe in his right and with palms wide, lifted the next log onto the stump with his left.

Purposely avoiding the thicker logs, he was able to pick up his pace and continue splitting. Once he ran out of smaller pieces, he was forced to once again put down his axe to grab the next piece. As he lined up this larger log on the stump and split it in two, his rhythm was interrupted by the sound of more crunching leaves.

Who could that be?

Turning to face the sound, it took him a moment to recognize Falahar in his thick winter coat, face partly covered by a cowl.

"Good morning Falahar. What brings you to our humble abode?"

Falahar kept his hands in close to his chest, pumping his legs as he stood in place.

"Good morning, Artimus, sir. I'm sorry to bother you on a day such as this. But Chancellor Ulagret requests you join him this evening for dinner to discuss an urgent matter."

There was a slight stutter in his words, the cold having quite the effect on the young man.

"An urgent matter? Aren't they all urgent?" Artimus asked, setting up another large piece of wood and splitting it in two.

"I suppose so. But I think he might actually mean it in this case. We had some visitors from Paxvilla this morning."

Artimus paused mid-squat, dropping the log he had just picked up and looking at Falahar.

12

"Paxvilla? It's been months since we've had any humans come here. Any idea what they came for?"

"I can't rightly say-"

"Best guess?" Artimus asked.

"Well, the rumor is that they want to establish more formal trading relations with Erathal."

Artimus nodded, picking up the log and placing it on the chopping stump. As he picked up his axe, he glanced back at Falahar.

"Will it be the usual dining hour for the Chancellor? And is my wife expected to join as well?"

"He's an elf of habit, so yes to the hour. And I'm afraid a yes for Savannah as well."

Turning back to the log, Artimus lifted the axe overhead and paused for a moment. He took a couple breaths before splitting the log and turning back to Falahar.

"Please let the Chancellor know we'll be there," confirmed Artimus, his tone flat.

"Urgo," came Falahar's expected reply.

Without another word, Falahar turned and ran back east, his steps heavy.

Artimus shook his head and considered his pile of firewood. He was not looking forward to telling his wife about their new dinner plans. Perhaps a few more logs would be helpful to ensure they'd have enough fuel for the winter.

Taking just a few moments to consider, he grabbed the next log and continued splitting away.

.=.=.=.=.=.=.=.=.

Erathal Castle
22 Aethra, 1087 MT - Evening

Artimus surveyed the dining room, a bit uncertain about the crowd that had been gathered.

A large flame roared in the fireplace, keeping those gathered warm despite the snowfall outside. They had been summoned to the Chancellor's personal dining room, which meant for a cozier and more intimate environment. Ulagret was seated in his usual position at the head of the table. Opposite of him was his wife, Zenith.

In all his time serving the kingdom, Artimus had never actually interacted with her outside of these formal dinners. In fact, he was quite sure he hadn't even seen her since the Republic had formed last year. So far, she seemed as introverted as any other time, silently sitting, and sipping her soup.

Savannah and Artimus sat together on one side of the table and next to them was General Zeidrich and his wife - Artimus couldn't remember her name. Did it start with a 'D'? Or was it a 'G'?

It wasn't important.

Across the table, Guildpac had been invited, along with the Senators of Trade, Agriculture, and Production. Up to this point, there had only been some small side conversations, but as they finished up their soup and the attendants brought in salads, it seemed the Chancellor was ready to begin.

"Ahem. I hope everyone is enjoying the tomato bisque. This time of year, soup becomes one of my favorite parts of the meal. But, if we are all sufficiently warm, I suppose it's time for me to get into our purpose for this gathering."

"As you've all been informed, we had some unexpected visitors this morning. It seems the people of Paxvilla, despite their rejections of our help in the past, are ready to start discussing some trading arrangements. Senator Verdana and I met with them earlier and I must say, I am intrigued by what they shared. Senator, would you like to share your impressions?"

Verdana, the trade Senator, put down her fork and nodded.

"I'd be delighted to Chancellor. First, it seems despite their lack of magical proficiency, the humans have been quite busy in these recent months. According to their representatives, they have built quite a considerable little town to the northeast. If their claims are to be believed, they already have a larger footprint than the nearby tribe of Dumner. And, while they have little of strategic value to trade, they brought along some interesting pieces from their artisans."

She paused, picking up her fork and spearing some greens and a small tomato.

"Further, they brought us these salad ingredients we eat tonight. They tell us Evorath's soil is much richer than what they are used to, and they expect by next spring to have quite the harvest to trade."

Golorin, the Senator of Agriculture, perked up at this. He had already started eating his salad and by his raised eyebrows and taut smile, it appeared he was enjoying it.

"If their methods are this effective and their quality this consistently good," he began, "perhaps trading for their agricultural processes would be worthwhile."

"A thought that had occurred to us," the Chancellor confirmed. "Which is why we knew you needed to be included in this conversation."

Unlike the others gathered, Golorin was new to the political process. So, he probably didn't catch the condescending tone in Ulagret's voice. Artimus made a note of it.

"Did they make any indication of what sort of goods they were in need of?" Worgoin, the Production Senator asked.

"Yes, which is why you were included in this meeting. It seems they are having trouble obtaining sufficient ore for creating tools. They chose a strategic location, close enough to the mountain to source stone, near enough to the river for water, and like all the forest, a space ripe with lumber. But it seems they are lacking tools and have limited expertise to set up a proper mining operation."

"You mentioned artisans. Do they have blacksmiths to work with the materials if we were to trade them?" Worgoin inquired.

The Chancellor nodded as he chewed a bit of his salad, closing his eyes as he swallowed.

"Yes, though I'm not sure we'd want to provide the raw materials. They are unfamiliar with mythril -apparently it did not exist where they are from. And while they have some smiths who can work with steel, I'd suggest from a tactical standpoint that we provide them with only specific tools. This way, we don't have to worry about them using the materials to create weapons. Wouldn't you agree General Zeidrich?"

The General appeared a bit distracted, looking off and to the left as he ate his salad. He snapped to attention at the mention of his name.

"Yes, I think that makes sense. While I don't see them presenting a serious threat at present, I'd advise caution. So, trading tools rather than raw materials makes more sense. Wouldn't those tools be more valuable anyways?"

Verdana nodded.

"Yes, we could definitely ask for more in exchange for finished goods. Especially if we are interested in them teaching us some of their agricultural methods, I could see this being the better way to go."

"This all sounds very fascinating," came the beautiful and familiar voice from Artimus's left. "But I can't help but wonder how my husband and I are supposed to contribute to this conversation, or to these trade negotiations."

Artimus dropped his fork and hunched over, covering the right part of his face with his hand. Based on the way the evening had gone so far, he was really hoping they'd trot through the evening without having to be involved. Was she trying to give them extra work?

"I'm glad you asked," started Chancellor Ulagret.

"Senator Verdana, do you care to answer our young druid?"

"Of course, Chancellor. Well, Mrs. Atyrmirid, while the humans brought these vegetables to sample and some jewelry from their artisans, everything else is just hearsay at this point. Rather than trust their village is in the state they claim, we'd like to send some representatives of our own to investigate.

"Since your husband is our head investigator and you're an accomplished gardener and druid, we thought the two of you would be the perfect candidates. We'd of course send along a Guildpac here with you as well to act as our diplomat."

This was sounding more and more like a nightmare.

As Artimus opened his mouth to object, Savannah reached under the table and squeezed his leg.

"That sounds like a wonderful plan. But, in my condition I'm not sure if we can venture through such weather as we have tonight."

"Of course, we can't," Guildpac interjected. "Which is why the humans are staying as our guests this evening. And we are scheduled to meet with them tomorrow to discuss a time for us to visit their town. Rest assured; we'll be waiting until the snow has softened a bit."

"How thoughtful," Artimus added on, picking up his fork to work on the salad.

He really hated winter.

## Chapter 3

Dumner Village
24 Aethra, 1087 MT

Yesterday, Dumner had gotten 12 centimeters of snow, a heavy but not entirely unexpected first snowfall. Early this morning, there had been some light flurries. But it seemed Evorath herself had blessed this day. As noon approached, the sun shone down and offered a pleasant contrast against the cold winter air.

Irontail didn't mind the snow, but he did appreciate the extra sunlight. The contrast of cool snow on the ground and warmth from above provided a pleasant setting for today's activities. Looking out at the turnout, he couldn't help but feel a strong sense of pride for all Dumner had accomplished over this past year.

He surveyed the field before him, which was filled with dozens of centaurs and an array of other species from across Evorath. Thrilled to see some satyr, trolls, and lizock in the mix, he surveyed the outskirts of the gathering where vendors had erected booths selling all manner of goods. Activities were being enjoyed and people were connecting -in no small part to Irontail's own efforts.

Proceeding up the steps to the stage, Irontail took his place in the center. As directed, a podium had been constructed in the center alongside a standing bell. Getting in position behind the podium, he grabbed hold of the rope and rang the bell. As it clanged out through the field, Irontail watched as those gathered focused on him.

"Welcome," he shouted across the field.

"On behalf of Dumner and all her people, I welcome you to the first annual Erathal Gratitude Festival. Regardless of where you come from, we want to take the opportunity on the 24th day of Aethra each year to celebrate all Evorath's creation and give Her thanks."

He glanced around at those who had gathered, noting some familiar faces along with some unexpected surprises. Tel' Shira had made it after all, and it looked like she brought along a couple guests. Not wanting to get distracted, he looked down, turning his attention back to his speech.

"It is truly a privilege to be witness to such a gathering. These past few years have been difficult for everyone here in Erathal forest. But we know Evorath would never forsake us. She even sent her Avatar to contain Death itself. And these past months have been a time of great healing and growth.

"Today, we can enjoy peace once again. My hope is that on this day each year, all people of Evorath will be able to gather for a day of peace and gratitude. Centaur, felite, lizock, elf, satyr, troll -all of us are children of Evorath. We remember this fact today and we celebrate all that we have to be grateful for.

"So, as you go about exploring these grounds and celebrating today, engage in conversation with someone of a different species. Get to know your neighbors here on Evorath and you might be surprised how much you have in common.

Tonight, we will end the celebration with a great feast. All are welcome to attend and share as we gather as one big family, as the children of Evorath."

He paused for a moment, looking around to the crowd, which had gathered in more closely to listen as he spoke. Turning back to his notes, he continued.

"It's a pleasure to see so many of you gathered today and I don't want to take up too much of your time. But, before I go, I must share something I am grateful for. And that is, of course, the support and effort I've seen in making today a reality. So many of you have worked to make today happen, and to each of you, I extend a heartfelt thanks.

"Notably among you, I must thank Chief Oogmut and the entire Oogmut clan for helping to clear the land we are celebrating on. I must also thank Lord Vistoro, who has been indispensable in raising awareness for this occasion. And let's not forget the illustrious sculptor Dioney, who created the statue of Evorath in our newly dedicated temple. Finally, I must make mention of High Priestess Persia, who will be leading a worship session this evening after the feast. I wish I could do more, but one thing I can do is give a heartfelt thank you to you all!"

Lifting his hands, he paused for a moment and was relieved when the audience began to applaud. Smiling, he lowered his arms and finished.

"So, thank you all. And thank you everyone who has gathered to celebrate. Now, I've kept you long enough. Enjoy yourselves!"

The audience applauded once again as he stepped away from the podium and left the stage. He was greeted at the bottom by none other than Lord Vistoro.

The lizock noble was wearing a heavy, purple robe with a hood pulled overhead. A round sigil engraved with a dragon crest held his robe tight. Wearing red mittens, he stood with his hands clasped in front of his chest, shivering as a slight breeze blew through.

As usual, he was flanked by two lizock. One a large, muscular bodyguard and the other an average-built female attendant. Both were similarly well-protected from the cold.

"Rousing speech from an inspiring leader," he said reaching up and placing his hand on Irontail's left arm.

"I have to admit, this day is turning out even better than I had envisioned," he continued. "Our vision of peace among all Evorath's children may be closer than we think. We're making history today my friend."

Looking down at Vistoro, Irontail nodded. He tried to maintain a stoic expression, but he could feel his lips curling into a smile.

"You were a big part of making today happen. When we met last year, I could never have imagined us getting here so quickly." Irontail always felt politicians spent too much time on flattery, but in this instance he was sincere. Vistoro had been shockingly cooperative in arranging this event and over the past few months his camp had become Dumner's predominant trading partner.

"I am but a humble servant of Evorath," Vistoro replied with a slight bow. "And Evorath needs more leaders like you."

"And like you," Irontail countered without pause.

Looking past Vistoro, he noticed Tel' Shira approaching their position.

"Speaking of leaders," Irontail continued, "I think we have another future leader approaching now."

"Quite a turnout, your festival has," Tel' Shira declared as she approached with an outstretched hand.

Accepting her handshake, Irontail nodded.

"It is more than I could have hoped for. But I can't take all the credit. In fact, Lord Vistoro here helped a lot with getting the word out. In many ways, this was more his festival than mine. Speaking of which, Tel' Shira, meet Lord Vistoro." He finished motioning to Vistoro.

Tel' Shira turned and extended her hand again. Vistoro removed his right mitten and shook her hand.

"A pleasure to meet you Tel' Shira. I believe Irontail was just complimenting your leadership abilities."

As Vistoro spoke, Silkhair trotted up. Irontail locked eyes with her and could tell by her intense stare that she had something urgent.

"If you'll excuse me," Irontail interjected before pulling out of the conversation.

"What's wrong," he asked stepping alongside Silkhair.

"Oh, nothing to worry about. There was a slight cultural conflict that broke out between a satyr and a felite at the temple. But the High Priestess was able to de-escalate it."

Perhaps he had misread her expression.

"Oh, well thank you for the report. Was there something else?"

"No, well, maybe," Silkhair twirled her long, blonde hair with her left hand, eyes darting side-to-side.

"What's on your mind?" Irontail asked. He recognized the pensive look on her face -this time for certain. She was a thinker, and something was weighing on her; a trouble Irontail knew all too well.

"Well, I am just wondering: if the Avatar isn't in attendance for this festival, how do we know what we're doing is really aligned with Evorath's desires?"

She was asking the right questions. Fortunately, this was one Irontail had the answer to.

"You know that I've had the opportunity to meet with the Avatar on more than a few occasions these past six months. In those meetings, he has expressed support for this occasion. I know you were even present for a couple of those meetings. Perhaps you didn't know, he has extended his personal blessings to High Priestess Persia to lead tonight's worship."

Silkhair shook her head.

"Right, but if he is so in favor of this Festival, then why isn't he attending? It's one thing to say you are in favor, but it's another to show up and share your support."

"I appreciate that sentiment," Irontail replied with a nod. "However, in this instance we must remember the Avatar has a mission of his own. We are called to serve Evorath in our ways and He is called in His. The Avatar's focus in this time of peace is in preparing his students and teaching them the ways of Evorath."

"And that makes sense," Silkhair countered. "But, if the Gratitude Festival was representative of Evorath's will, wouldn't it serve as a great example for his students?"

Irontail smiled. Perhaps Silkhair was more interesting than he gave her credit for.

"Remember, not everyone is in the same place as you or I. Those in attendance today are here because they already believe in Evorath's calling for peace and unity. You've met some of the Avatar's students. Can the same be said for all of them?"

Silkhair looked down, combing her hands through her hair for a few seconds.

"No, I suppose not. Many of them still seem disinterested in serving Evorath. Most of them would probably feel they have nothing to be grateful for."

"Then how beneficial would a Gratitude Festival be for those people?"

"Not useful at all."

As she said this, she looked up and smiled at Irontail.

"Thank you, Chieftain."

"No, thank you. I appreciate a centaur who knows how to ask a good question. Probably because I ask so many myself! None of us has all the answers. Was there anything else you wanted to discuss?"

"No, thank you again."

Irontail nodded and turned back around, stepping over to Tel' Shira and Lord Vistoro.

"The honor was all mine Lady Tel' Shira. I hope we have a chance to converse again soon."

Lord Vistoro and his attendants started back towards the main festivities, stopping for a moment as they passed Irontail.

"I'll take my leave to explore these festivities some more. But she is an interesting one indeed. Thank you for the introduction."

"My pleasure," Irontail said as Vistoro proceeded to walk away. He turned his attention to Tel' Shira.

"I can tell he enjoyed meeting you. I hope the feeling was mutual."

"Definitely. Mutual, the feeling was. Interesting philosophies, Lord Vistoro has."

"I like the word 'inspiring' to describe it. But yes, he certainly gets you thinking. About a month ago, Artimus and Savannah were in town for dinner, and they got to meet with

Lord Vistoro. Savannah and he went on for hours about liberty and the responsibility of Evorath's children."

"Fascinating discussion, that must have been. In attendance, are the elves?"

Irontail shook his head.

"I'm afraid not. At least not yet. Savannah sent word that with the snowfall and in her condition, they may not make it. But who knows? I have a feeling they'll be here before tonight's feast."

"Being physically limited, I cannot imagine. Right, I hope you are. Introduce you to my teammates, I must."

She motioned behind her to the two felites Irontail had seen from stage. The first was slightly taller than Tel' Shira with a calico pattern fur. The other was a bit shorter and had orange fur and black spots. They both wore simple leather jackets. The calico was closest to Tel' Shira, and she motioned to her first.

"Ri 'Lara, this is."

Ri 'Lara took a slight bow as Tel' Shira motioned to her orange teammate next.

"And Tar Lau, this is. Best Capabolo players, they are."

Irontail nodded to each in turn, smiling as he considered his words.

"It's a pleasure to meet you both. I've not had the chance to make it to the Confederacy to watch a match yet, but I hear you three are doing quite well."

"Honored to meet you, we are," started Tar Lau.

"Yes, to meet you, honored, we are," added in Ri 'Lara. "Perhaps make it, you can, for the finals."

"Finals? When will the match take place?

"First of Frozga, it will happen. Win, we will."

Tel' Shira smiled, her teeth showing as her teammates growled in agreement.

"I have no doubt of that," said Irontail returning the smile. While he was always happy to speak with Tel' Shira, he wasn't sure what else to say. And, after spending so much time this morning to ensure everything would go smoothly, he really wanted to go visit all the vendors and see how everyone was enjoying the event.

"So, uh, I was going to check out some of the merchants and make sure no one needs anything. Do you care to join me, or did you have plans of your own?"

Tel' Shira glanced back at her teammates before responding.

"Visit the temple, we plan to. Stay for long, we cannot. For training, leave before nightfall we must."

"Oh, that's a shame you won't be able to stay for the feast tonight. But I understand the need for training before your match next week. In that case, enjoy your visit here. And please find me before you leave to let me know. It was a pleasure to meet you both Tar Lau and-" Irontail paused, forgetting the other's name for a moment.

"And Ri 'Lara," he finished. "I wish you Evorath's favor in your upcoming match."

Both felite nodded and Tel' Shira took a light bow.

"Before we leave, find you I will. Take care, until then." Tel' Shira said.

Irontail nodded as they turned and took a step to the north before pausing. Though he had intended to start in that direction, he didn't want to prolong the conversation awkwardly. So, he turned and started south. As he trotted towards the southern edge of the festival grounds, he passed some centaur children, a group of elves, and a satyr couple. Continuing towards the border, he was delighted to see yet another pair of familiar faces.

"Artimus, Savannah," he shouted, waving his hands overhead.

Both elves looked around for a moment before spotting him. Savannah raised her hand and returned his wave. They both adjusted their course and started in his direction. As he neared, he observed that Savannah's belly had grown since the last time he saw them. She must have been nearing her due date.

Reaching their position, Irontail continued.

"I'm delighted to see you made it out! How was the journey from Erathal City?"

"The road seems so much longer in this snow. We were just happy the storm died down so we could come at all." Savannah paused, looking past Irontail and across the field.

"It looks like quite a turnout though! I'm really thrilled to see that so many are here to celebrate. I know I haven't been too involved, but I really appreciate what you are working towards here. Perhaps next year I can help more in preparing for the festivities."

She looked down as she finished, her hands held close to her stomach.

"I know everyone would be thrilled to have you more involved next year. I'm just glad we got such a turnout -that should ensure we are able to continue this new tradition next year. What about you Artimus?"

Artimus looked up, narrowing his eyes for a moment before widening them again and shrugging.

"I'll help by eating whatever food you have at the feast tonight," he joked. "Aside from that, perhaps I'll support some of these vendors as well. I don't suppose our normal guest quarters will be available though, will they?"

Irontail nodded. Since he had taken over as chieftain, the village had grown significantly. As part of that growth, he had constructed a tavern. This served to provide lodging for visiting guests from anywhere in Erathal.

"Of course! I was figuring you wouldn't want to go home in the dark. After all, by the time you arrived, you wouldn't get much sleep."

"Glad to hear it," Artimus replied. "Unfortunately, we won't be heading home tomorrow either. I'll fill you in on the details a bit later, but we've been tasked to visit Paxvilla tomorrow."

"Paxvilla?" Irontail gasped. "I didn't think they were inviting outsiders. Then again, maybe they just aren't inviting of centaurs. I attempted to open diplomatic channels a few months back and they made it clear they didn't want anything to do with Dumner."

"That's unfortunate," Savannah interjected. "But not completely unexpected. After all, they come from a world where they were the only sentient species. Maybe our visit tomorrow will be the first step to better integrating them in with the rest of the people here in Erathal."

"I'd certainly welcome that," replied Irontail. "Perhaps you'll have the opportunity after meeting with them to stop back in and letting me know how it goes."

Despite all the species present at today's Gratitude Festival, Irontail still felt a bit of a sting that he had been unable to get any humans to attend. As far as he knew, Paxvilla was the only human settlement in Erathal and having them to unite behind the cause of peace could go a long way. Aside from the dwarves and the barghest, humans were the only other species lacking any representation at today's festival.

"We'll see what we can do." Savannah said, rubbing her belly and looking towards the vendor carts. "For now, do you mind leading us to where we can get some food? I'm afraid this baby is demanding!"

"Oh, I-" Irontail looked around nervously. "We have all the food vendors set up over to the west there. Allow me to show you the way."

Not wanting to keep her waiting, Irontail started towards the food area.

## Chapter 4

Paxvilla, Human Town
25 Aethra, 1087 MT

Thoron snorted, trotting northeast along the road to
Paxvilla. Between the lack of wind and the afternoon sun, this
had to be the warmest day in over a week. But as Artimus
glanced over to Savannah, shivering in her fur coat, he wished it
could have been even warmer. It was still freezing, with no signs
of melting snow. Still, he appreciated the dry air and hoped it
would hold out a few more days.

He looked behind, making sure Guildpac was keeping up.
The bureaucrat was trailing a bit behind, but his brown draft
horse seemed to be handling the snow as well as Thoron. Artimus
had been concerned about escorting the less-than-skilled wizard,
but he had hardly said a word since leaving Dumner this
morning. If the weather were a bit warmer, this would have been
a downright pleasant ride.

They were approaching a bend in the road ahead turning
north. Artimus noted a sign to the right posted on an oak tree. It
read "Now Entering Paxvilla." Pulling back on the reins, he
looked back to Savannah.

"We should let Guildpac take the lead from here," he said
pointing to the sign. Savannah nodded, slowing down her own
mount.

As Guildpac pulled between them, he glanced over at the
sign and nodded. Allowing him to pull ahead, Artimus and
Savannah followed close behind as they turned around the bend.

At first glance, Artimus was a bit disappointed as they turned the corner and saw only trees ahead. Continuing along the road, he spotted palisades through the trees. They were still a good half kilometer away, and as they continued their approach, he could see they were in the process of building out these defenses.

The palisades looked crudely constructed, some gaps and uneven deployment apparent as they drew nearer. But at the center of these defenses, they had erected a large gatehouse. This appeared well-made, as if they had thrown together the palisades and started to build out more proper defenses afterwards.

"This may be a difficult negotiation, so allow me to lead the conversation" Guildpac spoke as they approached the gatehouse. "I'll give you a signal or call you by name if your input is required. Otherwise, please keep your thoughts to yourself."

"But what if they address one of us directly? Should we still stay silent?" asked Savannah rolling her eyes.

"By all mean, you can respond if they direct any questions your way." His unwavering monotone suggested he hadn't caught the sarcasm.

"Oh, that is a relief." Quipped Savannah. Artimus stifled a laugh, his eyes downcast as he shook his head.

With this exchange, they were coming up to the gatehouse. Upon their approach, Artimus spotted a bearded man peering through an arrow slit in the fortification. Coming to a halt before the gatehouse, the man called down.

"State your business in Paxvilla," his voice was hoarse.

"Good day, sir. Our presence here has been requested. We come from the Elvish city of Erathal and seek to tour your community in hopes of establishing trade relations."

"Aye, you're 'ere to see the Earl then. Please stand back as we open the gates."

The man stepped out of sight with these words and a few moments later the gate creaked open. It took about ten seconds for the gates to fully open inward. As the entrance was fully accessible, Guildpac started forward and both Artimus and Savannah followed just behind.

Looking up as they passed through the first set of gates, Artimus spotted a portcullis and noted the murder holes overhead. He hadn't realized how much depth this gatehouse had, but from inside it became apparent they knew what they were doing, leaving enough room for a good number of enemies to get trapped inside during a siege. Passing through the end of the gatehouse, however, he recognized they had not yet completed its construction. There was no second portcullis yet, and though there were hinges for additional gates, they appeared unfinished as well.

As soon as they were through the gates, Artimus started taking in as much as he could of his surroundings. These humans really had been busy.

The town opened into a huge clearing, many of the trees that once covered this spot torn down and replaced with all manner of structures. He noted the road continued, a clear path carved out ahead and forking to right, which seemed like a good place to start surveying the land.

He noted the palisades curved around and stretched for as far as he could see, suggesting they had encircled their town with this defense. There was a wellhouse not twenty meters northeast of the gatehouse where he spotted a woman and two children drawing from the well. Off in the distance, he saw a structure that he guessed served as the town stables. Judging by the familiar smell coming from that direction, he was quite certain in fact.

Glancing back to his left, he spotted a large wooden structure with a great many windows. Based on its location and size, Artimus guessed these were barracks of some kind. As he continued his survey, he confirmed this suspicion, spotting some archery targets and straw dummies deployed just north of these barracks.

They had reached the first fork in the road at this point, and looking ahead Artimus confirmed another town staple -a blacksmith. From this distance, he could see the smoke billowing up from the forge and hear the unmistakable sound of metal being hammered.

"We'll take yer horses from 'ere," the town guard instructed.

Taking a break from his observations, Artimus focused back on the moment at hand. The guard that greeted them at the gate had been joined by two others. Both were clean-shaven, one about the same height but portlier than the first. The other was a bit shorter and thinner. They all wore a simple red tunic with a symbol sewn on the front featuring a yellow shield and red cross in the center, complimented by an underlayer of chainmail.

The portlier guard grabbed onto Thoron's reins.

"If ye' would, sir."

Artimus nodded, dismounting Thoron, and walking over to help Savannah off her horse. Savannah took his hand and gave him a smile as she worked her leg over slowly to dismount. Sliding down the side of her horse, she looked at Artimus with wide eyes.

"After we get back home, I'm not getting on another horse until this baby is out."

"You won't get an argument from me," Artimus agreed as the portlier guard came over and collected Savannah's horse as well.

Turning back to Guildpac, it looked as if he had dismounted as well, and the shorter guard had taken the reins of his horse.

The original guard from the tower stood in place as the other two started leading the horses off towards the stables. After a few moments, this first guard spoke up.

"If ye would follow me to the Earl then. Eel be 'appy to 'ere you've arrived."

Now on foot, the three elves began following the town guard north along the path. They continued in silence, which was perfect for Artimus.

Looking around, he noticed a mill up ahead to the left. A donkey was pulling the heavy stone around and with his keen eyes he could see it was processing grain. An elderly man stood nearby with a cart full of grain, clothed in simple brown tunic and slacks. There was also a fork in the road heading west, where he spotted a plethora of people walking, but Artimus couldn't make out what buildings were in that direction.

Instead, they continued north on the path. As he looked around, Artimus noticed most of the people they passed tended to leave a wide berth. Some merchants had set out their goods to the east, a crowd gathered around their tables to look at the wares. Beyond them, he noticed an assortment of various sized structures, likely a residential part of town.

As they continued along the road, the number of people out walking steadily decreased. Just up ahead to his left, he spotted some tents and what appeared to be the start of some larger log structures. It looked like they were plotting out a foundation to build a sizable dwelling. But, as he directed his attention directly up the road, he realized they were nearing their destination.

While it had a long way to go, Artimus guessed by the considerable number of stones that this was the start of a castle foundation. More than two dozen men were working in this area, moving stone, chopping wood, and mixing mortar. Artimus noted these men were all formidable in stature, the least of them likely stronger than himself. From his observations thus far, it seemed humans had a small height advantage over elves as well.

Taking in the full view, he realized the palisades came to an end at this point. Then again, they weren't needed. It seemed the humans had opted to build right into the Runeturk mountains, hewing the stone from the source and building up their future seat of power right into the mountainside. They really had chosen a strategic location for their settlement.

Their escort skirted to the right, going off path and heading east. Shifting his attention in that direction, Artimus recognized their destination.

A longhouse of sorts had been built in this spot. Made of hewn pine logs stacked four meters high, they had constructed a sizable structure. With the solid construction and thatched roof line, it looked like a cross between elvish and centaur construction. This was undoubtedly where they would meet the Earl.

"If ye would wait out 'here, I'll announce ye to the Earl."

Guildpac nodded and Artimus brought his focus fully onto the matter at hand.

They waited for just a minute before the guard returned outside, bringing with him another man. This man appeared a bit more groomed than the guard and he wore a bright green tunic and brown pants. He was slender in build, but looking at his calloused hands and worn face, Artimus guessed he was an attendant of sorts.

"Well met!" he began, his voice surprisingly high pitched. "My master would like to bid you welcome to our humble town of Paxvilla. You may call me Gregory. And, if there is anything

41

you need while staying in our town, I would be delighted to provide it for you."

"Well met, Gregory" said Guildpac stepping forward and offering a bow. "I am high wizard Guildpac, a servant of Chancellor Ulagret of the Elvish City of Erathal. I have brought with me two of our people's finest to help assess trade possibilities with your people. These are Chief Investigator Artimus and the druid Savannah."

Gregory looked at each of the elves in turn, smiling and offering a small nod. "Guildpac, Artimus, and Savannah. It is a pleasure to meet each of you. Please, follow me."

Guildpac followed behind Gregory and into the longhouse. Artimus motioned for Savannah to go before him, allowing him to take up the rear as they stepped inside. Once inside, Artimus took a quick glance around. It appeared this central room took up most of the building, laid out as a great hall of sorts. A red carpet led from the entrance up some steps to a makeshift throne constructed of simple wood and left unadorned. A large fireplace roared with flames just a couple meters behind this seat, making up the rear wall.

Pillars lined the walkway, torches offering additional light and heat for the winter. Artimus stepped up his pace, taking place alongside Savannah as they approached the throne. Two guards stood on either side of the throne, both wearing chainmail and cross helms. But, unlike the guards outside, these ones wore a different tunic featuring only a green star in the center of their red garbs.

Artimus considered the Earl next, an average-built individual of medium height and nondescript features. Brown eyes, brown hair, and a clean-shaven face meant he appeared quite like many of the men they had seen on their way in.

His attire was what really set him apart. He wore a purple silk robe, adorned with custom embroidery along the chest and arms. Across his waist was a gold sash and draped over his shoulders a red surcoat. His right hand was adorned with an ornate ring and his left with three. And of course, topping it off was an ornate crown. While Elvish royalty had expensive style, these humans seemed to take a gaudier approach to fashion. Artimus couldn't help but wonder if this meant they were more authoritarian in their rule as well -a concerning thought.

As they reached the base of the steps leading to the throne, Gregory stepped to the left and motioned towards the elves.

"Earl of Paxvilla, it is my pleasure to present to you the delegation from the Elvish City of Erathal. High Wizard Guildpac, Chief Investigator Artimus, and the druid, Savannah. They have come to discuss matters of commerce with your grace."

Guildpac took a low bow, so Artimus followed suit, using his peripherals to see Savannah doing the same. He wasn't sure why he was so concerned -she was always a better diplomat than he.

As they stood up tall, the Earl spoke.

"Honored guests, I welcome thee to Paxvilla. It is our honor to have you grace these halls. While the accommodations may be modest at present, we hope to ensure your stay here is a pleasant one."

Guildpac nodded, extending his hands out wide.

"We are humbled to be here your grace. Our Chancellor Ulagret was delighted to receive your delegates earlier this week and has sent us to see what future trade relations we might be able to establish. Please, let us know how we might begin this process."

The Earl rose from his throne, Gregory stepping up and offering him a hand as he descended the steps.

"We would like to begin by showing you around our town. It may not be much when compared to your great city of Erathal, but we are proud with what we have built in these past few months."

"Just by our journey here, we have already seen much for you to be proud of. It would be a great honor to have you show us around the rest of town."

"Stupendous! Then you shall accompany us." the Earl declared, stepping past Guildpac and starting along the carpet towards the exit. As he did, the two guards who had been stationed beside his throne both followed behind.

Waiting for the Earl, Gregory, and his guards to pass, Guildpac followed behind and Artimus and Savannah took up the rear.

Once outside, the Earl took a deep breath and looked around. He motioned towards the stone workers to the north.

"You see we have started construction of the castle already. I believe these are referred to as the Runeturk mountains. We recognize this as a defensible position we can use to protect ourselves from the more savage creatures of this world. And as you can see, our men are quite skilled at working with stone. I see a future opportunity where we can trade from the spoils of our quarry."

Guildpac nodded, passing a quick glance to Artimus and Savannah.

"Yes, you have quite a large project ahead of you, however. I suspect you won't have any stone to spare for many years still."

"Your words are true," countered the Earl. "But us men have a habit of looking towards the future for opportunity. I do hope you will consider that as we survey what Paxvilla currently has and what opportunities we might off in the future as a valued trading partner."

"Naturally," replied Guildpac without missing a beat. "Even just knowing you seek a long-term trade relationship gives me hope that we can find some common ground to work on."

The Earl wore a wide smile, nodding his head as he looked at each of the elves in turn.

"Stupendous! Please follow us this way," he instructed walking off the road towards the tents and unfinished log structures Artimus had observed earlier.

"Like the castle, our servant quarters are a work in progress. But since the completion of our current lodging, we wanted to ensure our servants were better protected from the elements. We expect by next winter they will have fully furnished quarters to lay their heads. Of course, that is not why we walk in this direction. Instead, I direct your attention to the granary ahead."

He motioned towards a large silo sitting to the east. It appeared there were two more being constructed on either side as well.

"When we first started here, our priority was in ensuring we'd have enough food for our people. Fortunately, many of our people had farming experience and we were able to plant and harvest a generous amount of grain. We suspect this year it will be just enough for us. But next season we should have double the harvest, if not more. If elves enjoy grain as much as men, I'm sure you could use a greater supply."

Guildpac nodded, his lips tight and eyes downcast as he clutched his chin.

"Your agricultural methods in general intrigue us. To be able to produce this much grain in the short time you've been here is definitely of interest. And I can say that if you truly can double this harvest next year, we would be interested in acquiring some of your grain. Is that silo filled with grain?"

"Stupendous!" the Earl exclaimed. "And yes, the granary is filled for the winter. I'm glad you bring up agriculture in general though -we will certainly be visiting some more opportunities for that at the end of our tour. Please, follow me along to our next destination."

The Earl continued past the granary, proceeding through some uneven ground and weeds. Artimus was surprised to see how willing he was to trudge through the raw terrain. They continued south towards some groupings of carts and tents. From the looks of it, some merchants were set up around another path.

Glancing back east, Artimus noted the mill he spotted earlier, which meant this was the left fork they had passed on their way in.

"And here we have some of our fine artisans. They have proven to be quite resourceful. While we are new to your land, our people have grown closer than ever before. As such, our artisans have been able to produce more than enough for what we need. That means we have plenty of wares to go around."

Artimus looked at the assortment of merchants. There were a few carts selling a plethora of jewelry, one stand holding a wide range of pottery, an apothecary, and a couple merchants selling clothing and textiles. None of this was really needed by Erathal, but the unfamiliar designs would undoubtedly be of interest to many. Apparently Guildpac agreed, a thought that made Artimus feel a bit woozy.

"Yes, this is quite impressive that you have been able to create so much in so little time. While none of these goods are lacking in Erathal, I must say I am delighted to see so many original designs. Like this, for instance," he said picking up a cup from the pottery display.

"The simplicity of this curved handle and the tapered design -it is unlike anything I've seen before. I am certain my people would be interested in obtaining cups like these."

"Stupendous!" came the expectant response from the Earl, a smile stretching across his face.

"Alas, if you would grant me the opportunity next to show you a somewhat unorthodox trade proposal. Please follow me to the blacksmith."

Staying on the path, the party proceeded east, the clanging of metal growing louder as they approached. As with the merchants, who all seemed to remain quiet and keep their heads down, everyone they passed on the road kept a wide berth, avoiding eye contact with the party. Artimus wondered if the Earl had made some sort of decree to have people avoid the visitors.

Finally, as they reached the blacksmith, the heat from the forge a welcome touch in this winter air, the Earl stopped and motioned within.

"You see here two of our master blacksmiths. They are training young apprentices to take up the craft. But I'm afraid our resources are limited. While we've extracted some ore from the mountainside in our quarry efforts, we lack the tools or mining expertise to get enough materials for all we need to make.

"But I am no fool. No amount of grain, artisan crafts, or other agricultural goods are going to get us the materials we're looking for. That is why I propose, as part of our trade arrangement, we exchange some of our smithing services."

Guildpac looked as if he was considering the offer. His eyes downcast and hand stroking his chin, he looked at Artimus and Savannah before turning back to the Earl.

"We should discuss this for sure. But I am eager to see your farming operations. Erathal has no shortage of skilled blacksmiths, but we do have limited farmers. So, I am eager to proceed to our next stop on the tour."

"Stupendous!" came the familiar response. "Please follow me."

-=.=.=.=.=.=.=.=.=-

Artimus looked over to Savannah as they came to a stop. She closed her eyes and took a deep breath, her face tight as she exhaled. It was clear she was struggling, which left Artimus wishing there was something he could do. He didn't care what else the Chancellor asked for -Savannah would be getting a well-deserved leave of absence upon their return.

Dismounting Thoron, Artimus jogged over to his wife and grabbed her horse's reins. He extended his hand and helped her get off her horse. She flashed him a smile as she came to the ground. Standing upright with a wince, she adjusted her coat.

"I'm alright," she offered after taking a few steps.

Though he wanted a conversation on the matter, he knew it would have to wait. Glancing back to the others, he noted everyone else had dismounted their horses already. He looked around at the snow-covered ground, wondering how much they would really be able to gather from this trip.

"Feast your eyes on the largest farm in Paxvilla." The Earl stretched his arm out across the field before them.

With snow still fresh on the ground, the field was almost completely white, but as he looked more closely, Artimus realized there were spots of green sticking up through the snow.

"As you can see, our farmers anticipated the winter weather and planted some new crops in this field over a month ago. While our root cellars have been stocked with the fall harvest, there is cabbage, brussels sprouts, and a variety of other greens growing in these fields right now. Unlike the grain, we already have some vegetables we'd be ready to trade."

Guildpac nodded, steepling his fingers as he did.

"This is quite impressive. I must admit, we do not have such an ample supply of winter crops in Erathal. So, I'm sure we would be interested in trading for some of this. Do you have other farms in operation growing crops now as well?"

"We have a similarly sized field now being allowed to rest over winter. This field is where we harvested all the grain from. So, I'm afraid not at present. We do, however, have other citizens that have more recently joined the settlement who are working to establish new farms, including the introduction of livestock."

"This is all very helpful to know," replied Guildpac. "You have given my partners and I a lot to discuss. It has been a pleasure to see everything you have accomplished. Are there any additional stops along this tour that you would like to show us?"

"Stupendous!" exclaimed the Earl.

"This was our last stop on the tour, but my chefs are preparing a feast for us as we speak. So, if you would please return with us to the longhouse, we can answer any additional questions you might have. And of course, you'll get the opportunity to sample some of our finest cuisine."

Artimus really wanted to interject. If there was nothing else to see, why wouldn't they just head back home? Unfortunately, he already knew how Guildpac would respond.

"It would be our pleasure to sample some of your fine cuisine."

"Stupendous!"

# Chapter 5

"If you remember nothing else, I've taught you, always remember this intention Evorath has for her children..."

Zelag glanced around. He found it difficult to focus during long sermons like this and he sometimes wondered if he was the only one. Casandra seemed perfectly attentive, her eyes forward, a faint smile on her face as she nodded at this sentiment.

Looking to his left and in the rows behind, the Avatar's other students all seemed equally attentive, some perhaps even more so than Casandra. His newest student, a young centaur from the Dumner tribe, had wide eyes and curled lips, her mouth agape as she nodded along. Negla, the ever-dutiful satyr also seemed enthralled, smiling, and nodding along as she listened. And of course, the barghest brothers, whom Zelag still didn't trust, both looked on with tongues wagging.

Elves, felite, lizock, and all manner of others had come to gather as well. At the very back of the group, the elvish monk had his usual quill and parchment, recording every word the Avatar spoke. It was like He didn't know how to turn anyone away. Zelag didn't understand it.

Of course, there was one bright spot at this time of year. The winter weather was proving to be quite pleasant in this human form. He was a lot less sweaty this time of year than the summer and fall. And he was finding the absence of insects to be a major relief. Still, he wished the Avatar had something more interesting to talk about.

"…next time you find yourself in a similar situation, remember this. Only in accepting this will we help Evorath realize Her vision for Her children. Now, let's pause for a minute and reflect in silence. Hold your prayers in your heart and Evorath will listen."

Finally.

Zelag looked down, his eyes darting side-to-side. After about a minute of silence, the Avatar spoke up once again.

"Evorath, please allow us to serve you. May our wishes align with your own as we work towards the good of all your children. Let us disperse now and take time to reflect on what was shared today. Walk in Evorath's light."

Zelag darted up, looking at Casandra. She returned his smile, uncoiling and standing up tall.

"We really are blessed to learn directly from Evorath's own Avatar," Casandra uttered. "What did you think of the teaching today?"

Scratching the back of his head, Zelag diverted eye contact and looked up to the left.

"Oh, I thought it was fantastic. It's always great to be reminded how much Evorath cares for us. When we've lost as much as we have, it can sometimes feel like She isn't up there at all."

"I feel the same way," replied Casandra clasping his left arm.

Zelag looked back into Casandra's eyes, a warmth filling his stomach. He couldn't help but smile wide.

"Do you want to get some breakfast with me?" Casandra asked, still holding Zelag's arm.

"And have you show me how poorly I hunt again? I'm not sure if that's a good idea." He still hadn't quite caught onto the concept of humor, but he found Casandra responded well when he introduced levity to a situation.

Casandra chuckled, releasing his arm, and crossing hers.

"You don't hunt poorly," she started. "I just have an advantage you don't. What if I promise not to use my magic this time?"

"Not even to detect prey?" Zelag asked. "Because in that case, we might not even find anything worth eating."

Casandra shook her head, slithering back and wiggling her fingers.

"I suppose I'll still do that. But once we find something worth catching, I'll even let you have first crack at it."

Zelag considered the sling hanging at his waist before looking back to Casandra and smiling.

"Alright, you have a deal. Remember, I've gotten a lot better with this thing lately!"

"We'll see," she replied with a laugh.

Twisting around, she began slithering away from the camp. Zelag followed closely behind, but just as they were pulling away from the gathering, he heard a most unwelcome voice.

"Are you going out hunting for breakfast?" came the shrill inquiry.

"We'd love to tag along," the next voice followed, this one a bit less harsh, but no less unwelcome. It was the barghest brothers, Neman and Morn.

Casandra halted her march, twisting around to look their way. Zelag begrudgingly followed suit, turning to face the barghest. Their bright red auras were blinding, like a pulse of light disturbing a night sky.

"You think you two can stay quiet enough for us to ambush anything?" Casandra asked with arms crossed.

"Last time was a fluke!" Morn insisted, stomping his feet. The younger of the two brothers, he always seemed a bit more animate.

"Yeah, we've been practicing our stalking," added Neman with a nod.

"I don't know," countered Casandra. "I did promise Zelag he would get first crack at whatever we found. Think you can hang back until he gets his shot?"

"Of course," shouted Morn.

"We can hang back," echoed Neman.

Zelag clenched his fists, gritting his teeth as he held his tongue. He really wished Casandra wasn't so accommodating to these hounds.

"Alright, I guess it's settled then," she said. "We'll all head out for the hunt this morning. Are you two ready to go then?"

The brothers looked to one another, patting their fur before turning back to Casandra and nodding.

"Yep!"

"Urgo!"

Morn and Neman responded simultaneously.

Shaking his head, Zelag turned back around, fighting the temptation to slap these annoying barghest. Casandra was glowing as usual, her tranquil green aura providing him with a small sense of calm. Taking a deep breath, Zelag took a step forward.

As he did, he felt a tightening in his stomach, the hairs on the back of his neck standing on end. His entire body felt weak, like something was pulling on it from behind. It was a feeling he had felt before, but he couldn't remember when. He saw a frown form on Casandra's face as her aura darkened.

Following Casandra's eyes, Zelag turned towards the source of the strange feeling. His vision blurred momentarily as he did, an overwhelmingly bright aura causing him to squint. But it was his human eyes that were leading him to trouble. His entire body felt numb, butterflies in his stomach as a chill went down his spine.

He beheld a dryad, her bare figure calling to him. Remembering the words of the Avatar, he directed all his energy inward. His muscles ached and bones cracked as he used all his willpower to focus on the essence of a dingo. The form was one of the most familiar to him, the canine bone structure, the lean musculature, every feature of this nimble creature. Hair sprouted from every part of his body, thickening to fur as his vital organs shrank. The intense pain distracted from the overwhelming magnetism he felt from the dryad.

As he completed his transformation, the pain diminishing, he barred his jaws and backpedaled. With a whimper, he continued turning back towards Casandra and taking position by her side. Casandra lowered her left hand and patted him on the head, shifting her weight defensively as they both looked to the dryad.

Processing his thoughts was not quite as easy in this form, the smaller brainpower of the creature leading him to rely more on instinct. That instinct, however, seemed to be kicking in. His attention shifted to the elves in the audience, all of whom were enchanted by the dryad. Without thinking, Zelag darted to the nearest elf, clenching his jaws gently around the elf's ankle and pulled away from the dryad.

The Avatar stepped away from his conversation with Negla, jumping between the elf and the dryad. He nodded to Zelag before turning towards Casandra.

"Help restrain these elves."

Casandra nodded, slithering forth and gathering magic energy into her hands. While she channeled this energy to reform and clasp onto the other two elves' legs, Zelag continued gnawing at the first. This elf was lazily swatting at him, trapped in the perfect balance of trying to move towards the dryad but distracted enough that he was making no progress.

"Speak. What brings you to disturb my assembly?" The Avatar's voice boomed forth, his eyes burning with intensity as his aura grew, the color turning a deeper and more vibrant green.

The dryad's own aura seemed to diminish at this question, a somber yellow glow taking over.

"Death has returned to our land. Sisters Birch, Willow, and Beech have all been slain. Aeria and a coven of sylphids were also cut down. It seems there is a coordinated attack happening against all Evorath's servants."

The Avatar's face tightened, his eyes shrinking and mouth trembling. "Daughter Pine, is this true?"

She nodded. The Avatar lowered his gaze, a swell of magical energy flowing from the ground beneath him. His entire body was engulfed in green arcane energy as he closed his eyes. His body seemed to vibrate with the ground beneath him and in the next moment, his eyes shot open.

"He has somehow shrouded himself from me. But you are right…I cannot feel our sisters. And they are not the only ones who have fallen victim to Yezurkstal."

He paused, looking around at all those gathered and frowning. The Avatar reached out and clasped the dryad's shoulder. Zelag noticed energy transferring between the two as he did.

"I will meet you there shortly," the Avatar instructed as he released his hold.

The dryad nodded, the ground engulfing and swallowing her up. Though Zelag had experienced this sort of travel a few times with the Avatar, it still amazed him to watch the ground consume this dryad, her energy integrating directly into the ground before fading away. Though curious where the dryad was going, this was one time Zelag was eager to listen to the Avatar.

Releasing his hold on the elf's leg, Zelag backed away and glanced at Casandra. She had loosened her magical hold as well. All three elves stumbled, looking a bit disoriented as they worked to gather their bearings. Everyone gathered was looking at the Avatar expectantly.

"I ask that all of you leave for your respective homes. Travel together as much as you can. The wilds of Erathal are no longer safe. I will send word when the time is right for us to gather again."

Those gathered were talking amongst themselves, a roar of conversation breaking out. In his dingo form, Zelag was having trouble discerning anyone's voice. So, he focused on his human form, thinking of the smell, the shape, the complexity of being.

Intent on assuming the form, he felt his bones crack and reshape, organs expanding and rearranging. Fur turned to hair, darkening, and thinning around his body. He whimpered in pain as his fore legs changed into arms, his hind legs snapping back and forming knee joints. Gritting his teeth as those back canines transformed into molars, he completed the transformation.

Clenching his fists to relieve the final remnants of pain, he turned to see Casandra back by his side. She patted him on the left shoulder.

"Are you alright?" she inquired.

"Yes," he replied feigning a smile. "It gets a little easier every time."

Looking around, he saw the elves had already gathered their belongings. They were discussing the safest route to Erathal City. Zelag caught bits of conversation from others there as well. A lizock discussing with a couple felite on whether she might travel with them. Lizock, centaur, troll -they all were working to figure out the safest ways to get everyone to their respective homes.

Zelag nodded towards Negla, who approached the Avatar. Casandra turned her attention that way as well.

"I would like to stay with you," Negla spoke quietly, her words barely audible with Zelag's human ears.

"You must understand, the path I must walk is wrought with great danger. I cannot ask you to follow me," the Avatar's aura was bright and powerful, his words stern and eyes resolute.

"I understand," replied Negla. "But I don't have anywhere to go. I cannot return home."

The Avatar frowned, placing his right hand upon Negla's shoulder, and holding her gaze for a few seconds.

"You have home among Evorath's children," the Avatar started looking over Negla to Casandra.

"All those who are unsure where to go shall seek refuge in Dumner," the Avatar exclaimed, his voice silencing all other conversations. "I will send word ahead to their Chieftain and he will ensure you have food and shelter."

Zelag and Casandra exchanged glances before approaching the Avatar.

"Trust in Evorath, Negla. You will be safe in Dumner." Without pausing, the Avatar turned to Casandra.

"Casandra, you and Zelag will lead everyone. I have matters to attend to with sister Pine. Await further instructions from me in Dumner."

"As you wish, teacher," Casandra responded without hesitation.

Zelag wanted to object. But he knew it was pointless. Still, he couldn't ignore the feeling of dread welling up inside. That monster Yezurkstal had already taken his family away.

And thinking of him being free, he couldn't help but fear what might come next. Whatever it might be, he would stay with the one person he had left in the world.

He would be by Casandra's side.

## Chapter 6

Erathal News Article 101:328
Standard Commerce Code 139
By, Executive Magistrate Dervoir

With the new law going into effect on the first day of Pertga, 1088 MT, I was asked to write about Standard Commerce Code 139. If you are a merchant operating within the borders of the Republic, it is your duty to ensure you are in compliance with this new law prior to the end of the year. Please inquire with the Castle Legal Affairs Office with any questions and to receive your new Merchant License.

Standard Commerce Code 139: To ensure safe and fair commerce throughout the Republic, all merchants are required to hold a Commerce Safety License. This license ensures that all merchants are operating within the confines of the Standard Commerce Code. The cost of this license is set by the Senator of Trade and is valid for the term of 1 calendar year. Failure to maintain a valid Commerce Safety License will result in arrest for up to 30 days and a fine of no less than ten silver pieces.

As of writing, the standard cost of this license is set to five silver pieces. The local constabulary will be enforcing this new law at the start of the year, so make sure you get your license before it's too late.

-=-=-=-=-=-=-=-=-

Erathal City, Atyrmirid Residence
2 Frozga, 1087 MT

"Well, what do you think?" asked Savannah.

63

Artimus looked up from the parchment, offering a smile to his wife as he did. She really was an elf of many talents.

"As gifted a druid as you are, you may be an even better philosopher. Your critique of Aurelius's theory of societal order is especially intriguing. I suspect you have more to add to it, but your arguments so far are hard to deny. I'd really love to get a copy to the Avatar and hear his insights on the subject."

Savannah smacked her hands on the desk, beaming with enthusiasm as she leaned in.

"You really think it's that good? You sure you're not just biased because I'm your wife?"

Artimus leaned back, glancing her over for a moment and smiling wide.

"Well, my opinion may be a little colored."

"Stop!" she laughed, standing up straight and slapping his shoulder while shaking her head. "I just mean, do you really think it's worth sharing?"

"Of course!" Artimus chuckled. "No, I mean it. You know I'm not as well-learned as you, but at the very least I can say it's thought-provoking. I know we've discussed many of these things before, but the way you've laid it out over this past week -I don't know how you even got this much written!"

Savannah blinked, holding her eyes shut for an extra moment before nodding.

"I felt inspired. As you said, we've discussed these concepts so much. Especially considering what we've seen as

Erathal has transitioned to a Republic, it's really making me question everything I've studied. Take Aurelius for instance. He was ahead of his time for sure, but…well, you read it! I just think it's worth considering that maybe Evorath intended us to live differently."

"You definitely make a good case for it," Artimus said nodding. "But it's a radical notion having no central authority. I wonder if elves are ready for it."

Savannah frowned, scrunching her nose, and twirling some of her hairs in her fingers.

"I fear they may not be. But if you see where I'm coming from, I like your idea of sharing it with Evorath's Avatar. He'll be able to confirm if I'm on the right track. At the very least, with the way things are going under Ulagret's rule, I think some elves would start asking the right questions."

Pushing back from the desk, Artimus stood up and placed the parchment back. Turning around, he embraced Savannah. He rubbed the small of her back, giving her a light squeeze.

"I'm just really proud that you are going forward with this. I think we should take the opportunity to celebrate! This is sure to be the beginning of something great."

Savannah squeezed Artimus, returning his embrace and leaning her head into his shoulder. Pulling out of the hug, her eyes were glowing, smile wide as her lips quivered.

"Thank you. And I agree. Let's start by getting back to the fire -it's a little too cold in here."

Stepping through the doorway, Artimus held Savannah's hand and led her through. When they were both cleared, he closed the door and proceeded to the fire.

While they had lived in this home for a good eight months, neither of them spent enough time indoors to really worry about furnishing. This meant they had but one chair before the stove, a decision that Artimus was beginning to regret. With Savannah in her current state, she was the one who really needed a chair, but it would have been nice to be able to sit beside her.

Motioning for her to take a seat, he proceeded to the pile of wood next to the stove and grabbed a couple pieces. Dropping them into the active flame, he used the iron poker to push the wood around. Squinting his eyes, he used his hand to fan away the bit of smoke that escaped, watching the embers dance around as the older wood split apart, white pieces breaking off and falling to the side.

Closing the grate on the stove, he looked back to his lovely wife, who had taken a seat in the simple wooden chair.

"Is there anything I can get for you?"

"Hmm…now that I'm sitting here, I could go for a cup of tea. Do you mind putting on a kettle?"

"I suppose I can manage that," Artimus replied.

He walked to the kitchen, opening the center cabinet, and pulling out a jug of spring water. Twisting off the cork from the top, he retrieved the kettle, which Savannah had left out conveniently. After filling the kettle with water, he stepped to the left and opened the top cabinet there.

"Now which tea are you feeling?"

Artimus came from a much simpler background. So, tea from his younger life typically just meant one thing. He found after marrying Savannah that tea included a much wider range of options than he had imagined. She kept her teas, most of them grown from her own gardening efforts, in pouches marked with various runes. In truth, Artimus couldn't even tell what most of them were.

"There should be a bigger bag with a symbol that resembles a mountain with a little star in the center. That's my winter blend. You should make yourself a cup too!"

Shuffling through the bags, Artimus found the one towards the back and fetched it. He also pulled out the tea leaf insert they had purchased from the gratitude festival. It was a brilliant invention really, a small metal container that you placed inside the kettle with the tea leaves. This way, you didn't have to sift out the liquid from the leaves when you were done warming the water. Placing the leaves into this cylindrical container and closing the lid, he kept the bag in his hand as well and walked over to Savannah.

"This is the right one, correct?"

"You got it!" she exclaimed with a nod.

Returning to the cabinet, he replaced the tea bag and closed the cabinet door. Picking up the kettle of water, he returned to the stove.

"Do I put it in while the water warms, or wait until after it's hot enough?"

"You can place it in now." Savannah giggled. "One of these days, you'll be able to prepare tea without my guidance."

"Now why would I ever want to do that?" Artimus asked as he dropped the cylinder into the kettle and placed it on the stovetop.

They exchanged a look of understanding. As the kettle warmed, Artimus simply stood next to his wife, hands on her shoulders as they watched the flames in silence. After a few minutes, as steam started to rise from the kettle, Artimus left her side and grabbed a couple of mugs from beside the stove.

"Give it just another few seconds," Savannah instructed.

Artimus nodded, waiting a few seconds before grabbing the heat towel and lifting the kettle from the stove. He proceeded back to the kitchen with the cups in one hand and the kettle in the other. Placing both on the counter and proceeding to pour the tea, he looked back to his wife.

"Do you need me to add anything else to it, or is this blend good to go?"

"Good to go?" Savannah asked, tilting her head to the right, and raising her left eyebrow. "Yes, it is 'good to go' I suppose."

Artimus grabbed both mugs and strode to his wife. Extending his left hand, he waited for a moment for Savannah to take the cup. As she did, he smiled and raised the tea in his right hand.

"To a mild and uneventful winter."

"If toasts could come true," she replied, taking the mug, and sipping the tea. Her face softened as she took the first sip, letting out a sigh of relaxation.

With a shrug, Artimus took a sip as well. The primary taste was unfamiliar, a hint of sweetness hidden beneath a kick of spice. There was a dash of cinnamon, along with a touch of clove. The flavor was a bit overwhelming at first, but as he let it settle, it left him with a sense of calm.

Savannah smirked, lifting her mug again.

"It's good, isn't it?"

Artimus pursed his lips and nodded, pausing for a moment before responding.

"They say tea can only be as good as the elf who made it."

Savannah rolled her eyes before taking another sip and offering a simple "uh-hmm."

Once again, they both maintained silence. Enjoying each other's company as they listened to the crackle of firewood in the stove and enjoyed the warmth it offered. The tea was a great addition to the moment, its crisp flavor providing a comfort Artimus didn't know he needed.

After a few minutes, Artimus decided he'd continue the conversation.

"You know, there is another person that might be worth sharing your manuscript with. That Lord Vistoro fellow seemed to have some interesting ideas. Didn't he?"

Savannah looked up and nodded.

"You're right. I would really like to hear more about how his camp operates. It sounds like, despite his title, he might be embracing those same principles I'm writing about. I see why Irontail has been insisting we meet with him all these months now. After we have this baby, we'll definitely have to plan some opportunities to meet with him and discuss his ideas further."

"Yeah," Artimus replied. "I'm a little curious about that whole situation. Sounds like he gave up a lot leaving Lizock City."

"I can't blame him," Savannah responded. "We have it bad enough here with some of the nonsense laws, but the whole situation with nobility in Lizock City is downright blasphemous. Because they are 'chosen by Evorath' those born of noble blood are exempt from more than half the laws in their city."

Artimus closed his eyes and took a sip of his tea, pausing for a moment to enjoy the bouquet of flavor.

"Yeah, I really hoped our movement here in Erathal would spark some wider change. But it seems like this past year they've been passing more ridiculous laws restricting 'common born' from certain professions and activities. But even with the changes we've made here, it's still not a whole lot better."

"That's true," Savannah replied. "Though they are doing their best to disguise it, we both know Ulagret, and the Senate are trying to force a new caste system back on the city. I wonder if-"

Thud. Thud. Thud.

A frown overtaking his face, Artimus lowered the mug to his chest and proceeded to the door. He paused for a moment, looking back to Savannah as if begging her permission to leave the knock unanswered.

She shook her head.

Letting out a long breath, Artimus pulled on the door, opening it to reveal a couple familiar faces amidst the falling snow.

Casandra and Zelag stood outside, both shivering in the cold. All parties seemed in shock, a full five seconds of silence holding as they looked at each other.

"I -you were not who I expected," Artimus admitted pulling the door wider. "Please come in from the cold."

Casandra slithered over the threshold, Zelag hesitating for just a moment before stepping inside as well. Artimus immediately shut the door behind them.

"I wish we were here under better circumstances," Casandra spoke, shuddering a bit as the warmth from the fire hit her.

Eyes wide, Savannah stood up from her chair and looked at the visitors.

"Evorath help us. What brings you here?"

Zelag looked uncomfortable, his hands clasped behind his back as he rocked back and forth. Casandra appeared even more tense, her face tight and eyes narrow.

"Death is upon us," Casandra exclaimed.

71

It felt like the air left the room in that moment. A chill ran down Artimus's spine. Despite the ample heat from the stove, it was as if he was trapped in a block of ice. He could feel the hair on the back of his neck stand on end.

"You mean," Savannah started, her voice wavering. "You couldn't mean." She was choked up, tears in her eyes.

"He is," Casandra replied. She looked down, her shoulders slouched.

"That's not possible," Artimus objected, gulping down air as he tried to remain calm. "The Avatar sealed him away in that poor excuse for a fortress he built. He's no longer a threat."

It felt like the air in the room was diminishing, the room shrinking momentarily before expanding back to full size. After a moment of dizziness, Artimus maintained his composure.

"I'm afraid it is possible. We were visited by the dryad of Pine. She reported that Yezurkstal has escaped and is wreaking havoc on the forest. The Avatar is calling for us to gather in Dumner."

Artimus closed his eyes, taking a deep breath. This had to be a nightmare. His wife was in the final stretch of her pregnancy. His only job was making sure she was safe and comfortable. This couldn't be real.

"What can we do to help?" Savannah asked.

For a moment, Artimus imagined this was all a dream. He thought about the warmth of the fire, the subtle sweetness of his tea, and the brilliance of his wife's writing. But as he opened his eyes, everything came into focus.

"I don't know," Casandra said, a higher pitch to her voice. "But I do know your input would be most valued. He has called for us all to gather in Dumner to discuss. Irontail has been a gracious host."

"Have you spoken to Ulagret?" Artimus asked, the words leaving his mouth before he fully understood what he was asking.

"No, I'm afraid our pleas have gone unanswered by your government," Casandra replied without hesitation.

Artimus wished he was surprised. But truth be told…it sounded right. Even if they accepted a rule by majority, since Ulagret had reclaimed leadership over Erathal just a few months ago, he had never shown any respect for the opinion of the people. A republic, monarchy, autocracy -they were only different in name.

Artimus stood up tall, shaking his head and looking to Savannah, Casandra, and Zelag in turn.

"We won't get any help from the Chancellor," he said automatically.

He paused for a moment, looking around the room and considering the tension of the situation. There was a heavy weight on his chest, the concept of once again fighting against the enemy that had nearly killed him. No matter how much he wished he could stay out of it, he couldn't. He had to stand up and fight.

"Savannah is in no condition to fight. But we'll do whatever we can to support the Avatar," Artimus uttered.

"Then you must join us in Dumner," Casandra replied without hesitation. "The Avatar should be arriving any day now. He will have a plan for how to counter Yezurkstal."

"Then we shall accompany you there," Savannah said.

Artimus looked at his wife. She clutched her teacup, still half full of her winter blend. As he looked into her verdant eyes, he could feel her determination. There was no sense in debate.

"Yes, we will come," Artimus confirmed.

"Fantastic!" Casandra exclaimed. She looked around for a few moments before turning back to Savannah.

"I imagine you need to pack. Do you want us to wait for you outside?"

"Of course not," said Savannah rising from her chair. "You wait here while my husband and I pack for the journey."

Artimus wanted to object.

But there was a pit in his stomach. Though he wished he had an excuse, he couldn't come up with a reason to abstain. He had been there when Yezurkstal first revealed himself. Gharis and Verandas, the soldiers he had lost.

It was his responsibility. And if Yezurkstal had been freed from his prison, it was his job to put an end to it.

Yet, there was a part of him that was terrified. His wife was pregnant with their first child. She could not be involved in this conflict. No matter the cost, he needed to protect her and his unborn child.

As they proceeded to their bedchambers, he looked to Savannah. She had opened the chest of drawers, sifting through her clothing.

"Promise me," he began. "Promise me you will stay out of the fight. If you promise that, I promise I will do everything in my power to defeat Yezurkstal."

She paused, turning, and locking eyes with Artimus.

"I promise."

## Chapter 7

Dumner Village
4 Frozga, 1087 MT

Zelag looked around the room, wondering how much longer they'd be waiting. Though he had been here before briefly with the Avatar, it felt a little overwhelming now within the Dumner meeting hall. The unique underground structure glowed with life, its walls emitting a faint glow of green magic. Like the auras he saw around living creatures, he assumed this was something only he could perceive. But that glow coupled with the large crowd left him feeling a bit claustrophobic.

He was growing impatient, wondering how many more members they were waiting for. From the crowd already gathered, it seemed the Avatar had cast a wide net this time around. Oogmut, Aeria, Artimus and Savannah, Tel' Shira and an unfamiliar male felite, Neman and Morn, and of course Irontail and some other centaurs were gathered.

Beyond these, a pair of satyrs had arrived as well, male and female. Both wore simple leather armor and were equipped with sword and shield. More surprising than this, there was a dwarf invited as well, his great red beard host to a few grey strands. He wore a heavier, studded armor and beyond the large hammer slung over his back, he also had a few hatchets hanging on his belt. His aura glowed a dull red.

Rounding out the party, there was another barghest, his fur grey with age and left eye missing. He had red paint smeared across his face and wore a bone necklace along with a peculiar walking staff made from a gnarled piece of wood with what appeared to be the skull of some bird mounted to the top. He also wore an assortment of leather pouches around his waist. His aura was a bright, fiery red.

As usual, Zelag was seated next to Casandra. They had taken position next to the head of the long table on the right side. The Avatar himself had not yet arrived for the meeting, so most of the other guests were socializing throughout the large room. The clamor of so many voices further irritated Zelag's already overloaded senses, leaving him to sit in silence.

"Are you feeling alright Zelag," Casandra asked, her familiar voice cutting through the tension.

Zelag shook his head, keeping his eyes down.

"It's just a lot of people. And we should be out doing something, not just waiting in here for the Avatar."

Casandra placed her hand on his right shoulder, gently squeezing.

"I know what you mean. But we don't even know where Yezurkstal is. Erathal City seems to be hiding its head in the sand and you heard Tel' Shira earlier. None of her elders have had any visions about Yezurkstal, so they don't feel he's a threat right now. Without an army to march on his city, a full assault wouldn't have a chance of succeeding."

"I know, I know," Zelag murmured, rubbing his temples, and looking at Casandra directly. "I just wish I could face him myself -I would kill the bastard."

Casandra uncoiled her tail, standing up taller and removing her hand from Zelag's shoulder. Her eyes were wide and mouth agape.

"I didn't think you so reckless. You know what the Avatar said. There's no way we could hope to match Yezurkstal head on."

"Hmph. Maybe he's wrong. It seems all he ever wants me to do is practice 'feeling the essence of life'. If not for our sparring sessions," he said motioning between Casandra and himself, "I probably would still struggle with this body's basic movement."

Casandra shook her head, her usual green aura softening as she pursed her lips and narrowed her eyes.

"Zelag, I hope you understand how much I care for you. But you are always too harsh on our teacher. And you expect too much from yourself."

"I-" Zelag wasn't sure how to respond to this, so he paused with his mouth open. Fortunately, the Avatar proved useful for a change.

The chatter died down as the wall to the room opened, ground splitting apart to allow the Avatar through. But he was alone and it seemed his aura flickered between red and a strange shade of yellow. He wore a frown on his face as well. Something had gone wrong.

Irontail approached the Avatar first.

"We expected you to return with more company. What happened?"

"Death," the Avatar spat, his voice loud enough to silence the remaining conversations.

Zelag looked around -everyone gathered had turned their attention to his teacher.

"I'm sorry to have kept everyone waiting," the Avatar stated, his aura calming to a more stable yellow.

"The enemy continues to grow in strength. We've lost another powerful ally today. But I'm afraid we have no time to dwell on this. Please, everyone take a seat and we can begin."

The Avatar proceeded to the head of the table, Irontail following behind. Exchanging a quick glance with Casandra, Zelag straightened in his chair as she coiled herself to seated height. The rest of those gathered filled in the open spots at the table in short order.

While everyone was getting situated, Irontail placed a map at the head of the table. The Avatar took his seat there, while Irontail took a couple steps back, remaining on the left side of the table.

Zelag fought the urge to look at where each of the other guests were sitting, his attention remaining on the Avatar. He had never seen his teacher's aura so erratic.

"My actions earlier this year against Yezurkstal were shortsighted. I never considered the possibility he would break free. It seems not only did he figure a way out of his prison, but he has become more powerful and aggressive than ever before. While any mage on Evorath may access the magical energies all around us, he now seems able to transform and manipulate that energy. This is a power reserved for the gods, not one any mortal being has tapped into before.

"Four dryads have been slain -I have ordered the rest to flee the continent of Erathal for the time being. Of course, that's just the start of it.

"Death has seen its way around the continent. Nearly all independent settlements and small camps have been systematically eliminated. I've been trying to help facilitate the exodus of these settlements but I'm unable to predict where he'll attack next.

"With few exceptions, the Satyr have all left the main continent, retreating to their island in the west. There are no remaining organized Barghest settlements. Dumner is the last centaur village left in Erathal. Casandra may be the last living Lamia in Erathal."

He paused with this, looking to Casandra, and offering a subtle nod. His aura burned as he did.

"And when I went to recruit Mistress Pellera to our cause this morning, I found Death had defeated me yet again. She led the last organized tribe of Lamia in Erathal, and I arrived a day too late to help. Like the other settlements I've seen, it appeared deserted, not even a single corpse left behind.

"And this means Yezurkstal's army grows each day. Since the only major power willing to pledge support is Dumner, there is no hope in an attack on his fortress."

Irontail cleared his throat, speaking up only a moment later.

"Teacher, we may also be able to sway Lord Vistoro to our side. He clings to a rigid morality, believing it is never right to harm one of Evorath's children, no matter the perceived benefit to the greater whole."

"And he is right to do so," interjected the Avatar.

"Yes teacher," Irontail countered. "Which is why we need to help him understand that these demons and undead monsters are no longer Evorath's children. That part of them that was is long gone from this world. If we can make him see that, we'll have the backing of his camp, which may just tilt the scales in our favor."

"That may be so," the Avatar nodded.

"But we may also lose another half dozen hamlets, camps, or settlements of some kind while we work to mobilize. No. It's more important that we determine his next move.

"I have a plan to accomplish just that. Before I reveal it however, I wanted to discuss each of your roles in this process."

He started by looking to the barghest.

"Mojo, you are the most powerful shaman Erathal has ever seen. Your role is simple: help to disrupt and eliminate the undead horde. Irontail, you and your soldiers will be assisting

82

him in this endeavor, along with the magnificent Oogmut, the ethereal Aeria, and the nimble felite warriors Tel' Shira and El' Auro."

The Avatar looked to each of those he mentioned in turn, his impeccable timing allowing him to move his gaze at just the right speed. He would pause for just a moment on each of them before moving on to the next.

"We will also be relying on Keloth, who will muster the entire Keloth family to fight with our offensive forces."

"Aye," interrupted the dwarf, raising his right fist in approval. "The Keloth family recognizes the danger Yezurkstal presents us all. We will commit our full might to eliminating him from this land."

Zelag appreciated the directness of this dwarf. He studied his stout figure, his fiery mountain energy, his flowing beard, his dense bones, and his powerful muscles. The dwarven body had some definite advantages over Zelag's human form. Not wanting to miss anything the Avatar had to say, Zelag shifted his attention back to his teacher.

"While our offensive effort is important, we cannot leave Dumner completely undefended. The rest of you will remain behind in Dumner. Hopefully it will offer you a safe refuge. But if trouble should come, you have the protection of a small contingent of centaur guards and the rest of you are skilled soldiers.

"Veterans Pogo and Porra will have leadership over Dumner's defenses in our absence."

He looked to the satyr couple with this, both of whom were still in a standing position towards the other end of the table.

The male, Pogo, was a typical satyr. Small and stature, brown fur and brown eyes, he looked fairly unassuming. Porra, who was apparently his sister, was a full head length's taller than her brother. She had lighter fur and hazel eyes.

"They have the most defensive battle experience. Artimus, Savannah, and Casandra, you can offer insight into Yezurkstal, which should be invaluable should he make his way here. Once we know Yezurkstal's next target, I will strategize a battle plan for our offensive forces."

The Avatar paused at this point, looking around to the room. Zelag followed his gaze, noting everyone was paying attention. Was the Avatar forgetting about him?

"Now we come to the most important part of our plan. Tel' Shira, I understand your elders are not having any visions of Yezurkstal. I suspect this is Yezurkstal's doing. I am unable to gain any insight into his movements myself. But you have the gift of Evorath's foresight. Together, I think we can glimpse into the future and see his next conquest."

Zelag turned and watched Tel' Shira. She shifted in her chair, her aura pulsing, a sign Zelag recognized as nervousness. Despite this, he could see no change in her facial expression.

"Struggle with visions lately, I have. See Yezurkstal, I cannot," she stated, her words slow and deliberate.

"I understand," replied the Avatar. "But you will not be alone. Have faith in Evorath and I will ensure you have the vision we need to see."

Tel' Shira nodded.

"If wish, you do. Try, I will."

"And you will succeed. We will begin work tonight. In the meantime, we need to ensure everyone is ready for what lies ahead. If you are involved in the offensive, you must understand the danger we face. Even by himself, I fear Yezurkstal's new power makes him a match for most armies in Erathal.

"Based on his recent activity, his army is at least many hundreds strong. But I estimate the reality is much worse. He could have thousands of servants on his side. With numbers on his side, our advantage will be in the surprise. Yezurkstal believes we cannot track him, but Tel' Shira's vision will allow us to prepare.

"We'll also have the advantage of whatever defensive embattlements are available. When that time comes, just remember to leave Yezurkstal to me. He is much too powerful for anyone else here to involve a direct conflict with him. I will do everything in my power to contain him and keep him out of the fight. The rest of you will focus on taking out the undead."

How long would he keep droning on? It was bad enough that he was not bringing Zelag along for the offensive. But not even bringing him up in the planning was insane. No one else here had the kind of abilities he had. If he could study Yezurkstal up close, he could become just as strong.

"For now, I will give the floor to our host, Chieftain Irontail," the Avatar finished, motioning towards Irontail.

Irontail trotted to the head of the table.

"We have a welcome feast prepared for everyone. Those who haven't done so already are invited to take seats. Many of you have not had the opportunity to meet before today, so please take the opportunity to get to know some of your neighbors while my centaurs fetch the meal."

"You centaurs are vegetarians, are you not?" Keloth asked, leaning back in his chair, and raising his right hand.

"We are," replied Irontail. "But we have made sure to prepare something special for the carnivores among us."

Keloth nodded. "I'll be the judge of whether it's special or not."

Blocking out the conversation that immediately followed, Zelag glared at the Avatar, his thoughts falling into darkness.

## Chapter 8

Dumner Village
4 Frozga, 1087 MT

Smoke filled her nostrils, the sound of crackling wood providing a relaxed chorus to calm her mind. Under the cover of this hut, she stayed dry from the falling snow, the warmth from the flame keeping her fur temperate amidst the winter weather. With metered breathing, Tel' Shira prayed for a vision.

"Good," the Avatar's voice pierced her concentration.

"Keep your breathing and focus as much as you can. After this explanation, I will begin as I indicated. You may feel a tingling from Evorath's magic. Work to integrate it into your ritual. I believe this time I can clear through whatever interference is blocking you."

The Avatar placed his palm between her shoulder blades. The instant he touched her, the tingling began. It was a peculiar feeling, like walking through a massive spider web. Strands of magical energy coursed around her body, the tingling running down her back and through her arms and legs.

A new warmth began to emit from the pit of her stomach, a burn that resembled the feel one gets from consuming strong spirits.

3...2...1...

With continued focus on her breathing, the strange tingle diminishing as she exhaled. It happened in that moment, like being hit by a gust of wind. The dark of her closed eyelids was replaced with a blinding light.

As the light cleared, she saw a forest clearing. There were log homes in the clearing, their construction following felite design. It was a felite camp of some sort, young children frolicking in the open, an elderly felite couple walking through a garden. Various images flashed through her mind as the vision expanded.

She felt like a bird in the sky, looking down on the sizeable camp. There was a road to the north, a road she recognized. This had to be one of the new communities being built in central Erathal.

For a moment, her excitement of having the vision made her forget why she needed to see it. That moment came and went much sooner than she wished.

The vision narrowed in scope, zooming down to the southern border of the camp. A small felite played there, all black fur and running on all fours, she couldn't be more than a couple years old. A black and white felite ran to the girl, lunging over her.

Her perspective jerked again. The black and white felite - the girl's father, tackled an undead centaur. Turning to yell at his daughter, the warrior was engulfed by a hoard of zombies. They proceeded forth, sweeping past the black-furred child, and running through the camp.

No one was prepared.

The screams of innocent children, the smell of iron and blood, the sight of carnage, it was an overwhelming barrage of imagery.

Homes burned, felite slain…and then he arrived.

Yezurkstal stood within the aftermath, more than one hundred corpses surrounding him. He raised his right fist, dark magic pouring out and filling each of the fallen bodies. The energy flowed and pulsed, a moment of calm before it erupted and disappeared.

The undead felite rose, falling in line to follow their new master.

Then something unexpected occurred. The vision zoomed in, placing Tel' Shira before Yezurkstal. It was as if she was there, standing in form of Death and staring him right in the face. And he spoke, causing her hair to stand on end.

"It's of no consequence. You'll be one of mine soon enough, Tel' Shira."

Tel' Shira leapt out of the tent, heaving as she looked at her surroundings. Her heart pounded in her chest; eyes wet with tears from the vision she just experienced.

Was that real?

"What did you see?" the Avatar asked stepping out from the tent. "Do you know his next move?"

Tel' Shira looked with wide eyes, turning left and right before looking at her hands. They were trembling.

"A vision, I had. Death's next target, I know. Knows, he does too."

She tried to slow her breathing, clenching her fists, and opening them up a few times.

"What do you mean?" The Avatar inquired, stepping closer and looking her directly in the eyes. "He knows what?"

"My vision, he knows. By name, he called me. He said, 'you'll be one of mine soon enough'."

The Avatar blinked, staring blankly.

He shook his head.

"That is unsettling. But let's focus on what we can do from here. Where is his next target?"

They exchanged a nod, and Tel' Shira replied.

"A felite camp, he will strike. On the map, I will show you."

The pair darted to the central mound, the vines opening to allow them entry. They passed a centaur warrior along the way, sprinting past him towards the war room. Again, the vines to the doorway parted as they arrived, allowing them quick entry inside.

Keloth and Irontail were still inside, the pair standing at the head of the table and observing the map. They turned as Tel' Shira and the Avatar entered.

Tel' Shira pulled ahead, the two tribe leaders stepping back as she reached the map. Placing her index finger down along the road, she pointed to a spot in the center of the continent.

"Here, Yezurkstal will strike. A felite camp, stopped along the way, I did. On that day, no snowfall there will be. Depart soon, we must."

Keloth cleared his throat, stepping forward and glancing at the map.

"If this is where Death will be, I'll make sure dwarves are there to greet him. Chieftain Irontail, I take your leave."

He offered a nod, pausing for only a moment before marching for the exit.

"Fare well!" Irontail shouted as the dwarf left the war room. The three remaining warriors all exchanged glances.

"Before dawn, we must march," Tel' Shira declared, nodding towards the map.

"I will start preparations right away," Irontail replied without hesitation.

And he maintained that initiative, not even a moment of pause before he trotted towards the exit. Both still leaning over the map, the Avatar looked at Tel' Shira and smiled.

"I knew you could do it."

-=-=-=-=-=-=-=-=-

"Argh!"

Zelag braced himself, shifting his weight to his right leg. Parrying his opponent's blow, he reset his stance and backpedaled. Pointing the tip of his wooden sword towards Pogo, he took a deep breath.

"You won't win with caution," Pogo barked, leading with his shield and charging Zelag.

Realigning his sword to point the blade skyward, Zelag swung around to deflect the charge. He pivoted on his right foot, bringing his left behind to maintain balance. Catching his sword's rebound, he swung again, this time arching left to throw his opponent off balance.

Shuffling his feet, he took one more swing -an opening! Unfortunately, he was fully committed to following through. He held fast to his sword as his weight shifted forward. As he worked to regain balance, his opponent took advantage. Feeling the impact from his opponent's weapon, Zelag dropped his sword and cursed.

"You're improving," Pogo insisted immediately. "I have faced few enemies in battle who could match your skill."

"Yes, that was a great show," Casandra cheered from just a few meters away. She was beaming, wearing a toothy smile as she slithered to Zelag's side.

Looking at Casandra, Zelag's initial frustration seemed to melt away. As usual, her aura was calming, a smooth and steady warmth about her.

"This is the first time I've fought against an opponent with a shield," Zelag stated, bending over, and retrieving his practice sword.

He took a step back rubbing his right leg where he'd been struck.

"You really should be proud," Porra interjected, approaching the trio. "I saw the look on Pogo's face during that last barrage of yours. You almost broke his defenses."

"Maybe we should have one more go at it then," Zelag blurted, looking to Casandra before considering Pogo.

"I think maybe we should put off anymore sparring until morning," Casandra said. "It's late and Dumner's residents might not appreciate us making such a racket."

"Yes, and we should get some shut eye ourselves," added Porra. "But tomorrow morning I'll teach you some tricks of my own. My brother won't stand a chance once you've trained with me."

"I guess," Zelag said defeated.

Pogo and Porra both retrieved their gear, slinging everything over their shoulders and starting back south towards the village proper. Zelag stood with wooden sword and shield in hand, gazing off towards the mountains to the north.

"Have a good night," Pogo offered as they started towards the village.

"Yes, good night," Casandra replied, slithering up to Zelag's side.

"They're right, we really should call it a night."

"I think I'll stay out just a bit longer." If Pogo gave him another shot, he was sure he could have landed a proper blow.

"Do you want to be alone? I don't mind staying out and enjoying the evening with you if you don't mind the company."

Zelag considered Casandra's words. He hadn't noticed it, but her words allowed him to pause and really take things in. It was cold, snow flurries coming down sporadically. With the calm air and full moon overhead, the silence of winter did create an enjoyable atmosphere.

"I don't mind," Zelag muttered. "I -never mind. It is peaceful tonight."

An owl shrieked off in the distance, a light breeze passing by as the two orphans stared into the night sky. Despite the flurries, there were patches in the cloud cover above, bright stars complimenting the full moon. For a few seconds of silence, Zelag felt at peace.

The last thing he expected was to hear the hoarse voice of a singing dwarf. His rhyming lyrics causing pause.

"As the earth shook, the dragon roared. 'This treasure is mine, find your own hoard.' The dragon spoke, his eyes on fire. But Kelgen refused, knowing his desire."

Zelag and Casandra turned towards the raucous Keloth, who was trekking north on the road out of Dumner.

Keloth stopped cold, his eyes wide.

"Oh, I didn't know anyone was out this way," he remarked continuing towards the pair.

"You may not find me performing at any mead halls, but I do love that song. Sorry if I startled you."

He should be sorry. And for a moment, Zelag was ready to share his true thoughts on the matter. Fortunately, Casandra slithered forward and spoke first.

"You've no need to apologize Master Keloth. But, seeing you come this way I must wonder. Did Tel' Shira already have a vision?"

"Aye, she did. I am making my way back home to rally the family. So, you must excuse me for not sticking around to talk."

Keloth strode forth, continuing past Zelag and Casandra, turning to wave as he did.

"Are you heading back alone at this hour?" Casandra called after him.

"Don't worry your fiery head. There's plenty of dangerous creatures about at night, but none as deadly as me."

Smirking at that comment, Zelag put his hand on Casandra's left shoulder. As Keloth disappeared into the night, Zelag thought perhaps it was best to say what he had been thinking.

"Thank you for always being there for me Casandra. I don't know how I would have gotten through this year without you." He felt a tear forming in his right eye, sniffling, and wiping it away.

Clasping Zelag's hand with her right, she smiled and peered into his eyes.

"Getting to know you has been the best part of my year," Casandra responded after holding his gaze for a few moments.

And as they stood, holding one another's hands, and staring into the night sky, Zelag had some hope for the future.

## Chapter 9

Erathal News Article 101:332
A Peaceful Winter
By, High Wizard Guildpac

As snow continues to fall on this cold winter morning, it seems the perfect time to reflect on the peace we've enjoyed since Chancellor Ulagret has reclaimed his position as ruler of Erathal.

During that time, our economy has continued to grow stronger. It seems one cannot go anywhere in the city without witnessing new homes being constructed. A new tavern is being built in the central exchange district, we've increased trade with our lizock allies to the west, and new elves are becoming citizens of Erathal every week.

Beyond our continued peace here in Erathal, I have the honor of announcing an exciting development. Our human guests in Erathal have been working hard to establish a settlement for themselves at the base of the Runeturk Mountains. I was blessed to be able to tour their settlement and meet with their leaders.

During my time there, it became clear that humans and elves have a lot in common. We also have a lot we can teach one another. This is why we are seeking formal trade relationships with the human town of Paxvilla.

When winter is through and the snow has dried up, we will be looking to start construction on a new road leading directly from Erathal to Paxvilla. Further, your senators are working with the Chancellor to ensure everyone in Erathal can benefit from this new trade relationship.

I for one am thrilled to be a part of this great Republic of Erathal and excited to see where this will lead.

If you know anyone who isn't a daily reader of our fine Erathal News, I recommend you tell them to keep their eyes out for more exciting announcements. The world is growing smaller, and Erathal is sure to be the best place to live.

Long live Chancellor Ulagret, and long live the Republic of Erathal and the best city in all Evorath.

.=.=.=.=.=.=.=.=.

Felite Outpost, Central Erathal
6 Frozga, 1087 MT

The snow had stopped falling, but not before leaving a solid half-meter lying on the ground. Leading the war party to their destination, the Avatar marched ahead of the group. Tel' Shira didn't understand how, but he appeared weightless on the snow, as if he floated just above the ground with each step.

Come to think of it, he seemed completely unaffected by the winter weather. He wore no hat to cover his bald head, no gloves to protect his hand, and no coat to keep him warm. Instead, he wore the same, simple brown tunic since Tel' Shira first saw him. After this was over, she had a lot of questions to ask.

Tel' Shira marched forward, her light footsteps allowing her to tread through the snow more efficiently than most members of her party. El' Auro was just a meter behind, his larger frame and heavy spear undoubtedly impacting his movement. Still, it was apparent felites were much better equipped at trekking through snow than their allies.

Oogmut was somehow keeping pace not much further behind the pair of felite. His heavier weight caused him to sink into the snow with each step. But he remained determined, his eyes looking forward and face unwavering as he stomped along. Regardless of how fast he managed to move, he still looked like an elephant trying to navigate an obstacle course.

Mojo and Aeria had both taken up lone positions to the left and right, respectively. Mojo's black fur had a layer of snow dusted over, creating an aesthetic that Tel' Shira found inexplicably humorous. But he seemed to be handling the snow about as well as El' Auro. Aeria, of course, was floating along, seemingly unaffected by the weather.

The centaur army took up the rear, dozens of warriors, druids, and archers all ploughing through the snow like only a centaur (or horse) could do. They were a mighty force, one that Tel' Shira would not care to face. Of course, while she kept telling herself that they would overcome the inevitable number disadvantage, she couldn't ignore the pit in her stomach.

Seeing Yezurkstal up close in her vision was uncomfortable. It was jarring. It was terrifying.

As much as she tried to distract herself by keeping her eyes ahead and focusing on the mission, she couldn't deny the poignant sense of dread she felt when recalling the vision. That innocent black felite, the screams of anguish…she shuddered at the thought.

"I can see the tower ahead," the Avatar called back, rescuing Tel' Shira from her thoughts.

She squinted her eyes, focused on the road ahead. With the snowfall, the only reason they could even see the road was the fact that so many trees had been cleared out along the path. Following the Avatar as he swerved to the right, she spotted the tower as well.

There were a few sparse trees spread out along the path, barren of leaves due to the winter condition. Tel' Shira had passed through this camp on her way to Dumner, but the additional snowfall since then made it difficult to spot any landmarks. As they drew near, she could see the outpost's palisades coming into view.

Tel' Shira approached the Avatar, who had stopped about fifty meters from the camp's defenses.

"I think it's best if most of the army waits at this distance," he said, pointing up to the tower. Though she could barely see from this distance, Tel' Shira noted a couple archers in the tower with their arrows trained on the Avatar.

"Wise decision, that is. Approach, El' Auro and I will."

Tel' Shira waited a few seconds for El' Auro to catch up. As he entered her peripherals, she proceeded towards the outpost gate. It was flimsy, crafted by thin strips of oak; not something that would stand up to a serious assault.

The palisades themselves were a good enough deterrent to ground troops, but if Yezurkstal had the usual contingent of aerial demons, they wouldn't do much either. While she considered the different battle strategies they could employ based on these limited defenses, she noticed a felite walking towards them.

"Tel' Shira, El' Auro. To Sinterro Tower, I welcome you. Of your guests, wary we are."

The speaker was a grizzled, middle-aged male. His orange fur and thick maim gave him the appearance of a lion. Equipped with a simple harness holding two bastard swords, the barrel-chested veteran was a familiar face. Looking to the scar on his left shoulder and catching the gaze of his green eyes, Tel' Shira smiled.

"Nor Leon!" Tel' Shira exclaimed. "Months, it has been. Out here, I did not know you were."

Her large old friend smiled, extending his hand, and pulling her in for an embrace. As they separated, Tel' Shira regarded El' Auro.

"Faught together in Dumner, Nor Leon and I did. Experience against Yezurkstal, he has."

"Then welcome, will be his help," responded El' Auro in a monotone. He might have been a loyal ally, but he lacked a little in the personality department.

"Name I wish not hear, Yezurkstal is. Bad tidings, you bring I fear." Nor Leon gritted his teeth as he finished speaking, his eyes aflame as he looked past Tel' Shira and El' Auro.

"Avatar of Evorath, that is," Tel' Shira confirmed following his gaze. "Vision, I had. Approach your camp, Yezurkstal does. Send aid, Dumner does."

Nor Leon moaned, turning back and walking towards the gate. He waved his left hand ahead, nodding at the tower.

"Into the defenses, bring your party."

Tel' Shira nodded, turning back to signal the others. The Avatar was already approaching, the rest of the war party following behind.

As her allies made their way forward, Tel' Shira continued ahead. El' Auro stayed back, presumably waiting for the others.

Reaching the gate, Tel' Shira froze. A chill ran down her spine as she thought of her vision, slowly turning back to her allies to the west. Shifting her gaze just south, she felt a wave of déjà vu pass over. The young girl in her vision had been no more than twenty meters south of these palisades.

Closing her eyes and taking a deep breath, she turned and entered the encampment. The central tower sat straight ahead, but the clearing had its share of other structures. To her right, she noted the tavern, which she had stopped in just a few days before when travelling this way. On the left, there was a long house serving as barracks for the tower garrison.

While the tower itself must have housed additional troops, a barracks of this size meant there were no less than three dozen felite warriors stationed here. Aside from this, she spotted the town well a few meters ahead. The rest of the housing and resources were positioned to the north of the tower.

This entire camp had been built in just the last six months. Tel' Shira even helped with the early planning. Thinking of what was on the way, she couldn't help but shed a tear. Stifling those emotions, she forced a smile and continued towards Nor Leon.

He was standing just outside the entrance to the tower, chatting with a younger, black-spotted felite who had just come from inside.

"…prepared. Join me, have Su Lao."

"Urgo," the young felite replied before dashing back into the tower.

"Your leaders, in the war hall, join us, they should."

Tel' Shira nodded, pivoting around, and approaching the Avatar. As he made his way through the gate, she greeted him with a wave.

"In the war room, our leaders they request."

They waited while the rest of the army filed through the gates and entered the settlement. As they did, Tel' Shira spotted someone familiar peeking out from the corner of the tower. Black fur, small whiskers, and sheepish yellow eyes -it was the felite girl from her vision.

Her heart sank and for a moment she felt a knot in her throat. She released the breath she didn't realize she was holding and strode towards the child.

The girl jerked her head behind the tower as Tel' Shira approached. As the felite warrior turned the corner, the young child stood still, looking up at her with fearful eyes, her tail sticking straight out behind here.

"Fear not, friend I am. Your name, what is it?" Tel' Shira knelt as she asked, offering her right-hand palm up to the young felite.

"Luna Freya," the child muttered, her voice soft and unsteady.

"Unusual name, that is. Tel' Shira, my name is. Such a beautiful shade of black, your fur is. Live here with you, do your parents?"

The girl shook her head, casting her eyes down as she replied.

"My daddy, only. Not with us, my mom."

"Sorry, I am," replied Tel' Shira. "Though, fear not. Love you, your daddy does. Safe, you will be. Honored to meet you Luna Freya, I am."

Luna Freya looked up, locking eyes with Tel' Shira and offering a timid smile.

"Honored to meet you, I am," the girl replied, placing her small paw into Tel' Shira's.

Returning the smile, Tel' Shira stood back up and glanced behind her to confirm the others were ready. Seeing the Avatar looking her way, she knew it was time to go.

"Later, see you I will. Until then, be good."

Luna Freya nodded, spinning around, and running on all fours back towards the housing area of town.

Feeling a bit lighter, Tel' Shira joined Aeria, the Avatar, Irontail, Mojo, Oogmut, and Nor Leon at the entrance to the tower.

"Required for planning, are you all?" Nor Leon asked.

"In truth, I was hoping one more would join us. But I'm afraid he may not make it until later this evening. Know that beyond our numbers, we have at least one hundred dwarves from the Keloth family marching here now to defend this outpost. According to Tel' Shira's vision, we have at least until tomorrow morning to get our defenses prepared."

"Know this, how do you?" questioned Nor Leon.

"Early morning, my vision was. Just after dawn."

"Understood," Nor Leon replied, scratching behind his right ear. "To the war room, follow me."

He paused for a moment, looking over the party before proceeding into the tower. The initial room was small, no more than three meters wide. There were three doors in this atrium, one on either side and one straight ahead. Since Tel' Shira hadn't been involved in the tower design, she waited for Nor Leon to lead them forward. It appeared the door straight ahead was their destination.

Nor Leon opened the door and started up the steps on the other side. It was a narrow stairway, forcing the party to proceed single file up the steps. Tel' Shira stepped aside and motioned for others to proceed before her. Aeria floated through first, followed by Mojo and then the Avatar. Irontail and Oogmut both took pause, exchanging narrow gazes.

"Why don't you go on ahead," Irontail said looking to Tel' Shira.

Oogmut nodded. "The Chieftain and I might need to leave the strategy to the rest of you. These steps don't appear to be made with creatures of our weights in mind."

"He's right. But I have faith the Avatar can devise the best strategy for me and my warriors," Irontail added.

Tel' Shira tilted her head, considering the staircase. For a felite, they looked perfectly safe and accommodating. But considering the size of Oogmut's feet and the length of Irontail's torso, perhaps they were right. The steps were steep, and the curve of the spiral staircase created a sharp turn.

"Inform the others, I will."

Without delay, Tel' Shira sprang up the steps. It only took a few seconds for her to catch up with the rest of the party, who had reached the next floor.

They were in a small antechamber, like the bottom floor with doors on right, left, and behind them. The door to the right was left ajar and appeared to be their destination. With Nor Leon continuing to lead the way, the party followed just behind.

This had to be the war room. The exterior wall housed a long wooden display running most of the length of the room and holding a couple dozen short swords. The large table in the room held a map of Erathal, including the outlying islands.

Another familiar face greeted them at the table. Tel' Shira had to do a double take, almost not recognizing her. But there was no mistaking it -the marbled white and black fur with a star-shaped black spot around her left eye and a lightning bolt on her right arm.

Tel' Shira dropped to one knee as she beheld her childhood hero.

"Lady Tu Lora. To meet you, honored, I am."

Her elder felite rose, taking a slight bow and extending her right hand.

"Young warrior, rise. Necessary, this is not."

Tel' Shira rose to her feet at the command. Even her voice was powerful, a certain absolute authority attached to every word.

"Tel' Shira, is it not?" Tu Lora asked.

With eyes wide, she offered a toothy smile and nod.

"It is," Tel' Shira replied. "Come to help prepare for an attack, we have. A vision, I have had."

Tu Lora looked over the party and sat back in her seat.

"Discuss, we must. A seat, please take."

Hardly able to contain her enthusiasm, Tel' Shira walked around to the other side of the table and took a seat. The other party members followed suit, finding a place at the table.

This battle was sure to be one Tel' Shira would remember for the rest of her life.

## Chapter 10

Dumner Village
6 Frozga, 1087 MT

Zelag held his breath, squinting as he focused on the target ahead. Releasing the bowstring, he watched the arrow cut through the air and impact the outer ring below the bullseye. Lowering the bow, he looked at Artimus.

"Very nice," the elf offered as he approached.

"Do you see how the bracer helps? Doesn't hurt so much that way, does it?"

Nodding, Zelag held out the bow, offering it back to the ranger.

"Yes, it makes it easier on the arm. So, you bring both the bow and your sword into battle? It seems the bow is a much slower weapon."

Taking the bow from Zelag, Artimus retrieved an arrow from the ground and smiled. In one quick motion, he notched the arrow and released it. Not waiting for the first arrow to strike, he pulled a second arrow from the ground and fired it off.

Zelag blinked, cocking his head, and looking at both arrows sticking in the bullseye.

"When you get enough practice, your speed improves. Come have a look," Artimus instructed.

The pair strode to the target. As they got closer, Zelag realized the arrows were touching. The only way they would have been closer would have been if the second one split straight through the first.

"Practicing your speed is definitely a good idea if you want to use a bow in battle. In the heat of the moment, this sort of accuracy is only achievable if you keep your mind calm. You need to practice so much that it becomes instinctual."

Nodding, Zelag leaned in closer to the target and rubbed around the arrows. He wouldn't admit it, but he was impressed.

"Are you as gifted with a sword as you are with a bow?" Zelag inquired.

Artimus shook his head.

"I like to think I know my way around a blade. But the bow is where I stand out. I haven't won the last four Erathal archery competitions for nothing."

"So, you're the best archer in the forest?"

"I don't know if I can claim that title. But of the elves in Erathal, no one has been able to best me."

Despite his apparent humility, he seemed arrogant. He sounded so confident and sure of himself, like the Avatar. And the way his bright aura shined, a dull white light holding steady all around him…Zelag wondered what caused this sort of confidence.

"Care to test your swordplay against my own?" Zelag asked.

Artimus slung his bow over his back. His face tightened and aura flickered.

"I think I should go back to Savannah and make sure she doesn't need anything. Maybe before dinner this evening we can get in some practice. If you're looking for a new challenge, I'd suggest you check out the obstacle course they have here. It might be meant for centaurs, but it's not easy."

"Alright," Zelag spat. "Maybe I'll see what Casandra is up to."

"She's probably still with my wife. Why don't we walk back to the central mound together and see?"

Pausing for a moment to consider, Zelag nodded. Without a word, he started east towards the village. Hearing Artimus's footsteps behind was enough to confirm the elf was following.

He would have preferred to walk in silence, but of course Artimus had other ideas.

"I've been curious about something for a while," Artimus started. "Do you always maintain that human form? Even when sleeping?"

Glancing back, Zelag saw the smile on Artimus's face and the steady glow of his aura. He must have been sincere in his curiosity at least.

"Yes," Zelag replied. "So long as I stay in this form, my body pretty much works like a human's."

"But the armor you wear. Isn't that part of you?"

"No. It was when I first assumed this form. But I've learned to separate it. The Avatar had me make this armor, but Casandra helped in doing so."

Artimus's pace allowed him to move alongside Zelag as they walked. He looked over the young shapeshifter for a moment.

"How does that work if you change form into something else? Like something small like a bird? Or something large like a troll?"

He was asking the right questions at least. This was still something Zelag was struggling with.

"For simple armor like I'm wearing, I just absorb it into myself. It makes changing a bit more difficult, but that way I can transform. So, as I transform back into this human form, I must make sure I remanifest the armor in the right place. It can be really painful if I make a mistake."

"It sounds like the amount of training and discipline you go through to shapeshift is intense. I'm sure if you apply that same rigor to archery, you could give me a run for my money."

Zelag squinted, lowering his brow, and glaring at Artimus. Was he being sincere? That steady white glow around the elf seemed to suggest he was.

"Thank you," Zelag blurted. "You are an unusual elf, aren't you?"

Artimus laughed, a hearty noise that caused his aura to flare out, a hint of yellow pulsing around it.

"I don't think I'm that unusual," he replied. "But I'll take it as a compliment."

Zelag shrugged. What did he care how the elf took it? At least that allowed them to walk in silence.

It took a few minutes before they ran across anyone else. As they approached the village, a couple centaurs were heading the other way. Both equipped with bows and arrows, they were apparently heading out for some target practice themselves.

Avoiding eye contact, Zelag did his best to ignore them as they passed. He overheard them mumbling about something. Perhaps another centaur? It wasn't important. Unfortunately, it seemed Artimus took that as an opportunity to start up the conversation again.

"What has it been like living with the Avatar? I know Savannah and I were out there a few months ago, but I understand he's gathered a lot more followers since then. Are you still staying in a tent at his camp?"

Though he noticed people tended to respond quickly to questions when addressed, Zelag had also figured out a delay was not unusual. In this case, he delayed answering for the longest he had ever tried. Not wanting to press his luck, he responded after some delay.

"Yes. It's gotten a lot more crowded with all the newcomers."

"Oof. That must not be fun," Artimus replied immediately. "I'm sure some of them are not the easiest to get along with either. I guess if you have the chance to keep up your training, it's worth it though. Are you still getting as much time training directly with the Avatar?"

"No. He claims that until I master my transformation more completely, I need to practice that exclusively."

"What sort of improvement is he expecting you to make?" Artimus pried.

He didn't give up, did he?

"I said I can transform with simple armor. I'm still getting the hang of using anything with an edge -it's hard not to cut myself."

The young shapeshifter was hoping that would not prompt further inquiries. But alas, the elf was persistent.

"I see," Artimus said. "I suppose mastering that transformation with a blade is important for conflicts like this though. Otherwise, it means you're pretty much locked in that form while wielding a weapon, doesn't it?"

Zelag again delayed his response. He could see the tavern just ahead in the distance, so maybe if he waited just a few more seconds he could put an end to this elf's prying.

"Yes," he offered as they approached the tavern. "I bet Savannah will be happy to see you. Why don't you go on up to the room? If Casandra is up there, you can let her know I'm outside."

Artimus stopped and glanced at him for a moment.

"Alright. I will see you later," the elf said walking towards the tavern.

What a relief.

-=-=-=-=-=-=-=-=-=-

Artimus stepped through the tavern door, pausing for a moment to reflect before proceeding up the stairs.

Zelag really didn't like him. That much was clear. His body language, his tone, and even the way he answered questions were all indicative of someone trying to avoid conversation. Perhaps it was best for Artimus to let it be.

There were only a few others gathered in the tavern right now. The young centaur hostess behind the bar was chatting with a couple barghest -those two brothers the Avatar had brought along. Otherwise, the bar stools were empty. However, it looked like a couple of young centaurs were on the far side of the tavern as well, standing aside a high-top table and sharing a couple drinks.

The stairs to his accommodations were on the left, so he continued past the bar and up the steps. Wearing a grin, he once again thought about how odd these steps were made. Each step had to be at least 40 centimeters deep and only 12 centimeters tall. While he assumed this was to make it easier for the centaur to go up and down the steps, it made for a much longer stairway than expected.

Reaching the top, Artimus made his way down the hall. At his request, Irontail always made sure they could stay in the last room up top. This offered them just a little extra privacy, which made staying here a bit easier. With no one else in the hallway, he kept his eyes wide to take in any details he might have missed before.

The walls were still barren. Though the wooden doors broke up the monotony of the hallway, Savannah's suggestion to add some sort of art or decorations had so far gone unrealized. Moving past the second to last door before his room, he also noticed scuffmarks on the floor. It looked like they were from claws, which made sense considering the barghest brothers had been put in that room.

Arriving at the room, he knocked on the door out of courtesy and waited a few moments.

"Come in," his wife's voice came from inside.

With a smile, Artimus pushed open the door and stepped inside.

It was a simple room, no more than four meters by three meters. A single window was on the east wall, the shutters closed to maintain privacy and keep the winter cold at bay. A fireplace with a fire roaring in the north end of the room provided ample heat. In the way of furniture, there was a simple bed and two chairs, along with a small table between those two chairs.

Savannah was seated in one of the chairs, Casandra standing opposite her. They both turned to look at Artimus entering the room.

"How was the target practice?" Savannah inquired as he made his way to the fireplace.

Removing his winter cap, Artimus made his way to the fireplace.

"It went pretty well," he said rubbing his hands in front of the flames.

"Zelag really doesn't like me though," he continued looking to Casandra. "Any idea what I did to offend him?"

Casandra shook her head, glancing down at the ground as she did. Her face muscles tensed; her lips held tight for a moment before she replied.

"It's nothing you did. I'm afraid that's just Zelag. He's a special and caring person if you get to know him, but he's not too willing to get to know many people."

Her skin flushed a little as she spoke. She looked back at Artimus and peered into his eyes.

"He needs more friends though. So please don't give up on him."

Artimus faked a smile and nodded.

"If you think he's worth being friends with, I definitely won't disagree."

"Don't be coy Artimus," Savannah interjected. "I know you'll approach this like every challenge you face. You can't wait to solve the puzzle on how to get through to him."

Artimus shrugged.

"Well, I should go down and make sure Zelag doesn't get into any trouble," Casandra blurted.

She slithered to the door, retrieving her bearskin coat, and draping it over her shoulders. Artimus pulled open the door for her, allowing her to pass through. As she cleared the doorway, Savannah shouted behind her.

"Don't forget what I said!"

"I won't."

Artimus waited for her to slither away down the hall before closing the door and turning back to his wife.

"So," she started, "think he'll be coming over as a dinner guest anytime soon?"

With a chuckle, Artimus shook his head. He stepped over to the open chair and sat down opposite his wife. Taking a moment to admire her features, he smiled and held her gaze.

"Maybe by next winter if we're lucky."

Returning his smile, Savannah reached out and took his hands, giving them a squeeze.

"Casandra tells me he is the last of his kind. Can you imagine if you were the last elf left on Evorath? It's understandable that he would be wary of making any friends."

Lifting her hand and planting a gentle kiss on her knuckles, Artimus nodded.

"Of course, you're right, as usual. I will say, he seems eager to challenge himself, but he's also impatient. I don't think he was enjoying archery as much simply because he knew he couldn't best me. But he wanted to practice more swordplay. I'm still baffled how good he already is at either."

"Oh? I wonder if that has to do with the form he takes on. Chatting with Casandra made me think: what if when he transforms into a different body, he inherits the abilities that body already had?"

"So, the human body he imitates was familiar with a bow and sword, so Zelag is too? I bet the Avatar could confirm if that is the case. It would make some sense though. He's allegedly never used a bow before today and the only time he missed the target was when we went out to 100 meters."

"Yeah, the next opportunity I get, I definitely intend to bring it up to the Avatar."

Savannah looked down and touched her belly as she said this, her eyes widening.

"Someone is getting some movement in," she exclaimed.

Artimus looked closely at her stomach. Grinning ear-to-ear, he watched the faint imprint of a foot jut out from inside.

"Here," Savannah said grabbing her husband's hand and placing it on her stomach.

As their unborn child continued to kick, they remained in the moment, gazing into one another's eyes, and smiling.

## Chapter 11

Felite Encampment
7 Frozga, 1087 MT

The snow had stopped falling just four hours ago. A chill morning air blew through the clearing as the first signs of sunlight danced across the early morning sky. Irontail kept his gaze forward, his eyes trained south on the horizon. Tears formed in his eyes, the cool, dry air causing him to blink and hold his eyes shut for an extra moment.

If the attack was going to occur today, it would happen soon. And yet, as he stood clutching his club, his mind continued to race with thoughts of Dumner.

Tel' Shira had indicated that Yezurkstal knew about her vision. If that was the case, what was to stop him from changing his attack? Even if he was still coming here, maybe he would delay the attack until nightfall. Or worse yet, what if he decided to attack Dumner instead?

As these thoughts continued to pop into his head, the centaur chieftain tried to refocus his attention on the battle strategy.

He stood at the front of the charge, just outside the garrison's gates. His centaur warriors were in formation behind him, ready to charge at the oncoming army. His archers had joined the garrison's own, standing far enough back from the palisades that they could rain down arrows on the enemy as soon as they entered Irontail's line of sight.

Standing next to him on his left and right, respectively, were Oogmut and Mojo. The Avatar was standing alone, just a few meters in front of Irontail and the others. In the thirty minutes since they had completed their formation, he hadn't moved a centimeter.

The felite warriors were all remaining within the garrison. When the battle started, the arrows would rain, the centaurs would charge, and any enemies that broke through would then be addressed by the felite or the archers.

Unfortunately, since the dwarves had still not arrived, it meant they would be terribly outnumbered. According to the numbers missing from the villages already destroyed, the Avatar indicated the enemy would have them beat at least 2 to 1. That wasn't including potential demon allies.

But what if those numbers were to go after Dumner instead? Was there even a chance they would hold out?

Snorting and shaking his head, Irontail refocused ahead. Aeria had been sent to scout. So, if things worked according to Tel' Shira's vision, she would be arriving to warn them of the approaching enemies.

"Dwarves!" a voice shouted from behind. Irontail looked to the tower, where a felite was shouting.

"Approaching from the north, dwarves are."

Irontail looked back ahead, checking for any sign from the Avatar. As if by divine providence, he spotted Aeria flying through the trees in the distance. She soared through the tree line and landed next to the Avatar.

"His army approaches. But I do not see Yezurkstal among them."

The Avatar turned and glanced at Irontail and the others. His face was stern, eyes narrow and lips closed.

"Have the archers ready for fire," he instructed.

Irontail nodded, turning, and raising his right hand.

"Archers, ready your arrows!"

Another yell from the felite in the tower.

"With the dwarves, someone else is!"

Irontail glanced back up, his arm shaking as he watched the felite dart back inside. Rapidly turning left and right, Irontail kept watch for any signs of Yezurkstal's army then looked back to the tower.

Left and right. Another shout from the tower.

"A pale elf, it is. Lead the dwarves, a pale elf does."

Irontail blinked, his right arm frozen as he pivoted his entire body and looked at the felite in the tower. It was as if time slowed, his vision blurring for a moment as the realization washed over him.

"Irontail, focus ahead," the Avatar's voice cut through his disorientation, a divine clarity taking hold and allowing him to regain composure.

Turning back to face the south, he saw Aeria fly overhead towards the watchtower. A moment later, he watched as dozens of zombies broke through the tree line and charged.

"Steady," he waited a second more before dropping his arm.

"Fire!"

The sound of dozens of bows letting loose at once was followed up by a hail of arrows above. The projectiles soared through the air, raining down on the approaching army.

Centaur, lizock, lamia, human, elf, barghest -every sentient race in Erathal was represented in this undead hoard. And as the arrows impacted arm, leg, shoulder, hand…they had no effect. Even the few lucky shots that impacted these creatures in the head seemed to lack the power to put them down.

Shouts came from behind, the footsteps of felite redeploying. Irontail couldn't afford the distraction.

"Prepare your next arrow!" he shouted, holding up his right hand again. This time, he waited only a couple seconds, watching as the undead approached.

"Fire!"

He dropped his arm again. Taking hold of his club in his right hand, he closed his eyes and took a deep breath. Whispering a quiet prayer to Evorath, he opened his eyes and extended the club forward.

"Centaur warriors! We fight today in the name of all we hold sacred. Remember, these enemies are already dead. Their souls are gone, leaving nothing behind but a hungry husk of flesh. In the name of Evorath, the name of Life, we charge forth to declare victory over Death itself."

His warriors shouted, hollering cheers, and howling in anticipation. He held onto that moment.

"Whatever may happen," he whispered. "May I do your will."

"CHARGE!"

The thunderous roar of centaurs filled the air as his dozens of warriors charged forward. With clubs, maces, and spears, they charged their unholy foes.

As much as his mind was prone to wander, this was the one time where Irontail felt he could focus. Ignoring the other combatants, he tunneled in on the nearest enemy grouping.

Drawing near a pair of undead centaurs and a barghest, he clenched his left fist and held tight to the club with his right. Three, two…

As they entered range, he swung his club in an upward arch, landing a blow on the nearest zombie centaur's jaw. The monster's face caved under the force. While the arrows may not have been sufficient, it appeared a forcible enough blow to the head would do the trick. This first creature collapsed, landing to the side with a thud.

Allowing the momentum from his swing to continue, he held tight and brought the club around in a circular motion. The weight of the club helped ground him, allowing him to pivot and kick towards the undead barghest with his hind legs. As his hooves smashed into the creature's face, he once again felt the skull crushed from the impact.

Knowing he had no time to delay, he twisted his torso around and planted his legs. He grabbed the club with both hands, taking a swing at the final, undead centaur. With a roar of triumph, he landed the blow, caving in the side of the creature's head and leaving it to plop on the ground like the dead husk it was.

Letting out a war cry, Irontail brought his club over his shoulder and continued the charge forward. A heavier grouping of troops were just a few meters ahead, one of his fellow centaur warriors already engaging with the assortment of zombified humans.

Irontail crashed into the fray, leading with his forelegs, and stomping one down straight away. As he landed, he heaved his club forward onto another one's head, releasing it and allowing the weight to bring the creature down. As his club fell to the ground, he spotted one of the zombies grabbing hold of his ally's left, front leg.

Not giving the creature time to continue its attack, he reached with both hands and grabbed it by the neck. His chest bulged as he lifted the former man up and slammed him back to the ground. Still squirming to get back up, Irontail finished the attack with another stomp from his hind legs.

Bending to retrieve his club, he spotted an undead satyr from his peripherals. Clasping the club with both hands, he swung up to intercept the former satyr in the side of her head. His nearby ally let out a shriek of pain, bringing Irontail's attention back to the warrior.

Two of the zombies had somehow managed to climb onto his back. The first had blades planted in the centaur's shoulder and the other one, directly in his side. While the centaur struggled to reach his assailants, Irontail darted over, once again releasing his club.

Wrestling the blade from the second one's hand, he pulled it from his ally's side and plunged it into the zombie's skull. When this one fell to the ground, he grabbed hold of the first one and yanked him off. Holding both arms of this one, Irontail reoriented his foe and slammed him headfirst into the ground.

"Can you walk?" he asked his ally.

Another zombie, this one already partially mangled, leapt towards the two centaurs. Without flinching, Irontail pulled the other blade out of his ally's shoulder and jabbed it into the creature's skull.

"I can still fight," the other centaur muttered, slapping the side of his cheeks, and picking up the great sword he had dropped. He winced as he stood upright, his legs faltering.

"You've fought well," Irontail replied. "Retreat for now and have a druid tend to your wounds."

The warrior nodded, limping back towards the camp. As Irontail turned to retrieve his club, he found a more formidable foe ready to face him.

Two barghest approached, but they didn't appear undead. Instead, they looked like some of the mutated creatures Irontail had faced in the past, which meant they had been transformed by Yezurkstal instead of resurrected by necromancy.

As these hulking, black furred creatures approached, Irontail held tight to his club and squared his stance. They seemed to be stalking him, both slowly stepping towards him with claws ready to attack. Doing his best to ignore the bedlam around him, Irontail focused on their movements.

Ugly and stupid. That's what he would call them. And as ugly started stepping to the right, Irontail recognized their attempt to flank him. Not wanting to give them the chance, he kicked off with his hind legs and leapt forward. Club held overhead, he attempted to bait ugly into an attack.

Just as he hoped, ugly slashed, but using his own flexibility, Irontail twisted his torso and slammed his club down on ugly's head. Breathing a sigh of relief as ugly's attack narrowly missed, he lifted his club back up and turned towards stupid.

Stupid didn't give him a chance to reevaluate, leaping into the air and going for a takedown. In the split second he had, Irontail widened his grip on the club, using it as a shield and holding it up to intercept his lunging enemy. Maybe stupid wasn't so stupid after all.

He brought up his hands, grasping the club as he impacted to soften the landing. With all the beast's weight on his club, Irontail had little choice. Pushing with all his might, he was unable to avoid it.

The club slammed into his chest, causing his to gasp for air and stumble back. Fortunately, the barghest appeared hurt as well. As the two separated, Irontail once again found he was without his club. Pushing through the pain in his chest, the centaur chieftain yelled at the top of lungs and unleashed a straight punch.

Whacking the barghest on the jaw, Irontail took a moment to collect himself. Taking a deep breath and reaffirming his aggressive stance, he stood on his hind legs and kicked with both his fore legs.

Stupid recovered faster than anticipated, and that spelled trouble. As Irontail's kick was intercepted by an upheld arm, he felt something tug at his tail. Just a moment later, he felt a sharp pain in his right hind leg. Coming back to all fours, he swiveled around to see what he was dealing with.

A zombified felite had scratched his leg and two former humans had grabbed hold of his tail. His mind raced. What was his next move?

Letting out another primal war cry, he prayed he was strong enough and grabbed hold of stupid. Clasping the enemy's broken arm, he twisted as hard as he could.

It worked.

Flinging the barghest into the felite gave him enough time to buck on his legs, kicking both the two humans in his rear and taking them down in one movement. Ignoring the burning pain in his right hind leg, he scooped up his club again.

Catching a glimpse of the melee around him, his heart sank. There were at least a dozen fallen centaurs already, and hundreds of the enemy were closing in around them. Not able to dwell on it for long, Irontail focused back on stupid and the felite, who had both gotten back to their feet.

Though stupid had clearly broken the arm he used to block Irontail's kick, it didn't seem to slow him down. The beast approached Irontail again as its felite companion ran to the side. Two other felite joined the fight as well, all four enemies circling around Irontail.

While he did his best to follow them all, he was struggling to come up with a battle plan.

"Be gone!" Irontail looked to the voice coming from behind. It was Mojo.

The shaman hopped over a fallen centaur warrior and blew a puff of red powder from his hand. Spraying the powder in the face of one of the felite, he spun around and approached a second. This time, he reached into his satchel and pulled out what looked like a bone carved into a dart. Whispering something, he threw this at the second felite.

Irontail watched as both these felite fell to the ground unmoving. Seeing his attention divided, stupid took the chance to charge in again. Caught off guard, Irontail did his best to redirect the energy of his enemy's attack. He grabbed hold of the beast's broken arm and squeezed, pulling him around to throw him to the ground.

"Kick!" Mojo shouted.

Instinctively, Irontail brayed, kicking with his hind legs, and hitting something solid. Not having a chance to turn and confirm the foe was down, he continued squeezing stupid's arm, hoping it would be enough. Stupid howled in pain as Irontail wrestled him to the ground.

Holding fast, Irontail screamed and slammed his enemy to the ground. Mojo followed up by throwing another one of his darts. It landed in stupid's arm, causing his movement to cease.

"There numbers may be too great," Mojo said, coming alongside Irontail and examining his leg.

"I can heal that, or I can do one better. You want to really do a number on these foul creatures?"

Irontail considered the shaman's words for a moment. Dozens more enemies were closing in and the sounds of pain and terror filling the air didn't fill him with confidence.

"I'd like to put as many of these monsters down as we can." Irontail said. "Whatever you have, I'll take it."

Mojo nodded, reaching into another one of his pouches and pulling out a small, red berry. "I was saving this for a rainy day, but seeing how things are starting out, I think you could really use it. You should have at least ten minutes, but make sure you're near some friends when it wears off."

Irontail nodded, grabbing the berry from Mojo, and swallowing. It tasted terrible. Somehow bitter like arugula but with a touch of blood flavoring and a spongy texture. His body felt like it might catch fire as he swallowed, a burning sensation running down into his stomach. And a moment later, everything around him seemed to slow, like time itself was coming to a halt.

He felt powerful, his muscles bulging as the pain from his injured leg melted away. It was unlike anything he had experienced before, a casual numbness taking over as he surveyed the field. What appeared as a bedlam before looked like a slow-moving exercise.

Armed only with his fists, Irontail ran back into the fray. With the force of a falling Erath tree, he tore into the enemy ranks.

## Chapter 12

Felite Encampment
7 Frozga, 1087 MT

Tel' Shira waited from her position atop the barracks. Since the Confederacy hadn't sent any reinforcements, their numbers left her worried. Hearing the dwarves were on their way was a relief, but it seemed that relief would be short lived.

"Archers, ready your arrows!" Irontail yelled from just outside the gate.

"With the dwarves, someone else is!"

Arching her eyebrows, Tel' Shira looked at the tower. What was this felite talking about?

"A pale elf, it is. Lead the dwarves, a pale elf does."

Tel' Shira shuddered, a chill running down her spine. It felt like something was crawling across her fur, her stomach tightening as she opened her eyes wide.

"Fire!" Irontail yelled.

The archers released their arrows. But Tel' Shira had more important considerations. She looked around, leaping from her spot atop the barracks and landing on all-fours just behind the archers.

"Fire!" Irontail's voice boomed out again.

Sprinting to the tower, she arrived at Tu Lora's position.

"Tu Lora. Defend the rear, we must. Yezurkstal, the pale elf is."

Tu Lora's nostrils flared; her eyes narrowed.

"Into the tower, the civilians, we must escort."

"Nor Leon," she shouted to her left, "To the garrison's rear, lead our army. To the tower, evacuate the civilians."

Without a word, Nor Leon nodded and shouted to the army.

"Felite warriors, with me."

If there was one thing you could compliment about felite soldiers, it was their ability to adapt. As the order left Nor Leon's lips, the archers all slung their bows and assumed marching order. All the melee combatants readied their weapons just as quickly, turning to follow as Nor Leon dashed around the tower.

While the rest of the army marched, Tel' Shira took one last look back at the centaur warriors. Pausing for a moment to consider whether they could hold the gate, she shook her head and ran after the others.

Past the tower, many of the soldiers who had families had constructed cottages and large tents to allow their spouses and children to live in the encampment. Fortunately, the entire population had been brought to some of the larger of such cottages, so Tel' Shira started at the nearest one first.

She pounded on the oak door as she arrived at the first one.

"To the tower, you must evacuate," she shouted. "Only what you need, take. Go now!"

Without awaiting a response, she darted around back and towards the next cottage. She spotted a small orange, spotted felite peeking out the window of this one. Sliding to a stop at the door, she pounded again.

"To the tower, evacuate! Safe there, you will be."

Seeing the felite get down from the window, she nodded and proceeded east to the third cottage. According to the plan laid out, this would be where the rest of the families were gathered.

Admiring the crescent moon design on the door to this cabin, she knocked again.

"Evacuate. To the tower, you must go. Only what you need, take!"

Looking back towards the other two cabins, she spotted lines of felite children and their protectors marching out. While many might die to protect the camp, these ones would at least stand a chance in the tower.

Breathing a sigh of relief, Tel' Shira swiveled and ran north. It only took a few seconds to catch sight of the other soldiers, who were deploying near the back wall. The archers had taken position in firing rows and stood with their bows lowered, arrows at ready.

The rest of the soldiers had assumed a defensive position a few meters in front of the archers, standing with weapons ready towards the palisades.

With Yezurkstal on the other side, it wouldn't take long for the enemy to breach the barrier. Tel' Shira scanned the area, looking for any strategic position she could assume. She spotted the start of a wooden watchtower on the northeastern part of the wall. It wasn't much, not even reaching the top of the palisades. But it would do the trick.

Tel' Shira ran to the incomplete tower and scaled the side, looking back towards the rest of the soldiers. She focused on her breathing, readying herself for the upcoming mayhem. Looking to the central tower, she waited for further instructions.

"In position!" the felite shouted from the tower.

The archers all notched their arrows, aiming over the palisades.

"Fire!"

As the dozens of arrows soared overhead, Tel' Shira wished she could see the enemy. Dwarves were hardy foes, and if Yezurkstal had turned them into undead puppets, she feared the rain of arrows would do little good. Especially considering their small numbers.

Her heart pounded as the archers launched another volley. And another.

A moment of stillness.

The felite in the tower shook his head. Tu Lora nodded.

"Weapons ready!" she shouted.

Thud.

Thud.

Thud.

Tel' Shira winced in anticipation as the pounding turned to silence.

Snap.

Wood splintered and cracked, the makeshift walls exploding inward. Tel' Shira shielded her face as splinters flew by. As the dust settled, the thunder of footsteps followed. Dozens of undead dwarves charged through the four-meter opening in the wall.

Holding her ground, Tel' Shira watched as the first wave reached her allies. Some of the strongest warriors were positioned in front, including both Nor Leon and Tu Lora. Both demonstrated the ferocity of their kind.

Nor Leon moved like a tornado, both blades extended as he flew through foul foes, furiously flaying and frantically fighting forward. Tu Lora stood her ground, swinging her claymore and cutting through the enemy ranks as they advanced.

Tel' Shira held tight, waiting for her moment to pounce as other felites entered the fray.

Many of these soldiers had no real combat experience, and it showed. A gray-furred male lunged forth, stabbing one of the dwarves through the chest. He had but a moment of surprise before the enemy swung its mace around, caving in the skull of this inexperienced felite.

Another warrior charged in with her spear, skewering two dwarves at once. As she worked to maneuver around these foes, a third dwarf came in from the side, chopping her down with its axe.

She couldn't wait any longer.

Cursing, Tel' Shira leapt from her perch, flipping mid-air, and drawing her twin daggers. She landed blades first on a nearby dwarf, plunging them into the creature's skull. Withdrawing her blades, she kicked off the fallen enemy and pounced on the next one.

As this dwarf collapsed to the ground, she had no choice but to alter her strategy.

Ducking under an incoming axe, she yanked her daggers out and slid away from this new enemy. On all four, she leapt again, narrowly avoiding the axe-fall of yet another enemy.

Tracking both dwarves, she came to her feet and flung the daggers forth. One hit its mark, embedding into the first attacker's skull, and leaving him to slump over. The other enemy brought his axe around just in time, deflecting the dagger away.

Cursing her luck, Tel' Shira squared up against the dwarf, keeping her stance wide and claws trained forward. The dwarf ran in, swinging its axe overhead. With a smirk, Tel' Shira side-stepped the attack, twisting around and grabbing hold of her enemy's arms.

Leaping onto her foe, she reached down and grabbed an arrow that was embedded in the dwarf's shoulder. Shoving the arrow into the dwarf's left eye, she backflipped over him, throwing him to the ground.

Then she heard a noise that made the fur on her back stand up straight. Chills ran down her spine and as the ground shook. An earsplitting roar of agony coming from none other than her friend, Nor Leon.

She looked in horror as a black energy coated him. He dropped his blades, writhing as he let out the most primal roar. The onslaught of dwarves split paths around him, like water running past a massive rock in the river. Clutching his chest as he went to all fours, Nor Leon struggled to look up, locking eyes with Tel' Shira.

Her lips quivered as she saw the look in his eyes. Black overtook his bright green eyes, a sea of darkness taking over. In that brief moment before his mind was enslaved, Tel' Shira could feel his mental cry for help.

She dashed towards him, scooping up his nearest sword and holding it overhead.

"Sorry, I am."

She roared, plunging the blade into her friend's chest. Tears ran down her eyes and her face burned red hot. Her knees buckled as Nor Leon fell flat.

Picking up her friend's other sword, she gulped down air. A shiver ran down her back as she surveyed the field and locked onto her enemy.

Death.

There he was, the foul, disgusting monster.

Tel' Shira trembled. Pulling the sword back and eying her foe, she tried to remove herself from the situation. A stuttered inhale, followed by a deep exhale.

She cried out and charged forward, weaving through a dozen dwarves on her way to Yezurkstal.

Leaping with sword held overhead, she swung down at her foe.

In a flash, Yezurkstal brought up his own sword, deflecting Tel' Shira's strike. It was like she had just tried to strike a mountain, a shockwave sending her to fly back and crash to the ground. The sword landed somewhere out of sight. But her adrenaline wouldn't let her stop.

Brushing herself off, she rose from the ground and charged again.

"Die, you will!" she screamed, drawing her right arm back to claw her foe.

Yezurkstal smiled, holding out his hand and unleashing a bolt of black magic.

Tel' Shira's felite reflexes kicked in. Tracking the movement of this magic, she tumbled to her left, avoiding the attack.

Rolling back onto her feet without losing any momentum, she continued her charge. As she closed in on Yezurkstal, he held his sword up defensively.

Removed from her body, Tel' Shira let her instincts take control. She stepped in to attack, anticipating Yezurkstal's stab and tucking around it. Ducking under to avoid the follow up swing, she slid through Yezurkstal's open legs, claws out.

Digging into his left ankle, she slid past and pushed off the ground behind him.

Why was his blood so cool?

She didn't have much time to ponder this, or anything else. For as she readied for a follow up attack, she felt an invisible force enveloping her.

Her chest was tight. The wind was knocked out of her as she was hurdled through the air, a black magic coating her fur.

Soaring through the air, unable to move, she watched the ground beneath fly by. Further and further away from her enemy, and from the battlefield, she flew north towards the tree line.

Barely able to register the impact, she landed against a tree. Her whole body was numb, her head slumped over as she hung suspended against a tree.

What was this sensation?

Just before her vision faded, she beheld the jagged edge of a tree branch sticking through her torso. Unable to move as her white fur turned a dark crimson, she released what she could only assume would be her last breath.

# Chapter 13

Felite Encampment
7 Frozga, 1087 MT

"Begone!"

Irontail continued his rage, galloping through the enemy ranks with arms outstretched. Whatever Mojo had given him seemed to provide an endless supply of energy and strength. These zombies snapped like twigs beneath his augmented might.

But this next opponent might really put Mojo's berry to the test.

Irontail zeroed in on a what resembled a troll. It looked mangled and malformed -even more than the standard troll. It was at least 3 meters tall, giving it a definitive height advantage. This creature had been alive when it was transformed and now resembled some sort of ogre. The full steel plate armor it wore would surely make it a worthy foe.

Or at least Irontail suspected it would have under normal circumstances. There was no way it could stop him now.

Closing the distance, Irontail ducked under the ogre's right cross, tucking in and delivering an explosive upcut to the creature's stomach. The steel armor folded under the force of Irontail's enhanced punch. Staggered from the blow, the ogre stepped back and away, clutching at its belly.

Irontail didn't give it time to recover. Reaching up, he grabbed the ogre's head and snapped its neck. Shoving the dead creature to the ground, the centaur chieftain turned back to survey the rest of the battlefield.

Dozens of his warriors had been slain in the conflict, but dozens more were still engaged in combat against the menagerie of undead foes. Mojo was still dancing through the battlefield as well, resorting to using his staff as a bludgeon at this point.

Just as Irontail started pumping his legs to charge another group of enemies, his vision blurred. An ache in the back of his head radiated forward. It felt like spiders were crawling up his arms and legs.

His arms went numb. His legs felt like jelly.

"Mojo," he shouted at the top of his lungs. Or rather he attempted to. It sounded more like a hoarse whisper.

The battlefield began to spin, his stomach boiling as he lost balance and stumbled.

"To your chieftain," a familiar voice rang in his head, the sound distant, like an echo in his memory.

A moment later, two centaur warriors came to either side, grabbing their Chieftain to keep him upright.

Head bobbing around and vision fading in and out, Irontail felt like he was removed from his body, watching the scene from above.

"Take this," the familiar voice said. It had to be Mojo. A hairy claw waved in front of his face, depositing another berry into his mouth. Irontail crushed the berry, a sickly-sweet flavor like pure, concentrated sugar.

His eyes shot open, a sharp pain running down his back and into his legs. He moaned, his vision clearing up to confirm it was Mojo who gave him the berry.

"Bring him to the druids," Mojo instructed. "Tell them to treat him for poison."

Poison?

Irontail struggled to straighten his neck, walking alongside the two centaur warriors through the carnage. The ground was littered with so many -friend and foe alike.

He wasn't sure if it was the pain, the berry, or the sheer barbarity of the battle, but as they walked him towards the camp gates, his eyes began to water. The moisture turned full on tears. And before he knew what was happening, Irontail was weeping.

How could Yezurkstal have such a callous disregard for life? So much life thrown away, and for what?

He caught sight of Oogmut, who was wrestling with an undead centaur. There were a handful of corpses lying around him, a grisly scene that caused Irontail to wince. Oogmut seemed undisturbed.

Letting out a grunt, the troll headbutted his foe. As the centaur let go and stumbled back, Oogmut reached out and placed his hand on the creature's chest. A faint light started in his palm and exploded outward. The light pulsed through the body of the reanimated centaur, causing him to convulse and collapse on the ground.

Oogmut regarded Irontail.

"What happened to him?"

"He needs to be treated for poison."

"Poison?" Oogmut's eyes were wide, palms open as he held his arms wide.

The troll stepped over the fallen dead and grabbed hold of Irontail.

"You two go back to fighting these monsters. I'll take care of your Chieftain."

As the other centaurs galloped back into the thick of things, Irontail leaned on Oogmut, who was gathering energy. A faint green aura coated his skin, flowing into his right hand. Oogmut closed his eyes and placed the palm of his glowing hand on Irontail's head.

"This is Mojo's doing, isn't it?"

Irontail could feel the magic flowing into him, the hair on his shoulders standing on end. The pain in the back of his head was replaced with a tingling sensation. His vision sharpened and his legs stabilized.

Standing up on his own, he blinked rapidly. A pain flared in his chest, like someone plunged a dagger into his heart. He gasped for air and his vision went dark.

Blowing out the breath, everything came back into focus, and he locked eyes with Oogmut. The troll withdrew his hand from Irontail, the magic fading away.

"Never take something from a shaman without knowing what you're taking. That could have killed you!"

146

Irontail shook his head, holding his hands out front and looking at his fists. He reached up and wiped the tears from his eyes.

"I think it nearly did," Irontail mumbled, turning back to survey the battlefield behind them.

It appeared the worst of it was over, at least on this front. The couple dozen remaining centaur warriors were closing ranks, uniting with Mojo to take out the remaining groups of undead. But Irontail remembered this was not the only battle being fought.

"We should assist the felite," Irontail suggested. "Mojo and the others can take care of the rest of these. I take it the Avatar went that way?"

"Yes," Oogmut replied. "While you and your troops charged in, the Avatar and Aeria both joined the felite. I wouldn't try to get back into the thick of it if I were you though. The Avatar will ensure victory on that front."

"Maybe, but I'm not willing to wait around and find out. I'm going that way. If you think I need more medical attention, then maybe you should come as well."

Irontail started off, his hind legs buckling as he took the first couple steps. Shaking his arms at his side and stretching his neck, he paused and took a deep breath.

Continuing at a slow trot, he made his way through the gates and into the encampment. Oogmut came alongside him, keeping up with a steady jog.

"I guess there's no sense in fighting it."

The two made their way past the tower, the sounds of the centaurs fading as the struggle from the felites, and dwarves grew. As they approached, it was clear this battle wasn't going any better than the first.

A hole had been punched through the wall. And the field within the wall was filled with fallen dwarves and felites. The few remaining felite warriors were losing ground to the couple dozen remaining dwarves.

"Don't overdo it," Oogmut muttered, placing his hand on Irontail's shoulder.

Irontail felt a warmth coming from the spot, allowing his muscles to relax. His whole body still ached from whatever Mojo had given him. But as the warmth spread throughout his body, his muscles twitched. He had some fight left in him.

Marching towards the combatants, Irontail said a silent prayer. Oogmut kept stride with him, the lumbering troll wearing a determined look. Eyes forward and fists clenched, it appeared he was collecting more magical energy for the conflict ahead.

Recognizing the need for his own focus, Irontail locked eyes on the nearest enemies. There was a group of half a dozen dwarves engaged with a pair of felite warriors. The male felites appeared similar in stature, both around two meters tall with barrel chests and short hair. One had orange fur and black stripes and the other had brown fur with white splotches. Stripe and Splotch.

Each was fighting with twin short swords. They were struggling to parry blows of their attackers. And with each blow they deflected, they were losing ground. Looking just past them, Irontail saw a more pressing concern. A pair of axe-wielding dwarves charged towards the melee, looking to take the felites from behind.

"Evorath help me," Irontail murmured as he pumped his legs. Despite the effort he was exerting, he couldn't get up to a full gallop. But with a speedy trot, he made his way forward.

The battlefield was riddled with fallen soldiers on both side, which meant there were plenty of unclaimed weapons about. And Irontail saw one that would serve him well. As he closed in on this pair of dwarves, he slowed down to pick up a war hammer. Though his back protested, he pushed through the stiffness and lifted the mythril hammer into his right hand.

Drawing the hammer back, he resumed his charge. Reaching the first dwarf, he swung. His blow landed with a thud, caving in this first foe's skull. The second enemy adjusted his approach, squaring up against Irontail.

Normally, this wouldn't be a contest. But in his current state, the centaur Chieftain exercised caution. He waited, watching as his foe squeezed its axe and tip-toed around its larger opponent. Its skin was pale, an arrow sticking out from the back of its neck. Scowl upon its face and blood dripping from its mouth, it appeared rabid.

The two continued their dance for a few more seconds. Suddenly, the dwarf darted at Irontail. With a deep inhale, the centaur pulled back his hammer and held for just a moment. Blowing out his breath, he swung.

And with a thud, another foe was defeated.

Turning back to help Stripe and Splotch, he noticed Oogmut had already stepped into the fray. In fact, as he took count, Oogmut stomped on one of the former dwarves, crushing the profane little creature beneath his foot.

Only four of the zombies remained. And as they tried to regroup, Stripe took advantage of the decrease in numbers. He deflected a strike from one foe and while the enemy was off-balance, he leapt over the other. Landing behind this second foe, he swung his left blade, decapitating the enemy.

Irontail trotted into the fight, cocking his hammer, and swinging at Stripe's other dwarven foe. The dwarf dove away from the swing, rolling over and coming back up with its axe at the ready. With its attention on Irontail, Stripe moved in with a low swing, dismembering the creature's legs. It let out a shriek, stumbling to the ground.

Even with its legs missing, the creature seemed determined to continue its attack. Crawling towards Irontail, foaming at the mouth, the zombie growled. Irontail shook his head, bringing down his hammer to put an end to the creature once and for all.

Seeing Oogmut and Splotch had finished off the other two, the quartet all exchanged a quick glance and a nod. Without a word, Stripe and Splotch took off towards the next group to the north, which included four zombies driving back Tu Lora.

With her massive sword, Tu Lora seemed able to shield herself well enough. But they were pushing her back with every strike, looking to make a hole in her defenses. Irontail went to follow behind as well, but as he trotted towards her, he felt a sharp pain in his right, hind leg.

Stumbling, he reached out and caught on to Oogmut, who had come up to his side.

"You'd best sit the rest of this out. I don't have the time or energy to help you properly recover from this. It's amazing you were able to do this much."

Irontail shook his head.

"I am the Chieftain of Dumner. As long as I draw breath, I cannot sit by and watch as the battle rages."

"I can't stop you, but don't get yourself killed. Dumner needs you."

Irontail nodded, stumbling north towards the fray. Oogmut marched to the west towards an uncontested group of dwarves -it looked like there were five of them, fresh felite blood covering their armor.

As he moved forward, Irontail watched Stripe and Splotch step in and help Tu Lora. It didn't look like they would need his assistance, so he focused on the sound coming from the other side of the wall.

Making his way forward, he spotted the main event.

Just outside the camp's walls, the Avatar was locked in combat with Yezurkstal. A mere twenty meters away, but they may as well have been twenty kilometers.

The two were grappling, the Avatar holding onto both Yezurkstal's arms and squeezing. But something was wrong. The last time these two engaged in a physical conflict like this, the Avatar had a clear leg up. Now, it appeared he was struggling to hold Yezurkstal at bay.

Fortunately, he was not alone. As he kept hold of Yezurkstal, Aeria swooped down from above. She had a dagger in hand. Closing this distance, she jabbed at Yezurkstal's back. The dark elf moved just in time, dragging the Avatar with him as he pivoted away.

But Aeria's strike landed! She swooped away, leaving the dagger embedded in Yezurkstal's shoulder.

"Worthless feklar!" Yezurkstal cursed.

Irontail felt a tightness in his chest. The air around him seemed to thicken as he looked on. A dark energy enveloped Yezurkstal and the Avatar. The energy exploded out, sending a shockwave all around the pair.

As the energy struck Aeria, she fell from the sky. Screaming as she hit the ground, the Avatar stumbled back and held his hands out in front of his face. They were shaking.

Pushing through the pain, Irontail continued moving towards the conflict. He could barely feel his legs at this point, each step a chore.

Yezurkstal pulled the knife from his shoulder, coating it with dark magic.

"Meet your worthless goddess."

He threw the knife. It cut through the air and found its rest in Aeria's chest. She let out a final shriek, writhing in pain as she crumbled to dust.

"No!" the Avatar bellowed, his voice booming through the clearing.

Yezurkstal pulled his sword from his sheath, grasping it with both hands and turning back to the Avatar.

"You'll join her soon enough."

Irontail couldn't stand by and watch. He had to do something. But it seemed his willpower just wouldn't be enough this time.

He stumbled forward, heaving as he fell to his knees. His chest throbbed as he sat there helpless, watching the fight continue.

The Avatar's eyes narrowed as he clenched his fists and took a few steps away from Yezurkstal.

"Death really is a befitting name for you. That's how you escaped from your prison, isn't it? You no longer walk with the living. But you fail to understand the truth. Death can never truly defeat Life."

Bringing his palms together in front of his chest, the Avatar twisted to his right. He opened his hands, forming a triangle shape. A green mass of magical energy formed within his palms. As Yezurkstal lunged for a strike, the Avatar twisted back around, holding his arms out straight and unleashing a turret of green energy.

Yezurkstal was caught by surprise, the beam impacting his sword and tearing it from his hands. While he recoiled, the Avatar redirected hands, aiming directly for his enemy. The beam struck Yezurkstal in the chest, pushing him back.

The dark elf dug his heels into the ground as he struggled to bring his arms back down to block the Avatar's magic.

Managing to bring his hands up around the beam of green magic, Yezurkstal shoved towards the Avatar. Dark energy coated his hands and trickled out into the beam. As both warriors stood with arms extended, the dark energy began pushing back the Avatar's attack.

"If you are the best Life has to offer, Death will always win out."

Watching these two locked in their magical exchange, Irontail almost missed the dwarf coming up on his left. Spotting the foe at the last minute, he threw his arms up to block the attack.

His enemy's axe landing firm in his left arm, bone snapping as the blade was left embedded in his flesh. Letting out a holler, the Chieftain did his best to ignore the throbbing pain. He used his good arm to grab hold of the dwarf and pull him close.

With only one hand to maneuver, he used the last of his strength to slam the dwarf into the ground.

He did it again, and again until the dwarf stopped moving.

Letting the dwarf fall, he examined the axe in his left arm. There wasn't much blood, probably because the axe was lodged in there so tightly. But he couldn't feel a thing either, a complete numbness overcoming that left arm and radiating up to his shoulder.

Turning back to witness the Avatar and Yezurkstal's struggle, Irontail considered for the first time whether Death might win.

The Avatar was losing ground.

And the last thing Irontail saw before losing consciousness was the darkness overtaking the light.

## Chapter 14

Dumner Village
9 Frozga, 1087 MT

Snow had been falling all morning. And as the sun reached its peak in the afternoon sky, Artimus continued his watch from the eastern guard post.

A far cry from the watchtowers elves would construct, he discovered that Dumner utilized a kind of seeing spell in these strategic watch locations. It was a bit disorienting at first, his vision augmented to show a fully clear, 180-degree view. But as he stood guard, he now wished he could get this spell put on all elvish watchtowers.

Savannah was seated next to him, bundled up in her fur coat and a large wool blanket. She took a bite from her apple, the prolonged crunch reverberating through the trees. Artimus looked at her, smiling as he considered all they had been together over the past year.

"You sure you don't want one?" she asked, holding out an untouched green apple and smiling between bites.

"No, thank you. I'll wait until our watch is over in a couple hours. I really thought we would have heard something by now."

Artimus kept his eyes trained forward as his wife took another bite and nodded.

"We don't even know for sure when Tel' Shira's vision was. They may have just engaged Yezurkstal this morning."

As usual, she was right. She was always able to keep a level head in these situations, a quality Artimus had come to admire. But in this cold afternoon snow, the uncertainty was unbearable. And part of him wished he had joined the others in going to the felite camp.

"You wish you went with them, don't you?"

Artimus looked back to Savannah, his mouth agape. She took another bite of her apple, chewing away with a smile.

"Have you been studying some new form of mind magic I wasn't aware of?"

"No," she replied after she finished chewing. "But I know your face too well. And that expression is more than worry - you're thinking you should have been there to help. But you're wrong."

"Am I?" Artimus countered, pulling his coat tight tapping his foot. "How so?"

"First, one extra bow wouldn't turn the tide of that battle. Second, your place is here with me and our unborn child."

She took another bite, exposing more of the apple's core. As she chewed, Artimus considered her words.

"Of course, you're right," he replied after a few moments. "And there's no place I'd rather be than here with you. But that doesn't make waiting here any easier. Especially not with how cold it is!"

He stomped his foot and rubbed his arms. Taking a few hops, he looked back around.

"Perhaps I should start a fire if we're going to be out here in this wretched weather."

"We might not be here much longer. Look!"

Savannah stood up and pointed off in the distance.

Artimus's heart nearly flew out of his chest as he beheld their approaching allies. At this distance, he couldn't make out how many were returning, but he could see the slow approach of centaurs in the distance.

As he stood watching, he could also confirm Oogmut and Mojo were among the survivors, their figures unmistakable amongst the others. Continuing their march, it also became apparent they were bringing along surviving felite as well, with a handful of them interspersed within the ranks. It was difficult to tell much more from this distance.

"Go out and meet them. I'd go with you, but I finally got comfortable."

Smiling at his wife, Artimus started off towards the approaching party. He stomped through the snow as quick as he could, hoping forward and trying to avoid sinking too much into the heavy snow. The only problem with this approach was that he had to look down to mind his steps. But after a few minutes trek, he looked up and saw some familiar faces approaching.

Unfortunately, there were not nearly as many of them as he had hoped.

Oogmut was near the front of the group, his face downcast and eyes somber. It appeared everyone in the party had a dark cloud overhead. A few of the leading centaurs had strapped carts to their backs and Artimus's heart sank as he realized why.

These were simple supply carts, crafted of pine and measuring just about two meters long and less than one meter deep. They would typically be pulled by a couple horses or donkeys. But their haul was not typical. Instead, it appeared they were carrying back the injured.

This nearest cart contained a centaur warrior, blood staining much of his upper torso. And as Artimus looked closely, he only counted three legs. If not for shallow breathing and the faint moans of pain, he might have been presumed dead.

Trying to fight off a sense of panic, Artimus began moving from cart to cart. Each contained a felite or centaur who had sustained some manner of injury. He doubted any of them would fully recover from these injuries.

In total, there couldn't be more than a couple dozen centaurs still on their feet. And the felite walking with the convey appeared mostly to be civilians, many of them small children. And the more he looked at these survivors, their bodies scarred and bruised, the more his heart raced.

Just as he was ready to scream, he spotted the faces he was looking for. Near the rear of the march, he recognized Irontail and the Avatar. But that still left one person missing. Dragging himself through the snow, Artimus approached the centaur Chieftain, whose right arm was in a sling.

"Please tell me that she is going to be alright."

Irontail avoided his gaze, shaking his head and glancing back at his cart.

Artimus looked down. Tel' Shira lay mangled in the cart. Her brilliant fur, once white as snow, was stained a crimson red. Both her legs were offset, clearly broken from a forceful impact. And judging by the way she laid in the cart, that wasn't the only damage she had sustained.

"She's still alive," the Avatar offered, his voice laced with regret. "But her days as a warrior are done."

Artimus felt a knot in his throat as he looked upon his broken friend.

"What about Yezurkstal?" he asked, his voice cracking.

The group continued their march towards town, neither Irontail nor the Avatar offering an immediate answer. Just as Artimus was ready to pry, the Avatar finally spoke.

"I failed to defeat him."

Irontail regarded the Avatar, eyes heavy and wearing the frown.

"But his army has been decimated. Now is the time for us to go on the offensive."

The Avatar shook his head, his face downcast.

"We have already lost too many lives. I need to meditate on our next move."

Artimus recognized the look in Irontail's face. His eyes sagged and lips quivered. His doubt was understandable. And as they continued marching in silence with the rest of the survivors, Artimus couldn't help but wonder himself.

If the Avatar couldn't overpower Yezurkstal, did they even have a chance at victory?

Glancing back at the felites who had come along, Artimus took inventory. As he suspected, they all appeared to be civilians. Many carried sacks or dragged along small hand carts. Only a few were equipped with weapons of any kind. Most of them were children.

One of the children in particular stuck out to Artimus. It might have been because she was crying, or perhaps because she walked a meter behind the rest of the group. Or maybe it was the jet-black fur that covered her from head to toe. Whatever the case, he recognized the look of anguish.

Her tail dragged through the snow. She clutched a small stuffed toy resembling a fish to her chest. And her eyes were void pools of despair. He couldn't say why, but at that moment, Artimus felt it would be better if he walked alongside her.

Stopping his march, he waited in place and let the felites catch up to him. As the rest of the group passed by, he took position next to the little girl and matched her stride.

"What is your name?"

The girl startled, jumping back and shivering. Her eyes widened as she looked over Artimus from head-to-toe.

"Luna Freya," she replied sheepishly, her high-pitched voice laced with more sorrow than anyone that age should ever have to endure.

"My name is Artimus," the investigator said extending his hand to the girl. "It's really cold out here. Do you want to walk with me?"

Luna Freya glared at him, her whiskers quivering. She looked like she might burst into tears, her eyelids shaking as she opened her mouth.

"I. Don't know." She whimpered.

"It's alright. You don't have to be alone."

Tears welled up in her eyes and she leapt into Artimus's arms. Caught a little off guard, Artimus stumbled, his back flaring up as he regained his balance. Catching Luna Freya in his arms, he squeezed her tight and patted her head.

"I. Am. Alone." She uttered between tears.

"It's alright. You will be safe here Luna Freya. And you won't have to be alone again if you don't want to."

She nuzzled into his chest, and he kept her held tight. Walking back through the snow towards the guard post. Wanting to catch up with Irontail and the Avatar, he did his best to pick up the pace.

The head of the caravan had already made it into the village, but Artimus did manage to push through the snow and catch up with Irontail just as they arrived at the guard post.

Savannah was standing there watching as the first of the survivors went past. Irontail paused as he reached her, looking back at Artimus and the others.

"We're going to the central mound. We could use your abilities to help tend to the wounded."

"Of course!" Savannah blurted. She stepped forward and looked at Tel' Shira in the cart.

Her face flushed, her mouth dropping open in surprise. Irontail snorted, rubbing his eyes and starting towards the village center.

"Oh, no," she muttered, her eyes welling up with tears. Artimus stepped forward, shifting Luna Freya into his right arm, and pulling her to his side. He embraced his wife with his left, holding her close and crying tears of his own.

"She couldn't be in better hands," he offered.

Savannah squeezed him, sobbing as she did. He sniffled, trying to maintain composure for both his wife and for little Luna Freya. The cold air stung, his eyes feeling like they might freeze over.

After maintaining the embrace for a few more seconds, he pulled away and wiped his tears with his left. With another sniffle, he held Luna Freya up.

"I think Luna Freya here could use a friend. Maybe you can take her with you, and she can be there when Tel' Shira wakes up."

Sucking in a deep breath, Savannah wiped her tears and looked at Luna Freya. She paused for a moment, looking back at Artimus, and offering a faint smile.

"Hello Luna Freya. My name is Savannah," she wiped her face again, eyes glistening as she swallowed back more tears.

"Do you want to come with me? I think I could use the company."

Luna Freya looked up at Artimus.

"You come too?"

Artimus nodded, clenching his jaw and forcing a smile.

"I will come after I get someone to stand watch here. I must make sure the village is safe. But Savannah is my wife. She will look after you and make sure you are safe."

Luna Freya glanced at Savannah and nodded. Artimus held her out, allowing Savannah to take her in her arms and wrap her with the blanket.

The two elves paused, locking eyes, and holding each other's gaze for a moment. In that moment, they knew one another's thoughts.

Yezurkstal would pay.

## Chapter 15

Dumner Village
9 Frozga, 1087 MT

Savannah stood over her broken friend. She concentrated on the open wound in Tel' Shira's stomach, channeling magical energy to promote healing and stitch the wound shut. While the Avatar had stabilized her for transport, the felite warrior was still in bad shape. Focusing on healing her friend was the only way Savannah knew to keep the grief at bay.

While it was not actively bleeding, this large puncture required continual attention. Only one surviving felite had seen what happened and from the story told, Tel' Shira was lucky to be alive at all. As if being impaled weren't bad enough, the concussive force left her with dozens of broken bones, some of them shattered beyond repair. But Savannah refused to give up hope.

"Excuse me, Miss Atyrmirid," interrupted a feminine voice.

Continuing to pour magic into the puncture wound, she looked towards the source of the voice. It was Silkhair, a young centaur with light brown fur and flowing brown hair. She had greeted the returning war party and had been here tending to the wounded since they arrived.

"Please, Silkhair. Just call me Savannah. What is it?"

Silkhair blushed and took a slight bow. "My apologies Mi- I mean Savannah. The other patients are just resting now, but before I return to my work in the fields I wanted to see if I could get you anything."

Savannah nodded, keeping her eyes trained on Tel' Shira's wounds and continuing to pour out healing magic.

"Thank you Silkhair. I think there are a few things I could use. First though, I've not been able to fully clean the blood off Tel' Shira's fur. If you could fetch a pail of water to help with that, it would be great."

"I'll get one now," Silkhair exclaimed.

While she trotted outside, Savannah kept her eyes trained on her patient. Her hand started to tingle, a slight numbness beginning in her fingertips.

With a sigh, she released her spell. She couldn't remember the last time she ran into this problem, but it wouldn't do her any good to overdo it. Perhaps while Silkhair fetched water, Savannah could get some rest and recharge.

Since they were using the barracks to treat the wounded, the best source of magic was close by. Grabbing her coat off the rack and wrapping herself tight, Savannah went outside and shut the door behind her. The snow was still falling, but it resembled more of a light dusting than the steady fall from the early afternoon.

Keeping hands close to her chest, she stomped through the snow towards the central mound. Despite all the snowfall, the magic of this living wonder kept it free from cover. The pulsing vines moved about freely, and Savannah could feel the verdant energy calling to her.

168

Approaching the mound, she simply thought about entry. The vines responded, spreading apart, and opening a path for her to descend inside. Stepping down the steady slope, she let out a sigh of relief as the warm air hit her. Despite the freezing weather outside, this mound maintained a year-round warmth.

Opening her coat to enjoy the tepid air, she could already feel some of the latent magic around her. Just walking through these halls would help restore her magical reserves, but the baby in her womb demanded something a bit more. Stepping into the room on the right, she passed through the entry and looked around.

No one else was in the room, which was a relief. She didn't feel like socializing with anyone.

The room had tables set up on the three walls, along with some storage crates underneath them. The centaurs had laid out a variety of foods. For centaurs, this meant mostly fruits and vegetables. But right now, Savannah was interested in one of the baked goods.

Walking to the table on the right, she looked across the apples and berries that had been laid out. To the left of these, there were a couple loaves of bread. Taking the bread knife, she cut off a thick end piece -about six centimeters. If she were at home, she would slather it in some preserves. Since none were available, she instead grabbed a handful of blueberries.

With bread in one hand and berries in the other, she meandered out of the room, taking a single berry and following it up with a bite of the bread. It had a soft, spongy texture. While a bit yeasty for her taste, the subtle hint of rosemary provided for an unexpected delight.

For a moment, she almost let herself forget about how dire the situation was with Tel' Shira. But only for a moment.

Still, she recognized the importance of taking care of herself. So, she continued to walk deeper into the central mound, eating one berry at a time and following up with a bite of this delicious bread. While her stomach was filled with food, her body was absorbing more of the green magic so prevalent in this mound.

Getting about halfway through her snack, she took one more bite and turned around. While she might have needed this break, she also wouldn't allow herself to spend any more time away from Tel' Shira than was necessary. By the time she made it back to the entrance, she had finished the berries and the bread.

She looked down at her stomach, watching for the expected clamor of kicks. There was a light fluttering after she ate, something she had come to expect these past couple of weeks. With a gentle smile, she stood there for a few seconds enjoying this flutter before pulling her coat tight and willing the entrance open.

The abrupt chill of the outside air caused her to shiver as she stepped outside, the mound closing behind her. In the few minutes she had been in there, it seemed the weather had taken a turn for the worse. A steady snowfall greeted her out here, the wind causing it to fall sideways.

Not wanting to be exposed to the elements more than necessary, she hurried back to the barracks, keeping her hands tight within her armpits. As she arrived inside the barracks, she slammed the door shut and rushed over to the fireplace. She held her hands out for a few moments, letting the heat of the flames wash over her. Feeling a wave of relief from the cold, she opened her coat and returned to the entrance to hang it back up.

As she did, the door was opened and Silkhair marched back inside. She placed down the bucket of water and shook herself off. A smile on her face, she bent down and retrieved the water pail.

"It's getting so cold out there I might need a coat if it keeps up!"

Savannah grinned and nodded.

"Yes, it seems it just picked up again. I will definitely be happy to stay indoors until it dies back down."

"I might stay here as well, if it won't bother you. Should I warm this water?"

"Yes, please. And of course. It won't bother me," Savannah lied. She would have preferred to be alone, but she couldn't in good conscious ask someone else to sacrifice their comfort for it.

While Silkhair took the water to warm over the fire, Savannah walked back over to Tel' Shira's bed. The felite's breathing was shallow. So shallow that it was almost imperceptible. Upon close examination, one could only just see the slow rise and fall of her chest.

Closing her eyes, Savannah held her hands over Tel'
Shira, palms facing down. She took a deep breath, holding it for a
second before exhaling. Putting a small amount magical energy
into her fingertips, she probed her friend's wounds yet again.

Since before they had been married, Artimus had been
asking her to explain how this magic worked. While she could go
into detail about the discipline of using magic, she still hadn't
figured out an adequate way of describing the nuances of the
process. But when she used this spell, she could see images of the
injuries sustained.

Her mouth twitched as those images passed through her
mind. Both legs were fractured, ribs were cracked, and while the
puncture wound was done hemorrhaging, there was still at least a
two-centimeter gap in Tel' Shira's torso. Worst of all, she saw
what used to be vertebrae, shattered, and broken from the impact.

Returning to the moment, Savannah opened her eyes and
took a step back.

"You're going to survive this," she whispered.

"What was that?" Silkhair asked, approaching with the
bucket of water.

"Oh, nothing. Just talking to myself. Is the water ready?"

"Yes, it should be warm enough for us to clean her up.
Let me go grab some more clean rags."

Silkhair placed the bucket down and trotted further into
the barracks.

Savannah felt a soft jab in her stomach. She rested her hand in the spot, smiling as the child kicked again. Burdened by the current situation, she offered a silent prayer to Evorath. Perhaps they could put an end to Yezurkstal's terror before the child was born.

"Here they are," Silkhair said. "Would you like me to clean around the wound?"

Savannah shook her head.

"I'd prefer to do it myself. But if you'd like to help, I wouldn't mind you just holding up the bucket and rags so I can work on it more easily."

"Of course! I'll do whatever I can to help."

So Silkhair reached down and lifted the water pail in her right hand and held the rags in her left. With a quick count, it looked like there were four rags in total, which should be sufficient for now.

Taking the first one and dunking it in the water, Savannah swirled it around. Fully soaked, she removed the rag and wrung it out. She proceeded to dab around Tel' Shira's torso. Her fur was thoroughly matted with blood, so even though they had tried to clean it when she first arrived, there were still heavy deposits.

The warm water would hopefully help loosen it up a little and make it easier to clear out. Continuing to pat around the bloodied area, Savannah squeezed some of the extra liquid out, further dampening Tel' Shira's fur. She waited for a few moments before wiping some more, careful to avoid touching the site of the puncture directly.

173

After about a minute of this, the rag appeared to be turning crimson itself. So, she tossed it aside and repeated the process a second time. And then a third.

By the third pass, Tel' Shira's fur was looking less crimson and more of her snowy white color was showing through. There was still a tinge of red, but all the major mats had been cleared away.

Dropping this rag directly in the water pail, she grabbed the final one and worked on patting the felite's fur dry. As she did, she regarded the two rags on the floor.

"You can put the bucket over there now. I'll grab the rags when I finish up."

"Oh, don't worry about it," Silkhair objected. "I'll get them."

While Silkhair picked up the dirty rags and added them to the bucket, Savannah continued drying Tel' Shira's fur.

"Do you think she will be waking up soon?" Silkhair asked.

Savannah closed her eyes, taking a breath in through her nose and blowing it out slowly through pursed lips. Opening her eyes, she shook her head.

"I really can't say. The Avatar said she hadn't awoken since they found her. She could wake up today. But I've seen elves injured like this who took more than a week before they came back from it. A felite druid might be able to better tell.

They'd probably be better equipped to heal her too. But we don't have any of them here unfortunately."

Silkhair frowned, trotting to Savannah, and placing her hand on the elf's shoulder.

"It is unfortunate that none of the felite soldiers survived. I've never seen so many widows and orphans. But from what I hear, your friend is in the most capable hands."

With a couple more pats, Savannah finished drying off Tel' Shira and held out the rag to Silkhair. The centaur let go of Savannah's shoulder and took the rag.

"Thank you Silkhair. I hope you're right. I really thought the Avatar would have been able to do more for her. And for the others injured for that matter."

"I was a little afraid to ask, but do you know why he can't?" Silkhair questioned.

"I didn't get a straight answer either, but I suspect it's his nature. He was summoned to be a physical embodiment of Evorath's might. It seems his healing abilities are limited based on that purpose."

"I see," Silkhair stated. "I wasn't a member of the village when you performed the Xyrloom to summon him, but you were part of that ritual, right? Could you perform another ritual to summon forth an Avatar of Evorath's healing grace?"

Savannah twirled some strands of hair between her fingers and thought.

"Unfortunately, I don't think it would work that way. The Xyrloom is based on an ancient ritual that Evorath used during creation. But the ancient texts that describe it are incomplete. I think it's only through the blessing of Evorath that we succeeded at all."

"How do you mean?" Silkhair asked, leaning in with eyes wide.

"Like I said, the ancient texts are all missing elements. We had the Dryad of birch help us perform the ritual, along with eight of us druids to represent the eight species of Erathal forest. In the village I grew up in, we had scholars that devoted their lives to studying texts about the Xyrloom and they still missed the importance of having that diverse representation."

Savannah paused, glancing back at Tel' Shira.

"But one thing that is common in texts on the ritual is that it could be used to summon a protector. With all that in mind, the Avatar himself has stated he was sent by Evorath. So, while some who participated in the ritual might like to think they helped summon the Avatar, I look at it differently. We merely prayed and Evorath answered."

Silkhair looked down at the rags in the bucket, her eyes staying downcast for a few moments.

"I hope you're right. In case you are, I'll say some extra prayers for Tel' Shira's healing. Maybe that will be enough for Evorath to work a miracle."

Savannah smiled, stepping closer to Tel' Shira and placing her hand on the felite's forehead.

"It couldn't hurt. I just pray Tel' Shira will have the strength to move forward, whatever the future might hold."

As she said this, she noticed Tel' Shira's whiskers twitch. Looking closer, she recognized her friend's chest was expanding more than before. Leaning in to listen, she could hear labored breathing.

"What is it?" Silkhair asked.

"I'm not sure. Hold on."

Savannah held her hands over Tel' Shira's chest and channeled some arcane energy. With a faint glow of green around her hands, she placed them gently down and probed. Could it be?

Moving her left hand to Tel' Shira's forehead, Savannah transferred some of her energy into her friend. She stared intently, wishing Tel' Shira to awaken.

As Tel' Shira eyes opened, Savannah greeted her with a smile.

-=-=-=-=-=-=-=-=-

Tel' Shira opened her eyes. Her vision was blurred, faint shapes and foggy lights before her.

"*Where am I?*" she thought.

She couldn't move, her entire body numb from the chest down. There was an intense pressure in the base of her skull, just above her neck. Trying to lift her head only intensified this pain, like someone was jabbing a rod into her neck.

Realizing the futility of her attempt, she focused on clearing up her vision. Was that…Savannah?

Tel' Shira opened her mouth, trying to form words. Nothing but breath escaped her lips, but seeing the smiling face of her friend Savannah gave her hope.

Her vision blurred again, and the room spun. Feeling her consciousness slip away, she clung to Savannah's words.

"You're going to be OK."

## Chapter 16

Dumner Village
9 Frozga, 1087 MT

Irontail was exhausted, his legs wobbly and eyes heavy. His arm ached; the axe wound closed but the pain still lingering. As the Avatar entered the meeting hall, he did his best to remain attentive.

"Thank you for being patient," the Avatar said as he walked towards Irontail.

Artimus, Mojo, Oogmut, Casandra, Zelag, Porra and Pogo had all been assembled. While they sat around the meeting table, the Avatar proceeded to the front and took a seat next to Irontail.

"First, I want to say that I am sorry. I take full responsibility for our failure in this latest battle. Allowing the death of so many of Evorath's children is a shame I will bare for as long as I live."

"Excuse me," Oogmut interrupted, standing up from his seat.

"I think everyone here feels a certain responsibility for how the battle went down. But let's not waste time assigning blame. Had the dwarves been on our side, that battle would have gone completely differently. We need to address that first. How did Yezurkstal anticipate our moves?"

"I'd like to know how any creature on Evorath can command that much power," Mojo interjected. "We've all heard terrors of necromancers. But Yezurkstal commanded a number far greater than any legend. His army was far too well-coordinated."

"These are both symptoms of the same problem," the Avatar replied.

"There are two things to understand about this evil we've commonly referred to as Death. First, let's address what has changed, and the reason he was able to escape the prison I locked him in. Yezurkstal is no longer alive."

The room was filled with gasps, everyone exchanging glances. Pogo even let slip a verbal "what?"

"The exact mechanisms of how are unimportant, but he must have figured out a way to turn himself undead while retaining all his abilities. In fact, it seems his undeath has made him stronger. Others in Evorath's history have profaned nature and resurrected the dead. But no one has ever extended their own time on Evorath in such a manner. This is a new kind of necromancy, one with terrifying implications."

"How so?" Irontail asked.

"Necromancy is not a gift from Evorath. To tap into it, one must call upon the dark goddess Frogatha. As you know, Frogatha is also the patron of demons and mistress over demonic forces. The Demon Wars were Frogatha's attempt to destroy Evorath's beautiful creation. Since then, necromancers have popped up here and there, worshiping Frogatha and being granted her boon. But those necromancers never had the power Yezurkstal does."

"It makes sense that he can do necromancy" Mojo interjected. "After all, Yezurkstal is a servant of Frogatha himself."

"No, I'm afraid he's more than that," the Avatar replied.

"I have been a fool this whole time. Evorath sent me as a response to your Xyrloom just a couple years ago. My mission was clear: to stop Yezurkstal from destroying Her world. But there was a catch, which brings us to the second important consideration around Death. Yezurkstal's mother was an unwilling participant, a worthy servant of Evorath. So, when she was raped by a servant of Frogatha, the child she bore was something never conceived of before. This dark union created a contradiction so powerful that the seeds of discord were felt far beyond the shores of Erathal."

Irontail found himself leaning in, listening intently as the Avatar continued.

"Had someone intervened early on, it's possible Yezurkstal could have been brought to the side of Life. But Yezurkstal signed his oath to the forces of Death and sealed the deal with the blood of his own mother -the innocent blood of a servant of Evorath. This is what gives him such extraordinary power. While I am an Avatar of the creator Evorath, he could be, somewhat inaccurately, considered an Avatar of his own mistress, Frogatha."

"But Evorath is more powerful than Frogatha," Casandra jumped in. "Isn't that why Frogatha attacked this world to begin with? Because she was jealous of Evorath's power?"

"That's just a myth," Oogmut interjected.

"No, I'm pretty sure it's true," suggested Pogo.

"It's irrelevant," the Avatar asserted. "Yes, Frogatha is less powerful than Evorath. In the divine playing field, Life always conquers Death. But I am not Evorath any more than Yezurkstal is Frogatha. I am simply a servant, one of Her many Avatars. I therefore draw from Her power, but only so much as I was made to."

"Please don't say what I think you're going to say," Mojo interrupted.

The Avatar nodded, steepling his hands and looking around the room.

"In my prayers to Evorath today, it has been made clear. Yezurkstal has not come near to his full potential. Frogatha, a goddess of death and decay, could not create life. At least not in the sense we think of life. So, while Evorath created this world in her image, a world full of diverse life and verdant growth, Frogatha created a dark, pale world. The realm of the demons.

"Even her creations within that world are mere shadows of creatures. The reason demons vary so greatly in size and shape is a sign of how they have come to be. They are lost, twisted souls. Without the capacity to truly create new life, Frogatha takes these souls and molds them into her servants. But it was different with Yezurkstal. Yezurkstal has the spark of life that one can only get by being a child of Evorath. He got that from his mother."

"So, he is more powerful than you," Mojo blurted.

182

"No," the Avatar shouted. "At least not yet. But while I was designed to serve a singular purpose, Yezurkstal was appointed to be Frogatha's first true creation. He is her first true son. In theory, because of Evorath's spark within him, he could grow to become more powerful than the goddess he serves."

"Then we have to stop him now," Porra chimed in.

"Yes," echoed Pogo. "Before he gets too strong."

"But how are we supposed to accomplish that?" Mojo asked.

"We exploit his weakness," the Avatar offered, rising to his feet.

"And what, pray tell, is his weakness?" Porra asked.

"Put simply, me. It was clear in our last fight that he was eager to prove himself. He thought he had gained enough power to defeat me. And when I proved he couldn't, it pushed him to the point that I almost got the upper hand. In fact, it wasn't until all his army were defeated that he finally fled."

"That's true," Oogmut interrupted. "It wasn't until the felites, and I were ready to join the battle that Yezurkstal finally fled."

"Precisely," the Avatar responded.

"So what?" Artimus asked. "Are you suggesting you go after Yezurkstal alone?"

"Not exactly," the Avatar replied. "But before we get into the nuances of strategy, let me make one thing clear. No one is to try and attack Yezurkstal head on unless I give the signal."

Irontail felt a sting in his right hind leg. Rubbing the injury he sustained there, he felt a wave of dizziness. Without thinking, he shook his head and snorted, taking a few steps back.

"Are you alright Irontail?" Casandra slithered up to his side, holding out her hand for support.

"Yes, I'm OK," he said rubbing his temples. "Still just feeling a bit weak from the battle I'm afraid."

"Probably less the battle and more Mojo's 'medicine'," Oogmut suggested. "Can we agree not to utilize any poison berries this time around?"

Mojo jumped up from his chair and glared at Oogmut. "You should be thanking me," he barked. "Do you have any idea how much time it takes to grow even one of those bezo berries? Irontail would not have survived the battle if I hadn't given it to him."

"He's probably right," Irontail said, stepping back to the table.

"Enough!" The Avatar slammed his fist on the table, bringing everyone's attention forward.

"We have a real enemy, one that could tear apart our very world. Oogmut, Mojo. You are both sons of Evorath and you will behave as such."

The duo exchanged looks, holding their places for only a moment more before taking their seats.

"Good. Now, let's get to planning."

-=-=-=-=-=-=-=-=-

Tel' Shira opened her eyes, a sea of white spanning out before her as far as she could see. She was floating, drifting weightlessly through the abyss. Examining her outstretched hands, she felt disconnected from herself, like she had somehow been removed from her body.

Where was she?

She tried to remember what she had been doing. An image flashed before her -the fight with Yezurkstal. She had drawn blood and then…

No.

She had awoken.

Yes. She survived the fight. Savannah had been there in a room. But how did she get into this endless sea of white? There were no smells, no sounds. This must have been some sort of dream.

Floating alone, she began to glimpse vague images. A dark castle in the distance, two massive turrets and a large keep. An army of dark elves filled the grounds of the castle, hundreds - no, thousands in number.

The castle faded, slowly turning transparent before spilling back into the overwhelming white around her. As it faded from view, more images passed by. A black wyvern, a galloping unicorn, a man milking a cow.

It was overwhelming, a slew of seemingly random images. As quickly as they appeared, they faded back into nothingness.

She floated towards a wall, large iron gates opening to allow her through. It was a bustling town, the smell of salt water and fish filling her nostrils. There were people of all species; elf, dwarf, gnome, lizock, felite, centaur…this was unlike anyplace in Erathal she had seen before.

As this vision faded, a bright light appeared in its place. The light grew in intensity, causing Tel' Shira to squint. Trying to cover her eyes, she found that she could no longer move. She closed her eyes, floating helplessly towards the light.

"Fear not," said a voice.

It was unlike anything she had heard before. Sweet like honey and ferocious like a tornado, the powerful voice filled the entire space around her. As it spoke, Tel' Shira was held still in place, like she was snagged in some invisible net.

Slowly opening her eyes, she watched a figure emerge from the light. It was a feminine form, an hourglass figure with petite arms and legs. Of course, it was proportionately huge, at least twenty meters tall. It appeared to have long, flowing hair as well. But it was pure light, as if it was spilling through the white backdrop of her mind.

"Tel' Shira, my child. You have done well." The voice made her whole body vibrate, a tingling sensation running from the top of her head to her toes. It felt euphoric.

"Who are you?" Tel' Shira asked, unable to focus on anything else around her.

"You know who I am," the voice proclaimed.

"I am pleased with you, my faithful servant. But your journey has only just begun. The road ahead will not be an easy one."

Tel' Shira squinted, the light intensifying.

"Of me, what would you ask?" Tel' Shira inquired.

"Your time as a warrior is over. Your pain may never fully subside, but should you follow the path I have laid for you, your rewards will be plentiful. A new era must begin, and you must lead my children to live as I intended them."

"Know what to do, how will I?"

"Trust your visions. Through prayer and meditation, my path for you will be laid plain. But should you doubt or feel the way unclear, fear not. You are not alone in your calling. I have sent other servants along your path to aide you in your journey."

The light diminished some, allowing Tel' Shira to look upon the figure with eyes open. Her figure were still shrouded by the light.

"Start, how shall I?" Tel' Shira asked.

"Worry not. For now, simply focus on healing. It will take time to adapt to your new life. You will receive a sign when the time is right. Look for the arrival of the one with the dragon crest. He will help start you on your path."

The light intensified, the figure fading back into the light. Once again, Tel' Shira was forced to close her eyes.

A numbness took over her body from the chest down. Faint smells started to fill her nostrils. A mixture of straw and burning wood. She felt a strong pressure at the base of her skull as she opened her eyes.

It was the room she had awoken in earlier, but no one was around this time. Unable to move her limbs or lift her head, she felt tears welling up in her eyes.

*"Follow your path, I will."*

## Chapter 17

Dumner Village
10 Frozga, 1087 MT

Casandra held the chainmail out in front of her, raising an eyebrow as she looked to Zelag.

"Maybe we should just stay behind," she suggested.

"No way I'm sitting this one out," Zelag objected. "Think of the difference we could have made had we been there a few days ago at the felite outpost. Besides, I want to be there when Yezurkstal meets his end."

Lowering the chainmail, Casandra slithered closer to Zelag. While the centaur armory was somewhat limited in selection for the likes of Casandra, it seemed they had built up an unexpectedly large supply of weapons and gear for bipedal creatures like the human Zelag imitated. He was currently standing before a set of plate mail, inspecting a flagged mace.

"I share your desire for revenge. But we don't know what difference we might have made in that battle. For all we know, we would have been killed. Or worse yet, we might have caused others to be killed. Neither of us is exactly an experienced soldier."

"Pfft!" Zelag put down the mace and approached the nearby window. Casandra followed behind, looking out at the still winter air.

"I can't just sit around and do nothing," said Zelag.

Placing her hand between Zelag's should blades, Casandra shook her head.

"Artimus, Mojo, Oogmut, Pogo and Porra are all going to offer the Avatar backup. Will the two of us make much of a difference?"

"None of them can do what I can do though," Zelag replied. "My shapeshifting may be just what we need to ensure victory. Besides, I'm the one person Yezurkstal couldn't use his magic on. Maybe you should remain behind though."

"No way! If you are going, I'm going too."

Casandra glanced towards the armory entrance, the sound of hoof falls calling for her attention. The entrance split open, allowing Irontail to pass through. He still appeared worn down, his movements sluggish as he trotted towards the pair.

"Are you finding anything useful?" the Chieftain asked as he approached.

Zelag stomped back towards the plate mail display, picking up the flagged mace and holding it out.

"I might want to take this one. There's something about it that appeals to this form of mine. I could see myself using it to crush Yezurkstal's skull."

Irontail stepped over and extended his hand, palm up. Zelag hesitated for a moment before lowering the mace and allowing the Chieftain to take it.

Grasping the weapon, Irontail pulled it in close and inspected it. He took a step back and lifted it overhead, holding it for a few seconds before swinging it down in a figure eight. Swinging it a couple times in this manner, he finished by holding it upright and offering it back to Zelag. The young shapeshifter snatched it back, looking it over closely.

"It's a little light for a centaur, but it seems made well enough. If you can land a blow with it, I imagine it will do the job. I hope you don't have to try though."

"Exactly," Casandra interjected. "Remember, even if we do go along, our job is to stay in reserve until they need us. Hopefully the Avatar can take out Yezurkstal on his own."

"I understand the plan," Zelag snapped. "But I hope I do get to step in. I'd love nothing more than to see that scourge dead at my feet."

Irontail glanced at Casandra, his eyes narrowed. Though she wasn't very adept at reading centaur facial expressions, she imagined the tenseness of his face was a show of concern for Zelag.

"Be ever wary of revenge. It is more likely to consume you than it is to destroy your enemy," Irontail stated.

"What does that mean?" Zelag asked.

"It's a quote from the lizock tale of Slithero the Foolish from the druid Sissera. Legend says that she gave that warning to Slithero before he set off from Erathal to explore the lands to the south. According to the stories, he was seeking revenge against a dragon that had killed his family. But instead of getting his revenge, he led a ship full of his people to their doom at sea."

Zelag placed the flagged mace back in its display.

"I guess it's a good thing we're not traveling overseas," he said.

"I don't think that's the point," Casandra suggested.

She understood Irontail's concern. Zelag had always been a bit impatient, but lately it seemed that his desire to get revenge on Yezurkstal was starting to consume him. His temper was growing short, and he seemed obsessed with training and getting stronger. Perhaps it was best for him to remain behind.

"I understand what Irontail is saying. But I'm not a foolish lizock. And like you observed Casandra, we are following the lead of the Avatar."

Irontail marched over to the displays with chainmail, running his hand along the bottom of a set.

"Just remember to stick to the Avatar's lead," he said. "Casandra, are you going to take anything extra from here?"

"I don't know," Casandra replied, slithering towards the chainmail.

"I thought about taking a set of chainmail, but what is the point? If things go to plan, our only foe should be Yezurkstal. And will any of this chainmail really help against his magic or his adamantium blade?"

"You're probably right," said Irontail looking between Zelag and Casandra.

"If there is time, perhaps you can talk to Savannah. I know she practices enchanting items to imbue them with magical

192

protection. Maybe she can enchant your bearskin to help insulate you from Yezurkstal's dark magic."

Casandra smiled and offered a nod.

"I've spoken to her about her enchanting techniques before. I'm afraid nothing will really protect against the powerful magic Yezurkstal uses, but she has already helped me put some enchantments on it."

Irontail scratched behind his head and returned the smile.

"Ah, that's good to know. At any rate, I came here for more than just to check on your progress. The Avatar has called for everyone to the war room. The others should be there by now, so if you're ready, we can head that way."

Casandra looked back at Zelag, holding eye contact. He grinned and scooped up the mace.

"I'm ready to go when you are."

.-=-.=-.=-.=-.=-.=-.=-.=-

Artimus tapped his foot, sitting at the right corner of the war room table and waiting for Irontail to return with the others. Pogo and Porra were sitting on his left, and Oogmut had taken the seat opposite him. Mojo was across the room pacing, his eyes downcast as if he was deep in thought.

The Avatar was standing at the head of the table, just a couple meters to the right of Artimus. No one had said a word for the last few minutes, a palpable tension in the air. Preoccupied with thoughts of the injured Tel' Shira and his wife caring for her, Artimus was just relieved to have some peace and quiet.

His ears perked up as he heard foot falls just outside the room. The sound of shifting dirt followed, and Artimus turned to see Irontail trot in, followed by Casandra and Zelag. It looked like neither had changed their attire, but the young shapeshifter carried a flagged mace in his left hand. Not the most fruitful trip to the armory.

Mojo stopped pacing and looked at the trio. While Casandra proceeded to slither next to Oogmut, Zelag followed behind and sat beside her. Irontail remained back at the entrance, nodding towards Mojo. Returning the nod, Mojo followed behind and took the seat next to Zelag.

Everyone focused their attention on the Avatar, who was still standing silent at the head. He looked to be 1,000 kilometers away, his eyes looking up towards the ceiling and hands hanging loose by his side. Irontail broke the silence.

"Now that everyone is gathered, shall we discuss the plan?"

The Avatar stood unmoving. Artimus looked around, all those gathered exchanging confused looks. After nearly a minute of continued silence, he wondered if he should ask a follow up question.

"Thank you for coming," the Avatar finally spoke, his gaze still upon the ceiling.

"You've all suffered great losses at the hands of Yezurkstal. Evil like this was never intended to exist in Evorath, but you have all stepped up and fought to keep it in check. Know that the failure to defeat Death thus far is mine, not your own."

As he finished saying this, the Avatar adjusted his gaze. He looked directly at Artimus, then shifted around the room, looking to each of those gathered in turn. Though his face was blank and eyes unwavering, there was something about his gaze that lightened the air in the room. It felt easier to breathe, like some tension had been released.

Pogo stood up and raised his right hand.

"I think I speak for everyone when I say there's no sense in worrying about the past. Let's hear your plan to put a stop to this cancer once and for all!"

"Agreed," echoed Oogmut. "There are so few of my people left in Erathal because of that monster. But dwelling on the past does us no good. Let's end his terror."

The Avatar centered his attention on the map at the head of the table.

"Very well," he said pointing to the hájje fortress just east of Lake Algarath.

"We all know Yezurkstal has built himself a fortress here. And until the recent battle, an attack on that fortress would have been an impossible task. I hate to say it, but a direct assault would still undoubtedly fail. Fortunately, I don't believe we need a direct assault."

The Avatar reached over and grabbed the wooden figures Pogo had whittled over these past few days. They were a bit crude, but Artimus had to admit he found the one representing Yezurkstal to be a bit humorous. It was round and stunted, resembling a demonic pig more than the actual evil monster it represented. He started by placing this Death pig figure just north of Yezurkstal's fortress.

"I will coax Yezurkstal out from the safety of his home. He has put dark spells of his own on the place, so he knows I will not set foot inside his gates."

Placing his own figure down opposite the Death pig, he grabbed for Mojo and Oogmut's figures next. Artimus had been surprised Mojo hadn't objected to his figure, which simply looked like a feral dog. It was Mojo who asked the next question.

"How do you intend to get him to leave the safety of his fortress? And what if he has other defenses? What's to stop him from trying to attack from the safety of his walls?"

"His ego." Replied the Avatar matter-of-factly.

"Yezurkstal couldn't stand that I forced him to retreat yet again. And he hasn't been handling that fact too well. While it does seem he still has a few demons left over, I don't believe he'd leave his fortress undefended. Instead, when I issue him the challenge, he won't be able to resist facing me alone."

"Wait," Artimus piped up. "How do you know he hasn't been handling it well. And do you know how many demons precisely? Because that could affect our plans."

The Avatar smirked, an almost cocky arrogance in his eyes.

"When I realized he was ready to flee, I took the opportunity to place a tracking spell on Yezurkstal. I've been able to keep watch on his movements since then. He hasn't claimed any more minions for his army, so he's down to the handful of demons left at his fortress. I suspect those demons will stay inside the walls with Verandas to keep an eye on Yezurkstal's wives and children."

The Avatar paused, looking around at the group.

"That brings up an important point," Mojo started. "What are we to do about the other dark elves. His 'wives and children' as you called them."

"We will do nothing," the Avatar replied, his tone absolute. "They are victims as much as anyone else. And though Yezurkstal's blood might flow through those children, they must be given the chance to choose their own paths in life."

"But what if they decide to follow in their father's footsteps?" Porra asked.

"If and when that happens, we will deal with them accordingly. But let me be clear. No more innocent blood should be shed because of Yezurkstal. And his children are innocent."

Most everyone seemed to understand this, but Artimus noticed the way Zelag shifted in his seat. His eyes were downcast, and he wore a scowl on his face. His desire for revenge could prove detrimental to whatever plan they made. No one else said a word, so the Avatar continued.

"With that out of the way, let's discuss our plan of attack. I will draw Yezurkstal out of his fortress. If he is stronger than before and I need help, I will fall back to Lake Algarath. This way, if he does manage to overpower me, I'll have you all for backup."

Moving the figures for him and Yezurkstal next to the lake, he took Mojo's figure and placed it a bit north. He also deposited Oogmut's figure just west, placing him on the edge of Lake Algarath.

"Mojo, you will be there primarily to lay traps. I know you have some tricks up your sleeve, so on our way down there we'll discuss placement and strategy. The only circumstance you are to enter the fight is if I specifically call for your aid."

"Oogmut, you will be there primarily for support. There are few in Evorath that have the kind of magical reserves you do. I'll be relying on that to help bolster my own magic. More importantly, if others do have to enter the fray, you will use some of that magic to bolster their physical attributes."

The Avatar grabbed the final three figures, placing Artimus, Zelag, and Casandra a bit further east from the action.

"Zelag and Casandra, you are coming for two reasons. As much as we don't want to consider the possibility of defeat, the first reason is just that. Should I be slain by Yezurkstal, you two are to immediately flee. Return here to Dumner and warn Irontail of what has happened. Second, to offer protection and support to Artimus should Yezurkstal realize you all are there."

"Artimus, you are there to further ensure our success. Your skill with a bow is unmatched in Erathal. You won't get a signal from me, but if the opportunity presents itself, I trust your arrow will hit its mark. Whatever you do, aim for the head and only fire if or when Yezurkstal is positively unable to avoid your strike."

Artimus nodded.

"Aren't you forgetting us?" Pogo interjected.

"No," the Avatar replied. "Your insights have been invaluable. But I must ask you to remain in Dumner again. With such diminished numbers, your presence here could be a real asset to Irontail."

"We'll discuss any questions along the way," the Avatar continued. "For now, get your gear ready. Bring only the necessary provisions. Even in this weather, we should be able to make it to our destination in just a couple days march. I'll meet you all at the southern border in exactly one hour."

Without giving anyone a chance to object, the Avatar stood up tall and left the war room.

Not wanting to delay, Artimus followed closely behind, ignoring the chatter from the other gathered. He stopped at the entrance, locking eyes with Irontail and holding out his hand. Irontail accepted his handshake, clasping tight and maintaining eye contact.

"As we discussed?" Artimus asked.

"They will be safe," the Chieftain replied.

The two held eye contact for a moment more before shaking hands and exchanging a nod.

As Artimus left the war room, he felt a tear forming in his right eye. Would he ever see this place again?

**Chapter 18**

Lake Algarath
12 Frozga, 1087 MT

Yezurkstal stomped up the steps, ascending the northeastern watchtower. His boot falls echoed through the tower, a reminder of the cold emptiness of his halls. He had commanded Verandas to barricade his wives and children in the keep. Between his own magical defenses and the remaining demons at his disposal, they would be safe from harm there.

It had been five days since he was forced to flee yet again from that wretched Avatar. And in those five days, he had done nothing but replay the battle over and over in his head.

He had been so sure the addition of the dwarves in his army would turn the tides. But even with the extra zombies fighting with him, the Avatar's forces of evil had proven too powerful. Perhaps if Frogatha had granted him more demons to fight with, the battle would have gone differently.

No matter. His crusade was righteous, and his way was the only way to order in this world. That is why he had to persist.

Reaching the top of the tower, Yezurkstal contemplated another visit to the demon realm. Perhaps by now his goddess would have more soldiers to march in his army. Or perhaps he was thinking too small.

What if there were a way to turn the tide at scale? After all, the only beings fit to live in an orderly world were his fellow hájje. Thinking of all the minds he had touched and things he had seen, he wondered: had he been too impatient?

The chilling winter air made for the perfect weather to ask these questions. Looking north at the snow-covered trees, he wondered if he might need to revise his approach. It seemed only natural that his righteousness would secure him victory in warfare. But as he allowed himself to consider these past couple of years, he was forced to face the truth: failure.

His military engagements were not winning him this war. But the one place he did find success was in claiming his wives. Perhaps it was time to forget outright conquest and shift focus to building up his people.

Yes, that had to be the answer. If he worked quietly to transform elves into hájje, he would be able to build up his ranks without resistance. It would be a way to cleanse the world of the impure while bringing in more of the beautiful darkness.

But the time to admire his own brilliance was cut short.

"Yezurkstal," the infuriating voice of the Avatar rang out through the trees.

"I know you can hear me. If you truly think you have what it takes to defeat me, now is your chance."

Gritting his teeth, Yezurkstal's hands shook, and his brow trembled. Scowling as he searched for the source of the Avatar's voice, it felt like the temperature dropped ten degrees.

There he was. Nearly fifty meters outside his fortress walls, Yezurkstal spotted the pathetic bald creature.

Without a second thought, the dark elf leapt from the tower, soaring through the air towards the forest floor. Using his dark magic to cushion the landing, he stopped himself just short of the snow, hovering above the ground and glaring intently at the Avatar.

"I thought you too cowardly to come face me alone," Yezurkstal yelled across the distance.

Neither combatant moved, both standing and staring, separated only by fifty meters of snow and trees.

"And I knew you were foolish enough to accept the challenge," the Avatar replied, his voice booming across the distance.

"Feklar!" Yezurkstal spat, drawing his sword back for an attack. Not wasting a moment, the dark elf sprinted towards his foe, soaring forth like an eagle locked on its prey. He closed the distance in mere seconds, leaping up and swinging for the killing blow.

His blade cut towards the Avatar's face, but to his surprise it never landed. Instead, he felt his hands vibrate as his blade struck an invisible barrier, green energy lighting up in a sphere around the Avatar. Almost losing his grip on the blade, Yezurkstal back peddled and sheathed his sword.

"You hide behind the magic of your goddess. But do you think it can really stand against me?"

Focusing on magic from deep beneath the ground, Yezurkstal felt his body heating up. He focused the primal red energy into flame, forming a large fireball in his right hand.

Continuing to draw on the energy, he unleashed the flames, firing a torrent of fire towards his foe.

The flames engulfed the Avatar, roaring around the green shield of magic. Yezurkstal screamed, holding his hands as he continued to channel the flames.

"Die, you miserable cur!"

The snow around the Avatar melted, but despite his persistence, he still saw the glow of green resisting his flames. Perhaps a more direct approach was warranted.

Dropping his attack, Yezurkstal didn't wait even a moment for the flames to die away. Instead, he lunged forward, palm flat.

His hand burned as he touched the green barrier, the green magic repulsing his very essence. He could feel the magic trying to work up his arm, but he dug into the depths of his soul, pouring out his own dark magic and forming a barrier of his own.

As the burning sensation in his palm faded, he watched his dark magic spread out along the green barrier. It was subtle at first, like a small crack spreading across glass. But as he poured more energy into it, the crack spread, spidering out until the entire barrier shattered.

Yezurkstal hadn't anticipated just how much force it would require, but as the barrier broke, a shockwave sent him reeling back. Even the Avatar looked like he lost his footing, staggering for a moment before regaining his composure.

"Meet your end!" Yezurkstal spat.

In a single motion, he drew his sword and stabbed towards the Avatar.

Sinking into the ground, the Avatar ducked under the strike and disappeared into the charred soil. Yezurkstal pivoted, looking around for his foe in confusion.

With an explosion of dirt, the Avatar popped back up behind Yezurkstal. Before he could turn to confront him, the foul creature got hold of him. He slipped his arms through Yezurkstal's armpits, catching him in a full nelson. A vine simultaneously shot out from the ground, wrapping around his sword arm, and wrenching the blade from his grasp.

"You disgrace Evorath with your unholy magic. You are an abomination against the life of this world, and you cannot be allowed to exist here any longer."

Yezurkstal's stomach turned. What a sickening, vile creature. To accuse him of being an abomination?

There wasn't time to dwell on it. He felt a burning sensation overtaking his entire body. The Avatar was focusing his green magic and Yezurkstal didn't know how long he could hold out. His mind raced, trying to come up with some way to escape the hold.

As if an answer to his prayers, a new target entered the field. Just ahead, from one of the pines, a figure emerged. It pulled itself out from the bark of the tree itself, the feminine figure of a dryad.

"I have come to witness your demise," the dryad uttered as she strode towards the combatants.

"No!" The Avatar sounded desperate, his voice trembling. "Leave this place at once."

More vines shot out from the ground, grabbing to restrain Yezurkstal's arms. The heat from the Avatar's green magic diminished some, the introduction of this wildcard clearly throwing off his focus. Foolish, sentimental creature.

Opening his mouth, Yezurkstal concentrated his arcane energy into his very words. He had only done this once before, but there was no room for failure.

"Frozri," he muttered the ancient elvish word for death. The dark magic flowed out from his mouth, cutting through the air with his word.

With this imperceptible spell, his magic soared towards the pine dryad.

"NO!" The Avatar bellowed, letting Yezurkstal go from his grasp and darting towards the dryad.

He was too late.

As the sound of his voice landed on the dryad's ears, she shrieked in anguish. Her body began to swell, boils and welts covering her bark-like skin as she writhed in agony. A few moments later, she fell silent, dropping to the floor like a fallen tree branch.

Using his dark magic to loosen their hold, Yezurkstal wrenched himself free from the remaining vines and grabbed his sword. Preparing the blade, he gave the Avatar no time to react.

While his enemy knelt over the fallen dryad, Yezurkstal swung his sword overhead, slicing through the Avatar's right arm. Powered by his own dark magic, the blade cut clean through his foe's shoulder, dismembering the limb.

The Avatar seemed unphased, rolling over his remaining arm and springing to his feet. His dismembered arm flopped a couple times, the ground crumbling around the arm to absorb it back into the soil. Distracted by this, Yezurkstal allowed his enemy time to flee.

"Coward!" Yezurkstal hollered after his fleeing foe.

Sheathing his sword, Yezurkstal sprinted after him. He weaved through the pines, batting aside branches as he pursued his enemy. Despite his missing limb, the Avatar seemed unfazed, breaking through the tree line into a clearing.

Lake Algarath was visible to the west, additional trees surrounding them on the other sides. It seemed the Avatar was content to make his stand here, standing about twenty meters away and squaring off against Yezurkstal.

The dark elf stepped into the clearing, making each step deliberate as he pushed through the snow.

"Is this where you've chosen to die?" Yezurkstal asked.

"It's where I've chosen to end your existence. Though for you, death would not be a fitting description of it, would it? Since you are no longer among the living."

The Avatar's words were weak, his tone less forceful than before. Despite the labored sound of his voice, however, it seemed losing his arm was having a minimal impact on things. In fact, he stood perfectly upright and tall, his one remaining arm simply hanging by his side.

"Even with one arm, you think you can defeat me?" Yezurkstal cackled.

"This is Evorath's world. So, I am confident of the outcome. Then again, I'm also relying on your arrogance to give me time for this."

As these words left his mouth, the snow at the Avatar's feet exploded, sending vines up and attaching to his shoulder with the missing arm. The vines coalesced, molding into the shape of an arm. Within moments, their color bronzed, and texture changed, matching the Avatar's skin tone. With a newly formed arm, the Avatar stretched, opening, and closing his fist a few times as he stared down Yezurkstal.

What a foul trick.

"It is of no consequence," Yezurkstal replied with a smirk. "As you've observed, I am undying. My reign on Evorath will continue long after you have been forgotten. I will reshape this world better than your goddess could have even conceived."

While he spoke, Yezurkstal focused his hatred and anger. He pulled from deep within his soul to channel all the dark magic he could muster. The moonstone on his sword's pummel glowed as he reached into those reserves, pulling out every bit of dark energy it had collected over these past weeks.

If there was one advantage the Avatar demonstrated, it was his physical abilities. He was stronger and faster than

Yezurkstal, a fact the hájje didn't like to admit. Channeling this magic to permeate his body, Yezurkstal realized this admission was how he would win.

His muscles bulged and senses heightened as he focused on augmenting his abilities. The dark magic coursed through his veins, strengthening muscle fibers, reinforcing bones, and granting him more awareness.

He could sense the Avatar gathering more power as well, green energy pouring into him from the ground. Not wanting to give him more time to collect power, Yezurkstal made his move.

Surprising even himself with his speed, he dashed towards the Avatar. Pouring magic into his fists, he led with a right cross. Too slow to dodge, the Avatar stumbled back as Yezurkstal planted his fist in the enemy's jaw.

Following up with a left hook, Yezurkstal sent his foe reeling again, knocking him to the right. The Avatar brought up his hands to guard, but he was helpless against the hájje's barrage. Hook, cross, jab, cross, hook, and breaking back through the defenses, he planted an uppercut on the Avatar's jaw.

The force in his final swing was so powerful that it sent the Avatar into the air. Not giving him time to respond, Yezurkstal continued the assault with a roundhouse kick to his foe's stomach.

As the Avatar fell to the ground, he released his counterattack. Yezurkstal almost didn't see it coming, but as he prepared to draw his sword for the finishing blow, he caught sight of a tree branch swinging his way. Ducking under the attack, Yezurkstal stepped back and redirected his attention.

An animated oak tree. How original.

Its base had split, roots flinging dirt around as it clumsily stepped closer. The main branches on the tree reoriented as it moved, twisting around to form large, gnarled arms. While it lacked a distinct face, the lumbering oak seemed capable of tracking Yezurkstal's movements.

"You're getting desperate," Yezurkstal spat.

Rechanneling his energy, Yezurkstal drew his sword and coated the blade with magic. As the tree swung again with its now larger branched arm, Yezurkstal simply held up his sword to block and planted his feet defensively.

While the force was considerable, Yezurkstal's augmented strength allowed him to stand his ground. His blade cut through the wood like butter, the animated tree's branches falling harmlessly aside. With a grin, the dark elf performed a 360 swing, cutting straight through the center of the tree.

His magic made this too easy. At less than half its height and without its limbs for balance, the tree fell back, landing with a thud.

Before Yezurkstal could direct his attention back on the Avatar, vines shot through the snow and wrapped around both his ankles. Loosening his hold on the sword, he let the blade drop to point towards the ground. But before he was able to cut through the vines at his feet, more shot up and grabbed either arm.

For a moment, Yezurkstal thought he might be overwhelmed. But only for a moment.

As more vines shot up and wrapped around him, Yezurkstal allowed his blade to slip from his fingers and plant in the ground. He used the moonstone on the pummel as a conduit, releasing dark energy. His spell splintered like lightning, arching between him and the stone and obliterating everything it touched.

Within seconds, the vines withered and died down. The Avatar mistook this as an opportunity to attack.

Seeing his enemy's incoming fist, Yezurkstal swatted with his left, knocking the attack away while cocking back his right fist and moving into attack. Redirecting that arcane energy back into his right fist, he unleashed the most powerful uppercut he could imagine.

The force caused a shockwave, sending the Avatar reeling back again. Staggered and bent over, it appeared his enemy was finally stunned.

Not wanting to let the opportunity pass him buy, Yezurkstal held out both his hands, palms open.

"This is my world now," Yezurkstal spat.

Firing a stream of dark magic from his palms, he watched his enemy fall to his knees.

This would be the end.

# Chapter 19

Lake Algarath
12 Frozga, 1087 MT

Casandra watched in horror as Yezurkstal dispatched the animated tree with such ease. And as he tore through the vines, she couldn't contain herself.

Rising from her hiding spot just east of the conflict, she slithered towards the battle with great haste.

"Casandra, no! That's not the plan!"

She ignored Artimus, rushing towards the conflict with a silent prayer to Evorath. Yezurkstal threw another powerful punch, the shockwave from his attack causing Casandra to slow for a moment and stare in awe.

What sort of monster was he to command such strength?

Shaking off the shock, she continued forward. With horror, she watched Yezurkstal start his next assault, a stream of dark energy impacting the Avatar and bringing him to his knees.

"Come on," she muttered breaking through the clearing. The Avatar held his arms up defensively, the dark energy pulsing around his entire being. Despite the stoic look on his face, he would not be able to hold out much longer. His skin began to darken, the magic permeating into his body.

"Enough!" Casandra exclaimed.

She brought both her hands overhead. With a downward swing, she unleashed a large fireball. The fireball struck

Yezurkstal, flames engulfing him. Casandra watched in anticipation, grinding her teeth.

Yezurkstal's attack ceased, the river of black magic dissipating to leave the Avatar knelt on the ground. The flames burned -had she really done it? Still on his knees, the Avatar looked pale, his breathing labored.

"Casandra, you must…" he took a deep breath, clutching his left arm. "Flee."

Casandra narrowed her eyes, looking back at the flames surrounding Yezurkstal. She felt an uneasiness in her stomach as the fire died down, smoke rising from the seemingly unscathed body of her enemy. His face was red, clenching his fist as he turned to face Casandra.

"Your kind will be blotted from this world," he uttered.

Before she could process a response, Yezurkstal drew his blade and charged. He moved so fast.

Unable to keep up with him, she held out her hands and channeled all her energy into creating a barrier. A thin glow of green surrounded her as she offered up another prayer.

"No one can save you."

With those words, she looked down, the most intense pain overwhelming her senses. Her body went numb.

She watched as Yezurkstal's blade cut through her stomach, searing through flesh and bone.

Her vision blurred and the world around her faded.

-=-=-=-=-=-=-=-=-

Zelag ran after Casandra, struggling to keep up as she slithered between the foliage towards the battle.

Trudging through the snow-covered ground, he stumbled a few times, struggling to keep up. By the time he got into the clearing, it looked like Casandra had already made her move. Yezurkstal was on fire, flames engulfing the hájje as he ceased his attack.

But something was wrong.

Zelag could see the magic from the flames dissipating. And instead of Yezurkstal's aura weakening, there was a darkness growing around him. In his human form, Zelag felt a strange sensation, the hair on his neck standing on end as that powerful dark aura expanded, turning black as night.

It was like his aura was absorbing the magic from Casandra's attack, integrating into his essence, and strengthening Yezurkstal. Then, the unthinkable occurred.

Yezurkstal flashed across the clearing, drawing his blade, and cutting through Casandra.

No, it couldn't have been.

But it was.

Zelag stood helpless, his hands shaking and eyes watering as he watched Casandra being cut in half. Her upper torso fell to the snow, red blood flowing out and staining the white snow. Her snake-like tail continued to convulse, flopping around in the snow, and releasing more crimson blood.

A wave of dizziness and nausea overtook Zelag. He doubled over, releasing the contents of his stomach. His knees were weak, his face on fire.

He began to weep, falling to his knees and clutching his stomach. How did it hurt so?

"You're different," Yezurkstal's caustic voice hit his ears, causing him to wince in pain.

"But fear not. I'll take your pain away, whatever you are."

Zelag sobbed, wiping his face, and looking towards Death. A flash of dark magic swept over him.

He felt nothing. First his tribe, and now the one person whom he could relate to. This was too much.

Yezurkstal had to pay.

"NOOOOOOOO!"

Zelag roared, his voice cracking as he leapt to his feet, arms spread wide.

"YOU WILL SUFFER!"

He thought of the most terrifying form he could imagine a creature he had encountered years ago with his progenitor. While he couldn't remember the name, he remembered the essence. The pain of this loss was enough to bring that mental picture into his mind.

Focused on that colossal form, Zelag began to grow, his bones stretching and muscles bulging out. Below his arms, a second set of hands began to grow, his ribs separating to form tiny fingers. His skin began to harden, turning mahogany red.

Legs doubling in thickness and doubling again as his feet were replaced with massive hooves. Chest bulging and eyes spreading apart, he felt no pain. Just anger, a white-hot rage that fueled his transformation.

Reaching over four meters in height, his main pair of arms continued to grow out, large, sinewy muscles complete with massive claws. His hair had all absorbed back into his body, being replaced with the rock-hard skin of this powerful form.

Nose coming to a black snout, reminiscent of a barghest and ears stretching out into large circles. His smaller set of arms grew out as well, reaching out from his chest and forming fists as he stared down Yezurkstal.

"What in creation are you?" Yezurkstal asked as he looked upon Zelag.

"He is a Preajin, which is why your magic is useless against him." the Avatar said rising to his feet. "Of course, that form is a surprise to me too. That's a bulwark."

"I WILL DESTROY YOU!" Zelag proclaimed, his voice booming throughout the clearing. Even the trees trembled as he roared.

Yezurkstal took a few steps back, his dark aura diminishing, clouded in grey.

Heaving a final breath of sadness, Zelag had only one thing on his mind in this moment.

Kill.

He dashed towards Yezurkstal, cocking back his top arms while reaching forward with his lower pair. With his sword still in hand, Yezurkstal dodged to the left, swinging his entire body around to strike at Zelag.

The blade hit Zelag in the back, ricocheting off his skin. Though this form was a little unfamiliar, the pain from his loss seemed to be charging him. He reacted purely on instinct, twisting around and swinging his arms wildly.

His right fist connected, smashing Yezurkstal in the head. As the hájje stumbled away, he shook his head and held up his sword.

"Angry about your weak little snake friend?" Yezurkstal mocked Zelag with a grimace.

Zelag roared, his deep and powerful voice in this form still a bit alien, even to his own ears.

He charged again, clenching all four fists as he zeroed in on Yezurkstal. Just as he was about to strike, his foe vanished, leaving nothing behind but a puff of black smoke.

Unable to slow his momentum, Zelag barreled through and ran headlong into a pine tree. He snorted, striking the tree in anger with his top right arm. His fist tore through the bark, the tree cracking and splintering before falling with a loud thud.

Pivoting around, Zelag looked for any sign of his foe. If not for his unique ability to see people's aura's, he might have been harder to spot. But as he made it about halfway around, he spotted Yezurkstal's dark aura darting behind a massive oak.

Charging again towards his enemy, he ignored the cracking sound of another tree falling.

"Zelag, look out!"

He wasn't sure who yelled the warning. And he didn't realize why they yelled until it was too late.

Closing in on the oak, he watched as the tree tilted over and came soaring down at him. Without time to move aside, he held up all four of his arms and continued charging forth.

The tree was too heavy, the weight coming down on his shoulder and causing him to crumble underneath. But this form would not be defeated so easily.

He landed in the snow; his body embedded a half meter into the ground beneath. Despite the crushing weight of the tree, he felt nothing. The tree kept pushing down on him, its branches blocking his view of anything beyond.

Grunting, Zelag channeled his rage and pushed with all his might. He wasn't sure what was happening, but as he pushed, the tree began to glow a light green. And suddenly, it felt lighter.

With a triumphant scream, Zelag tossed the massive tree to his left. The branches still obscured his view, but without the weight of the trunk he was able to brush himself off. Pushing up from the ground, he tore through the branches and looked back around.

Yezurkstal was walking towards the Avatar, who was now standing, but still hadn't moved from his spot. Judging by their auras, the Avatar was still not in a position to put up a fight.

Which was just as good. Zelag wanted this more than he wanted anything.

"AAARGH!"

Zelag sprinted towards Death yet again, his lumbering form announcing his approach.

Death looked back at him and shook his head.

"You really want to join your worthless friend, don't you?"

With a smile, Yezurkstal held up his right arm overhead, palm facing up. A black energy emanated from his stomach up through his chest and into his palm. The energy expanded outward, forming a disc of black magic suspended above his head. As the disc grew, gaps began to form, and its purpose became clear.

It was a net. Realizing this too late, Zelag continued his charge, unable to alter course as Yezurkstal threw the magical trap. Running headlong into the net, Zelag found himself stopped in his tracks.

The net felt even heavier than the tree, the oppressive weight of this profane magic bogging him down. Unable to continue forward, Zelag fell to his knees. Try as he might, even his titanic strength in this form was insufficient to resist the heft of this trap.

"Good boy. Now stay there while I deal with this other pest."

Yezurkstal's voice was grating. Zelag tensed every muscle in this form, trying with all his strength to overcome the weight of the net. But the more he struggled, the more he felt pressed into the ground.

Zelag struggled to follow Yezurkstal, straining his neck to keep an eye on the hájje.

Yezurkstal had turned his attention back to the Avatar and approached with his sword drawn.

"*Zelag,*" the Avatar's voice sounded in Zelag's head. "*When I have engaged him, shift into something small and escape the net.*"

With a snort, Zelag tried again to push up, his rocky fingers driving deeper through the snow and into the ground beneath.

"Good idea to have the sword ready," the Avatar said, stepping to his left. "You wouldn't have stood a chance without it."

"I can tell you are at the limits of your power," Yezurkstal retorted, his arms wide as he continued forward. "But I've yet to touch my limits. Why don't you have your other companions come into the open. If they do, I'll lay down my sword and give you a glimpse of what real power looks like."

Recognizing his struggle was in vain, Zelag heeded the Avatar's advice, focusing on the form of a squirrel. That would be plenty small enough to slip through this net.

The pain from the compacting of his bones was excruciating. But he refused to make a sound, grinding his oversized teeth as his entire body crunched in on itself. Organs constricted, bones crunched, and skin softened. Like his initial transformation into this form, the pain of Casandra's death somehow helped speed up the process.

Within a matter of seconds, the net slipped harmlessly over his now tiny body. With a wiggle of his tail, he leapt out from under the net and scurried after Yezurkstal.

*"Good work. I will lock down Yezurkstal. While I do, take on the bulwark form again and grab hold of him. If you can get him in your grasp, he won't be able to escape."*

"I'll tell you what," the Avatar said out loud. "I'll have my friends come out after you toss your sword aside."

Yezurkstal released a shrill laugh, holding his sword overhead as if inspecting it. After a moment's pause, he flung the sword to his right, the blade spinning a few times before embedding itself in a nearby tree.

"Let's see. It's two of them, isn't it? If I'm not mistaken, they were both at the felite camp a few days ago? How you would be foolish enough to try and face me again is beyond me, but please, let us stop the games."

*"Now."*

Zelag started back into his transformation, focused on the form of the bulwark. Thinking of the intense mass and dense skin, he felt his bones extending again. Normally, he wouldn't even attempt switching so rapidly back and forth like this. In fact, he had never tried doing this many transformations in such a short period.

But as his hide hardened and organs grew, as his second set of arms split out from his body, all he could think about was the loss of Casandra.

The long days training, the moonlight conversations, and the looks they'd exchange during a particularly long Avatar sermon…they were all just memories now. It was this thought that fueled him.

While finishing his transformation, Mojo and Oogmut came into view behind the Avatar, both stepping into the clearing with their guard up.

"More foolish than I thought," Yezurkstal scoffed, holding out his right hand. His sword dislodged from the tree, flying in a flash.

The Avatar lurched towards the hájje. As Yezurkstal grasped his sword, the Avatar continued his approach, funneling green energy into both his hands. Yezurkstal chuckled, swinging his blade overhead towards the Avatar's head.

Both hands glowing with life energy, the Avatar swung his arms, clapping his hands on Yezurkstal's blade. For a moment, Zelag wasn't sure what would happen. But it seemed his teacher's magic was strong enough.

He caught the blade, locking his hands and encasing the sword in green energy. It looked like Yezurkstal was struggling, trying to free his blade. That was his chance.

Fully back in his bulwark form, Zelag lumbered forward and extended his arms. Leading with his larger set of arms first, he wrapped himself around Yezurkstal, squeezing with all his might.

"YOU'RE MINE NOW!"

## Chapter 20

Lake Algarath
12 Frozga, 1087 MT

Artimus tip-toed through the foliage after Casandra and Zelag. As much as he wanted to take off after them, there was no way he would expose his location. Praying Evorath would protect the two orphans, he notched an arrow in his bow, keeping his weapon at the ready position as he crept forward.

Staying behind the cover of the trees, he watched Casandra engage. He knew she had powerful magic, but this had to be the most impressive showing yet. For a moment, he even believed it might be enough to overpower Yezurkstal.

But then his heart sank. He turned away as Yezurkstal made his move, unable to watch as the lamia he rescued less than two years prior met her end. His eyes twitched, struggling to hold back tears. Now was not the time to lose focus.

As he lifted his head to continue observing, his heart was filled with hope yet again. He had never imagined Zelag had such power but watching him transform into a bulwark and charge Yezurkstal, he once again felt a glimmer of hope.

Watching the fight unfold, he raised his bow and kept his sights trained on Yezurkstal. If Zelag could just get a hold of him...

But he couldn't.

And as Yezurkstal caught Zelag in his magical net, the experienced archer lowered his bow, making sure to stay hidden.

The way things were going, this battle could very well rely on him and his bow. So, Artimus remained focused on his prey, locked in like an eagle on a rat.

He was so focused on finding an opening that he didn't even register the exchange between the Avatar and Yezurkstal. And he missed Zelag escaping the net.

When Oogmut and Mojo walked into the clearing, he widened his gaze, his heart beating fast as he noticed Zelag was once again assuming the form of a bulwark.

Artimus lifted his bow, eyes trained on Yezurkstal.

This was it!

Yezurkstal made his attack, and the Avatar caught his blade midflight. Hands encased in visible green magic, the Avatar managed to hold firm as Yezurkstal struggled to pull his blade free.

"You're mine now!" Zelag proclaimed as he grabbed hold of Yezurkstal.

The Avatar yanked the sword out of Yezurkstal's hands, immediately tossing it aside. Artimus followed the blade long enough to see it vanish beyond the lakefront, the resounding splash indicating it would be lost to the depths.

With all four arms wrapped around the hájje, Zelag appeared to have the upper hand. Yezurkstal stomped his feet, but his arms were completely locked down.

Adjusting his aim, Artimus considered the wind. There was a light easterly breeze, but at this distance it would have little effect on his shot. Unfortunately, as he pulled back on the bowstring, Yezurkstal jerked. The resulting turbulence caused Zelag to shuffle his feet, pivoting around and effectively blocking his shot.

"Come on," Artimus whispered under his breath as he loosened his arrow and lowered his bow.

He considered his options.

On one hand, he could step out into the clearing. It would give away his position, but if he hit his mark, it wouldn't make a difference. On the other hand, what if Yezurkstal did manage to avoid his shot? Or what if the pressure caused Artimus to miss?

With a pregnant wife and child on the way, he just couldn't do it. He had to survive. Instead, he shuffled to his right, hoping to stay out of sight but find a better angle to get a shot.

The opportunity was gone.

Refocusing on Yezurkstal and Zelag, he saw they had completely spun around, making it impossible to get a clear shot. Even restrained by a massive bulwark, Yezurkstal was somehow putting up a fight.

As the struggle continued, the two stumbled closer and closer to the lake. It looked like Mojo and Oogmut were both channeling some magic. They remained at the northern edge of the clearing, their eyes focused on the struggle and hands held out front.

Meanwhile, it looked like the Avatar was getting ready to make his move. He kept close behind the grappling match, continuing to track them. Could this work out after all?

Zelag continued pivoting, dragging Yezurkstal closer and closer to the lake. As he took his next step, Yezurkstal's head came back into Artimus's line of sight.

Once again, Artimus lifted his bow. Pulling back on the bowstring and steadying his arrow.

With one more step, Yezurkstal came fully into view, squirming like an earthworm. Zelag held strong, planting his feet, and squeezing the hájje. The Avatar joined the fray, jumping in and grabbing hold of both Yezurkstal's legs.

While he did, vines shot up from the ground, wrapping around the trio and holding them firmly in place.

This was his chance.

Blowing out his held breath, Artimus let his arrow fly.

.=.=.=.=.=.=.=.=.=.

Yezurkstal cursed as Zelag grabbed him from behind. Wondering how the shapeshifter had escaped his magical net, he focused on pulling in all the dark energy from around him.

Augmenting his own strength, he was able to prevent this bulwark creature from crushing him. But as the shapeshifter continued to squeeze, Yezurkstal's mind raced, searching for some way out of this predicament.

How did this creature resist his magic?

228

Shaking, flexing, contracting, swinging his head; Yezurkstal tried everything he could think to wrench free, but the more he struggled, the more constricted he felt. Channeling his magic into his skin, he attempted to force his way out.

Expelling this magical energy seemed to help, forcing his opponent to stumble about the field. As he continued his struggle, they stepped closer and closer to the lake. And then the Avatar stepped in.

With his sanctimonious hands and unoriginal manipulation of vines, he grabbed onto Yezurkstal's ankles and anchored all three of them in place. They couldn't defeat him by holding him in place.

Opening his mouth to mock their approach, Yezurkstal's eyes widened as he spotted an elf step out from the foliage to the west.

"Fekla-"

-=.-=.-=.-=.-=.-=.-=.-

Zelag held tight, squeezing Yezurkstal with all his might. All four of his arms wrapped tightly around his foe, he focused on nothing short of destruction.

Somehow, the hájje was holding on, his magic providing protection from the immense force Zelag applied. But this would not deter him. Zelag would squeeze until the job was done.

As he struggled to keep Yezurkstal in his grasp, he found they were moving closer and closer to the lake. With each move, he tried to plant his feet and hold firm.

Finally, facing directly west, the Avatar jumped into the fray. It seemed he grabbed for Yezurkstal, but more important, Zelag felt vines wrapping around his legs, effectively anchoring him in place.

He spotted Artimus stepping out from behind the trees, bow at the ready. Zelag smiled as he watched the elf's arrow fly.

"Fekla-"

The arrow landed with a thud.

Time stopped for a moment. Yezurkstal's aura vanished, fading away into nothingness as he ceased his struggle.

Not prepared for the lack of resistance, Zelag squeezed tighter. With a satisfying crunch, he felt his enemy crumble in his arms. Without the ability to fight back, Yezurkstal's body was crushed and broken.

Zelag held out Yezurkstal in front of him, looking over Death one last time. He realized just then that the vines had been loosened around his legs, and he was free to move.

"You. You were." Zelag tried to find the right words for the occasion. He wanted to express how much he loathed Yezurkstal and how he was overjoyed to see him dead. But now, he just couldn't produce the right words.

Zelag roared, twisting around, and throwing Yezurkstal into Lake Algarath.

The body landed with a splash. But Zelag didn't care to turn around. He had something else weighing on his heart.

Twisting his head, he searched for his fallen friend, Casandra. He took off upon spotting her, running southwest to where she lied. As he did, he began his transformation back to human form.

This time, the normal pain of a transformation crept back in. His bones ached as they contracted. The second set of arms pulled back into his body, the intense pain in his ribs slowing down his approach. His internal organs felt like they were being crushed as they shrunk down to the human size.

As his skin softened, he focused on separating the armor from his human form, allowing it to slip out from inside his rock-hard bulwark exterior. This pain was almost too much to bear, causing him to stumble and stop to complete the transformation.

It felt like someone was trying to extract his skeleton from beneath his skin. Like his bones were metal and a giant magnet was pulling them out. Grinding his teeth, which were just beginning to form, he kept his eyes focused ahead. As full color returned to his vision, he felt tears flowing from his eyes.

After a few more seconds of intense agony, he fell to his knees. Fully in human form, he wiped the tears from his face and ran to Casandra.

Her body was split clean in two, the elvish part of her torso lying to the right and her snake tail stretched out flat to the left. The snow around her was soaked with her blood, an expression of shock permanently stamped on her face, mouth agape and eyes lifeless.

Falling back to his knees, Zelag bent forward and laid his hand upon Casandra's face. His lips quivered, struggling to hold in tears.

But he couldn't.

Leaning over and embracing her lifeless body, Zelag sobbed.

## Chapter 21

Dumner Village
15 Frozga, 1087 MT

Artimus sniffled, using his handkerchief to wipe the tears from his eyes. Left arm wrapped around Savannah's shoulders, he kept her held tight to his chest. The thick, smoky air bellowed around, an apt setting for such a somber occasion.

The two stood on the eastern outskirts of Dumner, the entire village gathered for a memorial service to commemorate all who had fallen in the previous weeks. Along with the centaur villagers, Oogmut, Mojo, Zelag, Neman and Morn were all in attendance. Pogo and Porra had also remained behind, wishing to pay their respects to their 'fellow warriors' as they phrased it.

This entire site had been designated a memorial to honor those who had died fighting Yezurkstal. Irontail had mentioned plans for building a monument on the location, which would serve as a focal point for all the trees that had been planted.

After the battle in Dumner nearly two years prior, many of the warriors had already been laid to rest in this field. Now, dozens of new centaurs and felites were being prepared for the same honor.

The heat of all the pyres provided a welcome change to the otherwise miserable winter weather. But the smoke and smell of burning flesh was a bit difficult to stomach. Of course, that all paled in comparison to the real loss Artimus was feeling.

Casandra had spent no shortage of time visiting he and Savannah. Aside from the battle preparations and engagements they had fought in, she had eaten at their table. She was a dear friend, closer than almost any elf, excluding Savannah of course.

But her death weighed especially heavy on him. His own fear of dying and leaving behind Savannah and his unborn child kept him from acting. Surely, he could have done something differently. What if he could have intervened and prevented it?

Choking up as he inhaled, he gave Savannah a squeeze. She looked up at him, tears flowing from her eyes. Her right arm tightened around his chest, and she leaned in, clasping his right hand with her left.

Keeping his eyes focused ahead, he watched as the flames danced around Casandra's lifeless body. The fire would consume flesh and bone, supporting the cycle of life and leaving behind fertile ashes. When winter was through, these ashes would serve as the fertilizer for the planting of a new tree.

Like the trumpet of an elephant, Artimus turned back as he heard Oogmut blowing his nose. The troll had taken a position just a couple meters behind Artimus and Savannah. While Artimus had not known Oogmut all that well, he had apparently also spent quite a bit of time with Casandra, training her in druidic magic. This had left Oogmut in poor spirits since the final battle against Yezurkstal.

Mojo stood just to Oogmut's left. While he admitted to only knowing her a short while, he also wished to honor her departure.

Zelag was the odd the man out, standing a few more meters away to the right. Though he had shed plenty of tears after Casandra's death, he appeared quite stoic today. His arms were crossed over his chest, looking ahead as if staring past Casandra's funeral pyre. Expression blank and mouth unwavering, Artimus recognized the look.

He was still in shock, unable or unwilling to accept that Casandra was truly gone. At least, that is what Artimus believed it had to be.

Of course, this memorial was not just for Casandra. It was for the other centaur warriors who had so recently met their end at the hands of Yezurkstal. The surviving felite from their camp had come as well, bringing all their dead to the spot for this occasion. It seemed everyone involved found Irontail's suggestion of a common memorial site to be one worth pursuing.

Despite this, the elvish investigator couldn't help but dwell on the death of Casandra. There was something almost poetic about it. The smell of burning wood, the bodies of so many dead all painted an all too familiar picture. When Artimus and Savannah had rescued her only a couple years before, it was from the collapsing remains of a burning cabin.

Either way, Artimus turned back, listening to the crackling wood, and watching as the fire consumed his friend. Continuing to cry, Artimus tried to keep himself from thinking too much about the fight that led to her death.

About twenty meters away, a wooden platform had been constructed. Built from pine lumber, it measured about three quarters a meter tall, three meters wide, and two meters deep. A small pulpit was placed front and center, and as Artimus looked in its direction, he saw the Avatar had finally taken his place there.

Bald and unassuming, this two-meter-tall creature had really done it. He had led them to victory over Death.

And yet, Artimus couldn't help but feel a bit numb. Why hadn't the Avatar been just a little stronger? Why couldn't Evorath have granted him just a bit more power? Why had she allowed Casandra, such a young and innocent mage, to suffer?

Blowing his nose in his handkerchief and wiping the tears from his eyes, he looked up to the Avatar.

"Children of Evorath," the Avatar's voice boomed across the field, magically carried to ensure everyone present could hear him clearly.

"Today we honor the memory of the warriors who gave their lives to combat Death. These were our friends, our family, and brave servants of Evorath. For me to speak about them all would be an injustice to their memory, which is why instead of leading this service, I want to turn it over to their family and friends to speak on their behalf. Before I do, I make one decree.

"While nothing I say now can lighten the sting of our great losses, today will always be remembered as Victory Day: the day Life defeated Death. All of those who have died fighting Yezurkstal did so in service of Evorath. When you join them in the next life, you'll be able to share stories of how their sacrifices ensured your survival. So, remember today not as a sad occasion, but as a joyous one. For one day you too will join them in the Great Forest of Evorath to enjoy a great feast."

The Avatar paused, and for a moment, Artimus felt he was looking directly at him.

"And for those who survived, know that Evorath still has work for you to do here. Overcoming the loss of allies in battle is a long road, one fraught with guilt and pain. But know that you are not alone. I task all of you here to be there for one another as you deal with this pain."

Savannah squeezed Artimus. He looked at her, bags under her eyes and tears running down her cheeks. Offering a subtle nod and a momentary smile, he returned the gesture by squeezing her left hand.

"Now I turn the stage over to Irontail, who has a few words to say."

The Avatar stepped back, nodding towards Irontail before proceeding to the rear of the stage. Irontail trotted up, climbing onto the stage, and taking his place behind the pulpit.

"Thank you, Avatar. Before I say anything else, I will echo the Avatar's sentiment. We are all on this journey together. So, if any one of you needs assistance in the aftermath of everything, know that I am here to serve. Before I open the stage for others to share words about their lost loved ones, I want to say one thing as the Chieftain of Dumner, and as a child of Evorath.

"I had the honor of fighting alongside these brave warriors in the fight against Yezurkstal. I count each and every one of them as our most honored dead. Whether they were residents of Dumner or not, they shall be considered great heroes of Evorath."

Irontail trailed off, gazing out over the massive field of funeral pyres. It must have offered quite a view from that vantage point, more than one hundred pyres laid out in such a grand field.

But Artimus didn't envy Irontail his position. Dumner had been devastated by the recent battle. Whatever new challenges Artimus might soon face; they couldn't compare to the obstacles Irontail would come up against. At least that's what Artimus told himself.

"As I hand the stage over to our dear friend and elder Stonehair, remember this. We will honor the memory of our fallen brothers and sisters by bringing more unity and peace to the forest of Erathal. And now I invite the esteemed Stonehair to share a testament in honor of his son Oakfist."

Irontail stepped back from the pulpit, trotting off the stage and passing Stonehair on his way down. The two paused for just a moment, exchanging a brief handshake.

As Stonehair took the pulpit and began speaking, Artimus couldn't help but wonder how many would be taking to the stage. From the looks of it, a line was forming to the right of the stage, with at least a dozen already gathered -both felite and centaur. Hearing Savannah clear her throat and sniffle, Artimus looked back to his wife.

"We should. Someone should say a few words. Do you think Zelag would like to?" Savannah asked, whispering between tears.

Artimus nodded, casting a glance back at Zelag.

"I'm not sure he's up for it. I haven't heard him say a word since -" Artimus paused, clearing his throat. "Since Casandra was killed."

Looking down at Savannah and seeing her longing eyes, he forced a smile.

"I'll go over and see if I can coax him to say something."

With a squeeze of Savannah's hand, Artimus pulled away from their embrace and approached Zelag. His boots felt heavier with each step he took. Crunching through the snow, he came up alongside Zelag, who stood unmoving.

"I know it might not seem like it, but sharing a few words about Casandra might help. Everyone here should know how much she meant to you. And they need to know that without her, Yezurkstal would still be at large."

Zelag turned his head, a slow and deliberate motion. His eyes were like burning flames as he glared at Artimus. With a grimace, he stared intently for what seemed like hours before responding.

"Never say that name again," he spoke plainly. His voice was laced with hatred, an acerbic emphasis on each word. After holding Artimus's glare for just another moment, he turned back to Casandra's pyre.

For a moment, Artimus considered leaving it at that. But as he looked back at the flames and thought about Casandra, he knew he couldn't. She would want Zelag to move on and to have friends who would help him on the way.

"Did Casandra ever tell you about how she saved my life?" Artimus asked, stopping his sentence short to leave out the mention of Yezurkstal.

Zelag's mouth twitched, a subtle movement that a less observant elf might have missed. His eyes remained firm on the pyre.

"She was never one to back down from a fight, especially when it meant protecting someone she cared about. In a way, she saved us all back then. If she hadn't stepped in that day, Savannah and I would have never been married. And who knows what else might have happened?"

The young shapeshifter balled his fists, squeezing them as he continued to look ahead. His breathing grew a bit heavier as he maintained his silence. While the last thing Artimus wanted was to cause Zelag more pain, he recognized grief for what it was. Letting him stew in this silence could lead him down a much more dangerous path.

"No one was closer to Casandra than you were," Artimus continued. "But I know Savannah and I will miss her dearly. She was a special person, and we were blessed to be able to call her a friend. I think you would be the best person to describe that to everyone. But if you aren't up for it, I can go up there inste-"

"No!" Zelag interrupted, staring daggers at Artimus.

Artimus stood silent, holding the shapeshifter's glare. Again, the two held this gaze for what seemed like days. They heard nothing from the speaker on the stage, all sound muffled, and vision tunneled. After a few seconds, Zelag finally blinked.

"I should be the one to give testament," Zelag replied. "But."

Zelag's eyes began to water, his lip quivering. He scrunched his nose, as if attempting to stifle his tears through sheer willpower.

"If I do," Zelag continued. "I'm. I'm just afraid. I'm afraid to really let her go."

As these words escaped his lips, the flood gates opened. He gasped, sucking in a gulp of air before breaking into tears. His entire body shook as he began to sob, clasping his hands over his eyes.

Hesitating for only a moment, Artimus clasped right hand with Zelag and pulled him into a hug. Embracing the taller man, the experienced ranger only barely managed to keep his own tears in check.

Continuing to sob, Zelag held onto the embrace tight, stuttering his breath as he tried to regain composure.

"It's alright," Artimus murmured. "Holding it in will only make it worse. I know it doesn't seem like it now, but the pain will lessen over time. And you are never alone. You are always welcome with us."

Letting a few tears slip through, Artimus patted Zelag on the back with his left hand. He proceeded to pull it out back in front, wiping the tears from his face before pulling away. Seeing

Zelag continue to cry, Artimus extended his right hand again, placing it on the shapeshifter's shoulder.

"I know for sure that you are the one Casandra would want to share a testament about her. Do you want me to walk up to the stage with you?"

Gasping for more air, Zelag choked up on his tears and backed away. He rubbed both his eyes, wiping away the tears as his sobbing grew quiet. It seemed he had collected himself well enough, but as he held up his right hand and opened his mouth to speak, he buried his face back in his hands and resumed sobbing.

Artimus glanced over at Savannah. He wasn't exactly sure what he was hoping for. Perhaps it was that she would come pull him away. Or maybe it was that she would come over and offer something that would help calm Zelag. But as he caught her gaze, he knew he needed to do this himself.

"Take your time," Artimus suggested, stepping back in and patting Zelag on the back.

With a look at the stage, Artimus saw there were still over a dozen people lined up and waiting to speak. Right now, a young felite male was on stage. With orange fur and black stripes, the felite wore a simple, black shawl. It seemed he was up there talking about his brother.

Zelag reined in his crying, taking a few deep breaths, and wiping his eyes again. His eyes were red and swollen, tears still flowing. But his face curled into a faint smile.

"Casandra would probably make a joke about now," Zelag suggested. "She always found ways to cheer me up."

242

Nodding, Artimus ran his hand in a circle around Zelag's upper back and gave him a few more pats.

"She did have a great sense of humor," Artimus agreed.

Taking a few more sniffs and wiping his hands across his face, Zelag nodded.

"Alright. I'm ready to go up there."

"I'll be right behind you."

Artimus offered a smile, or at least the closest equivalent he could muster. He motioned towards the stage, walking alongside Zelag past Casandra's pyre and towards the pulpit.

The black-stripped orange felite stepped back from the pulpit and left the stage. While Artimus and Zelag stepped into line, a centaur stepped up to the pulpit. He looked young, his simian face stained with a red handprint on his right cheek.

While he spoke, Artimus leaned over to Zelag and whispered.

"Would you like me to stay here?"

Zelag rubbed his hands in front of his chest, his bloodshot eyes darting back and forth as he rocked.

"Yes," he muttered, offering a subtle nod.

The pair continued standing in line, taking a few steps forward when someone finished sharing their testament. Though Artimus tried to listen, he didn't fully register any of what the speakers were saying. Most of them kept their testament brief, sharing a positive anecdote about their lost loved one and affirming that they would see them again in the Great Forest.

One of the felites, a young white and black male did ramble for a bit. But he got to the point eventually.

It really reflected the impact this latest battle had on both the centaur and felite populations. Mothers, fathers, sisters, brothers, sons, daughters, uncles, cousins -some even spoke of losing multiple family members. The full impact of Yezurkstal would be felt for years to come.

Reaching the front of the line, Artimus looked back to Zelag. The young shapeshifter was muttering something under his breath, tapping his foot and nodding his head. He was focused, his eyes locked on the step leading up to the stage. But as he muttered, his face became flushed.

"What if I don't say the right things?" Zelag blurted just a little too loud. "How can I share a testament of Casandra and do her memory justice?"

Artimus stepped in front, looking directly into Zelag's eyes. He took a deep breath through his nose, deliberately exhaling from his mouth as he maintained eye contact.

"Zelag, believe me when I say you are the only one who can share Casandra's testament. Trust yourself as Casandra trusted you. You will do great."

Locking eyes with Artimus, Zelag nodded. Tears were forming in his eyes again, his mouth locked shut.

"Thank you," he spoke after a few moments.

"You're welcome," Artimus replied, stepping back behind his younger friend.

With a glance at the stage, he saw the felite stepping away from the pulpit and proceeding down the step. It was Zelag's turn to speak.

Providing a light nudge, Artimus directed Zelag onto the stage. As he reached the pulpit, Zelag looked back down at Artimus, who offered a smile and nod. With a slight nod in return, Zelag began.

"I am here to offer testament about the life of Casandra. While we may not have been related, Casandra was the closest thing to family I had left in this world. She was an orphan, her entire village destroyed by Death when he first made his move less than two years ago.

"The truth is, I didn't meet her until earlier this year when I found myself in the same situation. Because of Death, humans killed every one of my people. But when I thought I was alone and no one could understand me, I found Casandra."

Zelag struggled finishing that last sentence, choking up and sniffling. He wiped some tears from his eyes and continued.

"Even though she had lost everything just a year before meeting me, she gave me hope. She was so full of joy, always focused on improving her craft as a geomancer and always ready to listen. Over the months I spent getting to know her, I slowly started to feel like I too would be able to find peace. Like I had found a new family. But as I know many of you can relate to, that was all a dream."

He paused again, stuttering, and breaking into tears. For a moment, Artimus thought he might fall back into a full sobbing fit again. But after just a couple seconds, he wiped his eyes again and continued.

"Casandra was a direct pupil of Evorath's Avatar. She was so proud of that fact too, always ready to go above and beyond to serve Evorath. If there was a way, she could challenge herself, she'd find it. And if there was a person in need of help, she would be there to help.

"Honestly, it annoyed me at times the way she would find things to be cheerful about, even in situations where it didn't make sense."

With a sniff, Zelag flashed a brief smile and shook his head.

"A good example of this happened just a few weeks ago. Though we hadn't gotten snow yet, it was still too cold for a lamia to be outside for long. And even worse than the winter air, it gets even colder if you venture into a dark, damp cavern.

"So, when we stumbled upon the cavern, I couldn't resist. And Casandra couldn't say 'no' to an adventure. About fifteen minutes into our descent, we realized it was getting too cold to proceed. Of course, we decided to push on anyways, and Casandra did so happily, clutching her fur coat and shivering the deeper we went. After another twenty minutes, we spotted what looked like an opening to a larger cave. Unfortunately, we didn't realize the cave ahead had such unstable footing."

"I slipped and Casandra attempted to catch me. Instead, I dragged us both down and into the near freezing water. Her long hair and winter coat were both soaked, which meant she was in real danger of freezing.

"Many in that situation might have lost their temper. Some would have given up hope. But not Casandra. Instead, as she slithered out of the underground lake, she started laughing.

"Naturally, I asked her what she was laughing about. And she said it was because normally she'd be afraid for her life. But -
"

Zelag gasped, bringing his hand up to cover his mouth. With a sniffle, he wiped away some tears and pressed on.

"But she knew because I was there, she would make it through. Well, she did make it through that day."

Zelag paused again, taking some stuttered breaths, and clasping the pulpit. His knees buckled and eyes fluttered.

"I only regret that her faith in me was misplaced. Because I was also there when she died. And I will forever regret that I failed to save her."

# PART 2

*The Aftermath*

# Chapter 22

Dumner Village
16 Frozga, 1087 MT

Tel' Shira clenched her jaw. Squeezing her eyes shut tight, she focused every ounce of strength on moving her toes. In truth, she was still numb from her neck down. But perhaps with enough focus, she could get the muscles to respond. Or so she told herself.

The pain in the back of her skull had lessened. Perhaps not in a meaningful way, but now she was able to stay conscious through the pain at least. In fact, this very second marked one second more in her longest stretch of consciousness since the injury. And while this headache had her suspecting that could end any moment, she was committed to use all the time she had.

"Tel' Shira," Savannah's voice interrupted her focus.

Letting out a sigh, Tel' Shira opened her eyes and relaxed. Or at least relaxed as much as someone who had a metal stake planted in the back of their skull could relax. That's what it felt like. Like some large projectile was lodged in the back of her skull.

"What is it?" Tel' Shira asked, struggling to stay focused on Savannah.

"Artimus and Irontail are here with the Avatar as you requested. But is there anything I can get for you before I have them come in?"

"No," Tel' Shira winced, trying to shake her head; but instead, she felt a shooting pain. Like someone was twisting a knife lodged in her neck.

Rapidly blinking her eyes, Tel' Shira was shocked to see her vision clear up.

Savannah had placed her hand on the felite's shoulder. Seeing the shine fade from the elf's eyes, Tel' Shira forced a faint grin.

"Thank you," she muttered, a wave of relief washing over. It lasted only a moment, but Tel' Shira clung to that moment as long as she could.

While her pain dialed back up to full intensity, the three visitors filed into the room, filling the area around her bed.

"For coming, thank you," Tel' Shira whispered, her voice still too weak to speak at full volume.

No one said a word, but she took their nods and Irontail's nervous glances to mean she should continue.

"A vision, from Evorath, I was given. Explain, perhaps the Avatar could."

Tel' Shira proceeded to recount every detail of her vision, including the glimpses of creatures and people. With labored breathing and continual pain, it took her some time to work through all of it. While it all seemed so disconnected and chaotic, she hoped the Avatar would be able to make more sense of it. Finishing up her tale, she closed her eyes and took a deep breath. The pain was getting so intense it made her dizzy.

"Here, this should help a little more," the Avatar said, touching her shoulder.

Again, she felt a wave of relief wash over her, the pain in her skull diminishing to a dull headache. It felt more like someone was pushing her on the back of her head. And this time, it seemed to endure for more than a moment. In fact, as she opened her eyes, she noticed the pain was only slowly returning.

Before she got too comfortable, it was already becoming more intense. Like an invisible hand was poking the back of her skull harder and harder each second.

"Your vision is very telling, and I will happily recount it to the one with the dragon sigil when we discover who that is. However, I am afraid my service to Evorath leaves me limited in what I can reveal. And in all honesty, it limits me in what I know."

As the Avatar spoke, Tel' Shira pain grew worse and worse. By the time he finished, it felt like someone was taking a hammer and chisel to her head.

"Thank you, Avatar." Tel' Shira replied with a wince.

"There must be something you can reveal beyond that," Irontail objected.

"I can say one thing. You're only beginning to scratch the surface with your gift of foresight."

Artimus cocked an eyebrow as he looked at the Avatar. He glanced at Tel' Shira and with a straight face turned to Irontail.

"That gives us very little," Artimus suggested. "But let's forget about that for a moment. Irontail, remember your friend Vistoro?"

"Yes, of course. He has become a fantastic trading partner with Dumner and was instrumental in the planning the Festival of Gratitude."

"Well, when we met him at the Festival, he was wearing a dragon sigil," Artimus replied.

Tel' Shira closed her eyes, trying to envision Lord Vistoro. Fighting the pain, it took her a moment to recall the details.

"Right, you are," Tel' Shira exclaimed, her voice cracking as she spoke.

Savannah stepped over to the nearby table, grabbing a cup of water and bringing it back.

"Here, take some of this," she said, offering the water.

Tel' Shira tried to nod, a searing pain in her neck reminding her that even such a simple gesture was nearly impossible in her current state.

"Thank you," she said instead, squeezing her eyes shut and trying to push away the pain.

She opened her mouth, allowing Savannah to give her some water. As she swallowed, she opened her eyes and looked around the room.

Everyone's eyes were trained on her, looks of pity and remorse on each of their faces. Even the Avatar wore a frown, his eyes narrow and downcast.

"Deal with the future, I will, no matter what it may hold. Your pity, I do not need."

Exchanging glances, everyone around her shifted uncomfortably. Artimus averted her gaze, looking down at his feet. Irontail looked up, scratching the back of his head. The Avatar looked right at her, offering a faint smile. At least he pulled it together. But Savannah offered the most interesting reaction.

She looked straight at Tel' Shira, locking eyes with her and holding her stare.

"I don't pity you," the druid offered, her voice steady and eyes focused. "I admire your strength and your courage. I doubt anyone else here would already be so determined about the future. And I can promise that we'll all be here for you on your road to recovery."

"And more important," Artimus added, looking back up at her, "we'll be there to help you fulfill any job Evorath has laid out for you."

Tel' Shira attempted to smile, but she suspected her mouth wasn't quite cooperating. In either case, she knew what had to happen next.

"Summon Lord Vistoro, we must," she muttered, her voice a bit stronger than before.

"Yes, it sounds like that would be a good next step," Artimus replied. "I have to admit, I didn't figure him for an interpreter of dreams though."

"And you'd be right about that," came a voice from over by the entrance. Its muted tone, calm inflection, and smooth pronunciation was unmistakably lizock. And as the voice spoke, everyone else in the room turned to face it.

"Lord Vistoro!" Irontail exclaimed, his eyes wide.

"That is some timing," Savannah murmured under her breath.

The Avatar stepped away from Tel' Shira's bed, and Artimus proceeded to walk over alongside Savannah. With a space cleared, Lord Vistoro walked up to her bedside and looked down at her.

"When I received word from Irontail that you were among the injured, I had to come see you myself. I had a strange vision recently. While I consider myself a servant of Evorath, this was the first time I was visited by her, or at least a messenger of hers."

Vistoro glanced over at the others for a moment before looking back down at Tel' Shira and continuing.

"And in that vision, I was told to seek 'a brave warrior, forever scarred by Death, but pure as the winter's snow'. When Irontail sent the casualty report from the battle with Yezurkstal, I suspected you might be the warrior of my vision."

Tel' Shira's vision blurred for a moment. Blinking her eyes, she refocused. As her vision became clear, she was looking directly at the sigil upon Vistoro's chest. It featured the distinct visage of a golden dragon set over a jagged mountain peak.

Her chest felt heavy, like a centaur was standing on top of her. Unable to move her arms, her eyes widened, and she gasped for air. Wheezing helplessly, she felt like her lungs simply couldn't pull in the air.

Savannah reached down, placing her hand on Tel' Shira's chest. A moment later, the felite felt a pop in her chest. With a huff of air, she was able to breathe again.

"Of your dragon sigil, a vision I had," Tel' Shira whispered, her chest still heavy.

"Yes," the Avatar interjected. "Tel' Shira, save your breath. I will speak with Vistoro after this and share every detail about your vision. I suspect that is not what is important though."

"I suspect you are correct," Vistoro replied with a smile, his tongue darting out between his teeth.

"You see, I already have some clarity on Evorath's mission for us. For now, your only priority is -or rather should be- to focus on healing. It seems now may be the right time for me to share more about what I've been working on with our other friends."

Vistoro stepped back and looked around the barracks. After surveying the space, he turned back towards Irontail.

"Perhaps there is a room in your central mound where the rest of us can discuss matters some more? One where we could look at relocating Tel' Shira as soon as she is healed enough to move."

Irontail scratched behind his head, his eyes cast up to the ceiling.

"We could use the war room. Since Yezurkstal is no longer in the picture, I don't see any reason why we'd need it in the foreseeable future. I can have someone prepare a bed down there right away."

"That should work," Vistoro replied, his eyes darting around the room.

"Wait for answers, I cannot," Tel' Shira piped in. "Help me healing, knowing about the plan will."

"We really shouldn't be moving you yet," Savannah objected. "The puncture wound in your stomach is still not fully closed. You need at least a couple more days here."

Tel' Shira scowled, trying in vain to shake her head. She had fought many battles, won a Capabolo Championship, and had a vision directly from her goddess, Evorath. And yet, she felt so helpless. Being unable to move, or even to feel her lower extremities; there couldn't be a greater torture than this one.

If not for the lifetime of training and discipline, she might have broken into tears in that moment. Even with them, she felt intense emotional pressure. And for a moment, she noticed tears collecting in her eyes.

Closing her eyes and focusing on her breathing, she tried to diminish the pain. She focused on Evorath's words in her vision. If she was destined to live the rest of her life without the ability to move independently, she was going to do so with poise and grace.

Opening her eyes, she looked around at everyone waiting for her to reply.

"Understand, I do. Move, however, I must. Stabilize me for movement, I trust you can."

Savannah frowned, but as she looked at Tel' Shira, the felite warrior looked straight back at her. Peering into the deep green of Savannah's eyes, Tel' Shira hoped to convey just how important this was to her.

"We don't need to prepare a bed down there," the Avatar interjected. "Irontail, if you keep the path clear, I can move Tel' Shira myself. Savannah, you can follow behind. Once we have her situated down there, the two of us will work to ensure-"

"Wait a minute!" Savannah interrupted, slapping the table next to Tel' Shira's bed.

"I can't believe I didn't think about it before," she exclaimed, looking at Artimus before turning to the Avatar.

"Avatar, I've seen you move through the very ground beneath us. You have the ability to move directly through Evorath at unbelieve speeds, don't you?"

"Yes, I can travel to any of Evorath's forests in short order."

"Perfect! And can you bring objects back with you when you travel to other destinations?"

The Avatar tilted his head and narrowed his eyes.

"Small objects, yes."

"Yes!" Savannah looked like she might explode from excitement.

"I know we've never visited your camp," Savannah started, her voice laced with energy. "But Casandra told me you have pertga orchids that grow there. I know they aren't normally in bloom this time of year, but can you stimulate one to grow and bring it back here?"

"You know that would kill the plant to force its growth in this kind of weather," the Avatar replied with a frown. His voice was much more timid than usual.

"One pertga orchid is a small price to pay! If I had one of those orchids, we could cut weeks, or even a full month off Tel' Shira's recovery."

Tel' Shira's eyes widened. She took a deep breath, pulling in air through her nose and holding it while she closed her eyes. Slowly releasing the breath through pursed lips, she opened her eyes again. Though she couldn't tilt her head, she glanced to her right, staring daggers at the Avatar.

"You're right," the Avatar replied, looking into Tel' Shira's eyes. "But to be clear, Tel' Shira, I want you to understand that this is not some magical panacea Savannah is talking about. I'll go fetch the plant now, and I trust Savannah will regale you with the legend of the pertga orchid."

"Of course," Savannah replied with a nod.

Not waiting for any other responses, the Avatar turned abruptly and walked out of the barracks.

Vistoro and Irontail both stepped closer to Tel' Shira's bed as Savannah explained.

"Truth be told, I've never gotten to work with a pertga orchid before. They only bloom in the month of Pertga. But what many don't know is that the month was named after the flower, not the flower after the month.

"As I'm sure you all know, pertga is the ancient elvish word for 'birth', or more accurately, for 'new life'. The orchid was named this word because of its amazing healing potential. But like the Avatar mentioned, stories of the pertga's healing power also include a fair amount of warnings."

"First, I won't keep you in suspense Tel' Shira. I don't believe it will do anything to help repair your shattered bones or restore any nerves. How much you recover from that is in Evorath's hands."

Tel' Shira closed her eyes and sighed. As she did, she felt another sharp pain in her neck. Her whiskers twitched as the pain pulsed throughout her head. It lessened after a few moments, leaving behind a continuous, dull headache.

"But according to the texts I've read, when the pertga orchid is ground into a paste, that paste has tremendous regenerative qualities. Legends tells of people who suffered near-fatal sword wounds, including wounds to the heart, lungs, or other vital organs. With paste from the pertga orchid, those people not only survived, but they were able to make full recoveries within a matter of weeks.

"From the stories, the magical qualities in the plants are unparalleled anywhere in Evorath. They work to stimulate tissue regeneration at a level that far exceeds anything I could do with magic alone. In fact, if the stories are to be taken at face value, the paste itself will meld into your skin and actually transform itself to replace the missing tissue that you lost."

Savannah paused, looking right at Tel' Shira with a nervous smile. With jaw tightly clenched and teeth exposed, her eyes told Tel' Shira there was more to the story.

"The potential downsides, what are?"

"There's no downside in the traditional sense. In other words, it should certainly heal you. But it's said to be a most painful experience. So painful, in fact, that some who have received it claim it was worse than the actual wound. Not only that, but some mentions of the pertga orchid say the pain can be so intense that if it's used on too severe an injury, it can kill the recipient."

"That sounds like a pretty severe downside," Vistoro interjected, his reptilian voice stressing the 's' sound a bit more than usual.

"It is," Savannah admitted. "But there in the dozens of texts that mention the pertga plant, only a few have indicated that potential. And some scholars argue its because the original wound was just too severe to recover from. Either way, I think if anyone is tough enough to endure the pain, Tel' Shira is."

Tel' Shira smiled, and this time she finally remembered not to even bother trying to nod. "Worth any risk, it is."

"Then I guess Savannah and I should begin preparations," the Avatar spoke, his voice coming from the entrance to the barracks.

"Oh my! You really do travel fast," Vistoro exclaimed.

"Are we sure this is a good idea?" Artimus asked.

"Yes, I also am wondering whether this is the wisest course," Irontail added.

"When not in my condition, easy to wonder it must be," Tel' Shira replied.

"Oh, I didn't," Artimus started, holding up his hand. But he stopped himself, casting his glance down and nodding. "You're right."

Irontail remained silent, simply nodding along with Artimus.

"Good," Tel' Shira said. "Ready to begin, I am."

## Chapter 23

Dumner Village, War Room
17 Frozga, 1087 MT

Irontail snorted, flaring his nostrils as he looked across the table at Oogmut. The war room table was heavy enough, but the way this troll stumbled about made the task even more cumbersome.

"Let's just take another left here," Irontail instructed, jerking his head to the right.

"Wait, your left or mine?" Oogmut asked.

"I'm motioning with my head," Irontail replied. "Your left."

"Oh, right. Where from here?"

"Just straight from here," the Chieftain replied. "There's a storage room down this hall."

"Very good," Oogmut replied. "I'm eager to get back in and learn more about this new settlement Vistoro has been working on. Do you really think Tel' Shira's vision was instructing her to live there?"

"It does sound interesting," Irontail answered.

While he hadn't had many extended social occasions with Oogmut, Irontail had discovered over the months working with this troll that talking was one of his strong suits. And for Irontail's preferences, that meant he talked entirely too much.

"But would you really be ready to give up your position in Dumner?" Oogmut inquired.

"If it's Evorath's will, yes. But I'm not convinced yet that I am meant to walk the same path as them. Perhaps my role in all of this is to stay here in Dumner."

"Perhaps, yes. I know your rule here has helped Dumner prosper more than any centaur village in Erathal has ever before. But if Evorath is calling for this sort of unified city, I wonder what larger implications that has for all Her children."

"Hopefully these next few days will help all of us get a clearer picture of that," Irontail replied. "It's just through there."

Oogmut paused, craning his neck, and looking behind.

"That's just a wall."

"Like the other passages here, it will open for you as you approach. Just trust me."

Squinting, Oogmut took a cautious step back, followed by another. Just centimeters away from it, the wall split open, allowing him to pass through.

As Irontail cleared the threshold, he looked around at the piles of junk scattered about. He hadn't been here in over a year, and by the looks of it, no one had organized anything since then. The massive number of random artifacts was not something he really cared to deal with.

"This looks like a treasure trove!" Oogmut exclaimed. "Do you keep an inventory of everything in here?"

"No, just step to your left a bit and we'll put it down," Irontail instructed.

Finally, Oogmut took a direction without questioning it, taking a few steps to the left and stopping.

"Here is good," Irontail confirmed.

The pair lowered the table and Irontail stretched out his neck. Cracking his knuckles, he glanced around at the scattered piles. His people had a habit of keeping anything they found, and this room was the repository for it all.

"Would you mind letting me rummage around here before I leave Dumner?" Oogmut asked, also looking around.

"No," Irontail replied, turning back towards the exit. The lighting was dim in here, the fungus on the ceiling providing a photoluminescent glow. But there were no active candles, which likely contributed to the disorderly mood of the space.

"But let's get back to the war room. We don't want to keep them all waiting."

"Right you are!" Oogmut replied. "I'll follow right behind you."

Irontail stepped back outside, walking down the hall towards the main passages. Right, left, left, right, and back to the primary hall. Once there, they just had to travel a few more meters. The entry to the war room spread open, allowing Irontail and Oogmut passage through.

Everyone else had already been gathered, including the Avatar's two barghest students (whom Irontail had not expected).

Tel' Shira was in her bed on the east side, to the right of the entrance. Chairs had been set out haphazardly around her, allowing everyone to face the western wall. Lord Vistoro and the Avatar stood beside this western wall, engaged in conversation.

The other attendees included Mojo, Zelag, Morn, Neman, Porra. Pogo, Artimus and Savannah, Silkhair (at Savannah's recommendation), and finally Oogmut and Irontail. Silkhair, who was standing by Tel' Shira's bed, looked at the duo as they entered the room. It seemed everyone's conversations were dying down, ready to discuss the business at hand.

"That didn't take long at all," Lord Vistoro exclaimed, smiling towards Irontail. "So now that we are all gathered, shall we dive into it?"

Most of the attendees simply quieted their voices and nodded. Oogmut proceeded to the rear of the room beside Silkhair. Irontail maintained his position by the entrance and offered a nod. Pogo, as usual, felt the need to comment.

"Yes, let's hear it!" he pumped his fist and looked around with a toothy smile, somehow extending the word 'hear' to sound like it included three syllables.

"I appreciate your enthusiasm," Vistoro replied with a straight face, his voice belying his words.

"With that start, let me begin by getting everyone up to speed. For those who were involved in discussions yesterday, please bear with us while we go back over all the foundations."

Vistoro paused, smiling as he looked about the room. Irontail wished he could skip this part. Having been involved in the hours of conversation yesterday, he would have preferred to go right into the details.

"Great! Most of you already know about the outpost that I have helped build to the west. About one hundred lizock and I left our oh-so-creatively-named Lizock City in the hopes of establishing a community. What you may not know is that we never intended this new community to be exclusive to lizock.

"On the contrary! The vision for our outpost is to create a free haven for all Evorath's children to live in peace. In fact, the reason I set off on this task was because I received a vision from our goddess. And it pleases me to know that our esteemed friend Tel' Shira has also received a vision that compliments my own.

"We both know from the details of our respective visions that we are meant to work on this outpost together. And we believe all of you gathered here can play an integral part in our vision. The vision of a future Evorath not divided by race, but united by our common love of Evorath and all her creation."

Mojo stood up from his seat, glancing around with a look of uncertainty.

"If you're trying to convince me to swear my allegiance to some new nation, I think it's best I just step out now. You know I prefer to live my own life. I fought against Yezurkstal with you, but I am content finding my own way in the world."

"Mojo, my friend," the Avatar replied, his deep and authoritative voice calm and even toned. "Please trust me and hear Vistoro out on this. I assure you what he is proposing is in line not only with Evorath's will but will also fit your lifestyle better than you might think."

Mojo raised his eyebrows and nodded, but he remained standing.

"Mojo, I actually appreciate that perspective," Vistoro continued. "In fact, I believe it offers us the opportunity for a perfect example. Artimus, you know the laws of Erathal City quite well, do you not?"

Artimus shook his head and then looked directly at Vistoro. "I do, yes."

"Of course, you do! It's your job to enforce those laws. So, tell me Artimus, knowing some of the substances Mojo has on his person, if our barghest friend here were to make his way to Erathal's city proper, what would you have to do according to those laws?"

Artimus's face flushed, his mouth forming a nervous grin.

"Well, I've been known to turn a blind eye, but according to the letter of the law, Mojo would have to be arrested. He's carrying several prohibited substances."

Mojo looked at Artimus, baring his teeth.

"Mojo, is that not the reason you prefer to avoid the whole concept of nations?" Vistoro asked.

Mojo let out a light growl, his voice subdued, but filled with aggression.

"Partly. I also find the concept of ruling over anyone else to be unsettling. I serve Evorath, not some king, queen, chancellor, or whatever other despot wants to claim power over me."

"And in the time you've spent with the Avatar, I know you can take confidence in that stance," Vistoro continued. "Which is why we are not building a new nation. There are no rulers and there will be no rulers. What we are building is a community of Evorath's followers here on her creation. Nothing more, nothing less."

Irontail was watching everyone's reactions closely, and he noted Oogmut, Neman, and Morn all had their attention piqued by this statement. Since no one interrupted, Vistoro continued.

"I'll defer to the Avatar for a more theological explanation but let me make things a bit clearer. There is a natural law handed down to us from Evorath. That law can be boiled down to, at its most basic level: love. Love Evorath, love yourself, love your neighbor."

"Going only a centimeter deeper, we understand that love calls us to work together to spread Evorath's kingdom. A kingdom that was torn asunder by demonic forces and the evil influence of Frogatha. Those influenced brought disease, death, theft, murder -you name it!

"But what we forget about the ancient Demon Wars is that when those wars were fought, there was no distinction between races. Indeed, some of the greatest battle chronicled are stories where centaur, satyr, felite, elf, dwarf, barghest, lizock; when we united and combatted the forces of evil. Because that was Evorath's design!

269

"After the war was won, Evorath's children lost their way. We separated into different nations, forming kingdoms, confederations, republics -regardless of the name, the system was the same. Some get prestige, power, and influence. Others are relegated to a life of servitude."

Mojo held up his right hand.

"And how is what you are building any different?" he asked.

"The answer lies in the name: Marftaport. Like the elvish roots of the word, I am suggesting a settlement where there is no worldly authority. Instead, we all answer only to Evorath. We all follow only Her law."

Mojo narrowed his eyes, looking around and taking a seat. Irontail was just happy they had gotten down to the core of things.

"Alright, I am listening," Mojo muttered.

"Indeed! I knew the idea would sit well with you. Like Oogmut, you have some experience in community structured this way. Of course, without getting too much into the weeds, I also know that there are many questions. But before we go any further, does everyone understand what we are proposing?"

There were some murmurs that went out and Irontail noted Zelag sitting expressionless in the corner. But otherwise, people seemed to be understanding. Pogo was the first to respond.

"I think this is all a grand idea," he said. He stood up, holding his arms out wide. "And when we return home to Satyr Island, you can be sure we'll share the good news that others are catching on. But you must know this is already how satyrs live."

Irontail cocked his head to the left, raising his right eyebrow. He hadn't known that. And judging by the confused looks on others gathered, it seemed he was not alone.

Savannah raised her hand next. Artimus offered her help as she stood up. She was clasping the right side of her belly.

"I feel it worth adding that I have been discussing these concepts with Artimus for some time. I've even started writing down some of these ideas. So, while I'm uncertain about the logistics of moving to Marftaport, I can assure you that the three of us will be making said move as soon as we can manage it."

"Yes! That is the enthusiasm I'm looking for," Vistoro replied with a smile. "And we'll talk more after this meeting about what you're writing."

Savannah smiled, slowly lowering back into her seat before Vistoro continued.

"With that in mind, I'd add that we also have discussed moving Tel' Shira to Marftaport. I will be delighted to bring her along when I travel back in a couple days. But I have spoken entirely too much. Please, Avatar: I know you have plenty to say yourself."

Taking a step back and offering a slight bow, Vistoro motioned to the Avatar.

"Yes, thank you Vistoro. First, I want to make it clear that this plan aligns well with Evorath's vision. Having you work together and build a community like this is a step forward for all children of Evorath. And while I will not be moving my camp, I want to make it clear that you will have my support."

He paused, looking directly at Morn and Neman.

"And while I will be maintaining my ministry, I would like for some of my students to move onto the next stage. Morn. Neman. I would ask the two of you move your tents and relocate to Marftaport. Growth means they require strong backs to help build, and the two of you can surely contribute. More important, there is much you can learn from Vistoro, Tel' Shira, Savannah, and the other residents of this free settlement."

Morn and Neman exchanged glances, pausing for only moments before simultaneously nodding. In unison, they turned to the Avatar and offered a simple "Urgo!"

"Excellent," the Avatar replied, turning to Zelag next.

"Zelag, you will continue your training with me for the time being. I'm afraid there is no one else in Evorath who can help you with your unique abilities as I can. But in due time, I hope you will join the others in Marftaport as well."

Irontail watched the young shapeshifter closely. Even at the mention of his name, he seemed despondent. But as the Avatar finished, Zelag did offer a nod.

"Porra and Pogo, I hope the two of you will not just bring news back to your island. I hope you will also let others know that there is now a community where, should they wish, other satyr can once again return to Erathal and live peacefully alongside members of Evorath's other races. And if not, I hope they will consider opening trade with the newly established port."

Pogo stood up, but before he opened his mouth, Porra rose and held up her hand.

"I can assure you teacher; we will do as you say."

This was the first time Irontail had heard Porra speak. While her reputation as a warrior proceeded her, the stories never mentioned how melodic her voice was, every word coated in honey and sweet to behold.

"I know I can count on you two," the Avatar responded. He glanced at Mojo and Oogmut next, looking back and forth between the two.

"And now I return to my dear friends Mojo and Oogmut. I will not command you to do anything. But I will encourage you to embrace this new opportunity. I know both of you have suffered greatly at the hands of Death. Both of you are also well known among your people. I see Marftaport as a new beginning for the surviving trolls and barghest of Erathal.

"Rather than being scattered throughout the continent, this could provide a haven for you to live and grow. Your people could safely repopulate without fear. Not to mention, both of you have great wisdom that could benefit the residents of Marftaport."

"I'll consider it," Mojo replied. "But I'm not ready to say, 'yes' just yet."

"I cannot promise full-time residency," Oogmut interjected, "but I will definitely be honored to help build up the town."

The Avatar beamed with enthusiasm, his eyes bright and smile wide as he turned next to Irontail.

"And you, chieftain Irontail. You and Silkhair are in the most difficult positions. I would love to see you and all of Dumner join Marftaport. But I know that your people are so absorbed in their tribal traditions. Therefore, I must ask you to make a sacrifice."

Irontail glanced at Silkhair. She looked at him in the same moment, the two locking eyes for a moment. Blushing, she turned back to the Avatar.

"I understand," Irontail replied, looking at the Avatar.

"If I were to ask Dumner to abandon the attachment to their elders and to me as their chieftain, it would be chaos. And if I were to leave, to step down, I know someone would take my place and lead my people back down the wrong path. So, I accept the challenge that lies ahead."

The Avatar took a bow, folding in half and holding that position for a few moments before rising back to full height.

"You honor us all, Irontail. Your journey will not be easy, but over time I know you can transition your people to understand Evorath's way. While you work to ease Dumner into a natural relationship with Evorath, I know you will maintain close ties to Marftaport. Together, Dumner and Marftaport, and my own camp of students will help shape this world into what it can be."

To Irontail's surprise, the Avatar looked directly at Silkhair next.

"And Silkhair, I have a special task for you. While I don't wish to put you on the spot, I want to say this in front of everyone. I would invite you to join me at my camp. You understand Evorath's will better than you know and Dumner needs priestesses like you."

Silkhair's face flushed, and her eyes widened. With a slack jaw, she looked around the room for a few seconds before looking back at the Avatar.

"Are you asking me to study directly under you?" she asked sheepishly, her voice rising in pitch with each word.

"More than that." The Avatar replied. "I am asking you to become a high priestess of Evorath. I am asking you to help inspire all the centaur of Evorath and teach them the true path."

"Then I humbly and graciously accept," Silkhair replied, folding her hands at her chest, and offering a deep bow, which she held for at least five seconds.

"Then it's settled!" Vistoro exclaimed, clapping the Avatar on the back.

"Yes." The Avatar exclaimed.

"All of you gathered today will lay the foundation for the Legacy of Evorath."

## Chapter 24

Erathal City, Southeast Residential District
22 Frozga, 1087 MT

Artimus looked inside his former workspace. Even with the room emptied, it was a small space. Only just over two meters by two meters, it served its purpose well enough, but he had to admit to some amount of excitement over his new accommodations.

When Savannah had insisted, they make the move to Marftaport as quickly as possible, Artimus was less than thrilled about the proposal. While she was out getting whatever she could from the garden, he was stuck doing all the heavy lifting. Not that he wished Savannah to help; in her condition, he couldn't believe she was able to do so much work outdoors.

Ready to let go, he took one final glance into the workshop before closing the door. Growing up in Erathal City, Artimus never imagined he would be living anywhere else. And while this home was new since he and Savannah married, he still felt a strong attachment to this place and what it represented.

In the back of his mind, he couldn't help but wonder whether this was the right decision. And holding onto the iron knob just a moment longer, he considered the rough texture, remembering this would all be left behind.

At the recommendation of Vistoro, they still hadn't informed Chancellor Ulagret. Artimus looked to his right, looking at the desk and considering the letters Savannah had written to announce both their resignations for service. Under the laws of the Republic, they had every right to tender such resignation, but Artimus certainly didn't want to be there when Ulagret received them.

To the right of the desk, he had carefully stacked all his fletching materials, along with his current supply of arrows - excluding those with his bow and quiver, which were left just inside the front door. In addition to his crafting materials, he had secured a small wooden crate and stored Savannah's parchment, quills, and inkwells within.

Tucking the simple wooden chair back under the desk, he considered the fire. The crackling of the logs and fresh smell of burning timber always seemed a comforting sound. And though winter was coming to an end and the temperature was rising, the ongoing roar of the flames ensured the home remained warm enough to work without the need for a coat or jacket.

Of course, it was odd to see a completely barren mantle. The fireplace looked out of place, only a simple iron poker left sitting next to the roaring flames. While they may not have lived here long, it was the first home he and Savannah had lived in as a married couple.

"Alright Artimus," he muttered to himself. "No time to think about 'what might have been'."

Shaking his head, he walked into the kitchen. Most of the cooking supplies had already been laid out on the counter. The main kettle, the peel for the oven, and the other fire tending supplies was added to the mix. Alongside this was the assortment of wooden plates and clay bowls. It looked like Savannah had pulled out her various mortars and pestles as well: stone, wood, and her new bronze one. Perhaps one day he would have Savannah explain why she needed three different ones.

The emptied cabinets had been left open, so he proceeded to the nearest unopened cabinet. Crafted from an oak right here on the homesite, these simple cabinets were a gift from Cabal. After discovering his deception, Artimus had since looked upon them in a less favorable light. It would be one part of the home he didn't mind leaving behind.

Pulling out both the clay mugs and wooden cups, Artimus arranged them on the countertop. He proceeded to open the drawer beneath, removing the cutlery and placing them in the wooden cups for transport. Reaching under the counters, he pulled out a couple of crates and started placing everything in them.

He started by placing the kettle in the crate, adding the mortars and pestles directly into the kettle next. It only took him a few minutes to fill up this first crate with the rest of the items. He finished by squeezing the oven peel in on its side, the handle sticking up. Picking up this crate, he walked over to the desk and other supplies, setting down the first finished crate from the kitchen.

Just as he was turning back to the kitchen, his process was interrupted by a light knock on the door.

"Come in," Artimus instructed after a brief pause.

Pushing through the door, Falahar stepped inside. He wore a black wool coat and held a small box in his hands.

"Good afternoon, Lieutenant! I know you said you'd come by to drop off those letters, but I wanted to stop by myself and wish you safe travels."

Artimus considered Falahar for a moment. He seemed rushed, his breath rapid and shallow. His face was a bit pale and despite his forced smile, the experienced investigator could tell there was something more to it.

"Thank you Falahar," Artimus replied, reaching down, and grabbing the letters of resignation.

Walking over to the younger elf, he extended the letters. He looked straight into Falahar's eyes.

"Is there something else? Something I might be able to help you with?"

Falahar shook his head, avoiding eye contact.

"Oh, I brought you a little going away gift," he lifted the small box, giving it a light shake.

"It's really more for Savannah. It's some of that seasoning mix she liked, the one my grandmother makes. I figured she'd want it on hand."

Artimus nodded, accepting the box with his left and handing over the letters with his right.

Falahar took the letters and held them up vertically.

"I'll make sure these get into the hands of the Chancellor," Falahar stated.

Though his breath was leveling out, Falahar kept glancing back, as if he was expecting someone else to come through the door.

"Thank you Falahar. But are you expecting someone else?"

Looking back at the door, Falahar cleared his throat. He turned back to Artimus with a nervous smile and shook his head.

"Yes. I mean no. Well, I'm not supposed to say anything. But I think you and Savannah should get out of the city as soon as you can."

"Why?" Artimus asked without pause.

"I'm sorry!" Falahar blurted. He was sweating, his eyes darting around the room.

"About what? Slow down, take a breath, and tell me what is happening." Artimus grabbed Falahar's arms, looking him square in the face.

"After you stopped by yesterday and told me about where you were going, I could help but share the idea with some of the other castle attendants. But Guildpac. He overheard me talking about Port Mift- about Mirfta-"

"Marftaport," Artimus interjected.

"Yes, about Marftaport. When he confronted me, I refused to tell him about you and Savannah. But I didn't realize how persuasive he could be. I swear, I didn't want to tell him. But for some reason as he pressed, I just couldn't help but tell the truth."

281

"It's the one type of magic he can actually use effectively," interrupted a beautiful voice from the doorway. It was Savannah, standing with a crate full of roots, seeds, and other gardening odds and ends.

Falahar jumped, clutching the letters tight as he swung around and look at Savannah. He bent over, holding his knees and heaving.

"You startled me," Falahar exclaimed. "A type of magic?"

"That's not important," Artimus interjected.

"Yes," Savannah added. "Please, tell us why you are here."

Standing upright, Falahar closed his eyes and let out a long breath.

"Guildpac forbade me and others in the castle from even thinking about leaving the Republic. They said if we did, we'd be branded as traitors. And this morning, I overheard him talking about the two of you. I think they intend to make an example of you both. The sooner you can get out of here, the safer you will be."

Artimus looked at Savannah, locking eyes with his wife and holding her stare. She was resolute, a glint in her green eyes. They exchanged a nod.

"Falahar," Artimus said looking back at their young friend. "Please help Savannah get the rest of our items gathered here."

He motioned to the items he'd gathered thus far.

"I'll fetch Thoron and see if I can get another draft horse and a carriage from the stables. Savannah, can you get a message out? I know the transport wasn't supposed to arrive until this evening, but maybe we can ensure we meet them on the way."

"Go," Savannah replied, stepping forward and motioning outside.

Striding towards the door, Artimus paused and looked back at Falahar. "Thank you," he uttered before heading outside.

The brisk air caught him by surprise, the urgency making him forget how cold it still was. With a shiver, he took a deep breath and started off to the east. Running at a full sprint, he worked his way through the residential district towards the stables.

Only small collections of snow remained, leaving patches of dead grass and small deposits of frost where the snow had fallen. In the months getting married, this area had seen notable growth, with new houses being finished almost every week.

He passed by an assortment of small cottages, but fortunately none of the other residents. Keeping mental notes of all the obstacles and potential terrain advantages, he kept a steady pace. The cool air stung his face, his ears feeling a bit numb.

Ignoring established paths, he took a shortcut through some of the remaining forest. Most of the trees were barren due to the winter snowfall, which also kept the foliage at a minimum. This made it easier for Artimus to weave through the trees and come out on the other side in the open field.

The stables were just up ahead, Thoron's specific stall only about twenty-five meters away. Before retrieving his trusted destrier, he needed to pay a visit to the stablemaster.

Walking down the central path, he passed the pole barn where the unused carriages and wagons were stored. It appeared there were a few options available. Knocking on the stablemaster's door, he looked towards the stables.

These were the only stables for the southeastern residential district and consisted of about a dozen structures, each with eight stalls. The two closest ones housed horses for rent. Listening carefully, he could hear rustling from the nearest stalls, another hopeful sign.

"Enter." The raspy voice of the stablemaster sounded from the other side of the door.

Pushing himself inside, Artimus glanced across the room. Not much had changed since he was last here.

The stablemaster, Ornathorn, as indicated by the gilded nameplate on his desk, really loved horses. Aside from the intricately carved horse silhouettes in his mahogany desk, he had two brass busts of horse heads situated on a shelf behind him. Above this shelf, he'd hung a painting featuring a field full of wild horses. And of course, both side walls were decorated with additional pieces of art, all centered around horses.

Perhaps the most unusual piece was the sculpture standing to the right of the room. Made from used horseshoes, this horse sculpture was some sort of abstract installment that Artimus simply couldn't understand. Then again, art was never one of Artimus's interests.

Ornathorn himself was quite a distinct figure. Just over 1.6 meters tall, the wizened old elf always wore a large-brimmed, bright-colored hat and matching vest and scarf. Today, it seemed his color of choice was fuchsia. His thin gray beard and matching gray hair were always perfectly groomed, and his overlarge spectacles gave him quite a distinct profile.

Eccentricities aside, Artimus had been here enough time to know the drill. Proceeding to the single chair on the left side of the desk, Artimus took a low bow to Ornathorn before sitting.

"Ah, Lieutenant. Are you taking Thoron out for a ride this afternoon?"

Artimus smiled, shifting in his seat, a futile attempt at getting comfortable.

"No, sir. Though, I would like to take Thoron out. I'd also like to rent a draft horse and a carriage."

"A carriage rental? I guess there's a first time for everything. When would you like to have this carriage available?"

Artimus ground his teeth, keeping his lips shut tight.

"The sooner the better. I'm afraid I was a bit careless and forgot to come in, but I had promised Savannah a romantic adventure this afternoon. With the baby due next week, we wanted to take one last time to just relax and enjoy ourselves."

The stablemaster raised his eyebrows, rifling through some parchments and murmuring under his breath.

"You'll need a coachman then I suppose. I might be able to get som-"

"That won't be necessary!" Artimus interrupted. "I mean, excuse me Ornathorn. I appreciate your understanding, but I'm looking for an intimate ride, so I'll be my own coachman. So, if I can just get Thoron, an extra draft horse, and the carriage, I can be on my way."

With a gasp, Ornathorn rifled through his papers and shook his head.

"Oh, my. You know I must follow procedures on this. You must be a licensed coachman to rent out and operate one of our carriages."

Fighting the instinct to roll his eyes, Artimus took a deep breath in through his nose and blinked a few times.

"You know that I am qualified to operate a carriage," he said with eyes closed. "So, I'll be happy to fill out whatever extra form I need to."

Opening his eyes and looking directly at the stablemaster, Artimus made a conscious effort to smile. He was worried his frustration was showing through. But it seemed he was winning Ornathorn over.

Scrunching his face, the old stablemaster gazed up at the ceiling. With a low groan, he pulled out a piece of parchment and dipped a quill in his inkwell.

"Strictly speaking, you must know it's against the law to rent out a carriage to an unlicensed coachman."

Artimus leaned in and whispered.

"I'd consider it a personal favor."

It was dishonest. And Artimus had never used his position like this before. But with his family's future on the line, he didn't have the luxury of considering the larger implications. It was a broken system, and he was getting out.

Leaning back, Ornathorn pulled out a parchment. Dipping his quill in the inkwell, he scribbled a few details in the center and then jotted something else at the bottom of the paper. He offered an exaggerated wink and slid the parchment across the desk.

"So, I will serve as your coachman this afternoon. Please sign right here that you agree to the terms of the rental."

Smiling, Artimus took the quill and signed his name on the agreement.

"Excellent!" Ornathorn exclaimed, taking the contract, and blowing on the ink.

After a few seconds of this, he rolled it up and dropped it in a bin behind his desk.

"Now, I'll just need six silver pieces and I'll get your horse and carriage ready. You're welcome to fetch Thoron while I get the rest into the staging area."

"Six pieces?" Artimus asked, raising his eyebrows.

"I'm a bit pricier than the standard coachman," Ornathorn replied matter-of-factly, a devious grin plastered on his face.

"Of course, you are," Artimus said, reaching into his coin purse and pulling out the six coins. Dropping them on the desk, he stood up and walked outside.

Taking a deep breath, he closed his eyes and focused on the familiar smell of these stables. The subtle scent of composting hay mixed with horse manure might not have been pleasant, but it was oddly comforting. And with the uncertainty of his immediate situation, anything familiar and predictable provided comfort.

As he walked towards Thoron's stable, he found himself thinking through potential scenarios. Hopefully Falahar provided enough warning that he could get the carriage back home and have everything packed up within the hour. But being on the road wasn't enough.

If they were to go on the road towards Marftaport, it meant they'd still be within the borders of Erathal City for another few hours. That would leave them vulnerable to potential capture much longer than he'd like.

On the other hand, they could flee directly east and be outside the city limits in under an hour. That would mean looping back around off road, however. Should Ulagret order them pursued, they'd also be without any potential support for a much longer time -potentially a full day.

While not completely unexpected, the whole situation reinforced just how important it was that they leave immediately.

The idea of punishment bestowed on anyone because they desired to move to another settlement was appalling to Artimus. He would be much happier knowing his child would be born in a place where people were free to come and go as they pleased.

Arriving at Thoron's stall, Artimus brought his thoughts back to the present. Thoron stepped up to the door, neighing as he peered down at Artimus. With bright eyes and an eager nudge, the loyal destrier looked down at his rider.

Artimus smiled, reaching up and scratching Thoron under his chin. Scratching around, he grabbed the door with his left and opened it up.

"I'm afraid I came here in a hurry and didn't bring along any treats. But I promise when we get back home, I'll get you something. We're going to greener pastures, my friend."

Thoron nickered, nuzzling Artimus as he stepped out of the stall. Embracing his trusted companion, the ranger offered a light pat and scratched behind Thoron's ears.

"I must ask of a favor of you though, my friend. I know you're not fond of pulling a carriage, but Savannah and I have a journey to make. Can I trust you to pull your weight?"

Thoron snorted, nodding his head towards the stable exit. Though Artimus knew he didn't fully understand spoken language, he believed there was an understanding of intent. Of the horses he had owned over his lifetime, Thoron was truly a unique and special horse.

"I knew I could count on you. Let's get to it."

Artimus placed the halter on Thoron, securing the straps and giving him another pat. Walking beside his trusted horse, he exited the stables. They walked back towards the pole barn, where Artimus spotted Ornathorn leading a brown draft horse. If there was one positive thing Artimus could say about the stablemaster, it was that he was efficient.

As Artimus approached Ornathorn and the other horse, he grabbed hold of Thoron's halter. Though he trusted Thoron, he didn't know how the other horse might respond.

Staying back, Artimus waited while the stablemaster secured the draft horse to the carriage. The horse appeared docile, standing in place while Ornathorn secured all the necessary straps and latched the buckles. He snorted a couple times, tapping his front right hoof as he was fully attached.

"Go ahead and bring Thoron over," Ornathorn suggested, waving to Artimus.

With a nod, Artimus continued into the pole barn, bringing Thoron up alongside the other horse. The two sniffed at each other, exchanging a nicker before Thoron got into place. While Ornathorn proceeded to get Thoron hooked up, Artimus took a closer look at the carriage.

It was about three meters long by two meters wide. With a dark stain, the pine construction was simple in its design. Smooth lines and no unecessary frills, the front wheels looked to be about two thirds a meter in diameter and the rear wheels looked closer to a full meter.

The front of the carriage had a simple bench seat, which is where both Artimus and Savannah would sit. The rear compartment was left open but provided enough sitting room for four additional occupants. While it might prove a bit difficult, it was just wide enough that he could fit their chest of drawers between those rear benches. Getting all their crates secured might prove a bit of a challenge, but with some creativity it should prove sufficient.

"Alrighty!" Ornathorn exclaimed. "It looks like Thoron and Boron will get on like bees and daisies. If you have Boron and the carriage back by tomorrow mid-day, those six silver pieces will cover it."

"Thank you Ornathorn. I will make sure to return by then."

Though he felt a little guilty for the lie, he did plan to make sure the horse and carriage were returned. He just wasn't certain about the timing.

As Ornathorn stepped aside, Artimus climbed into the carriage and took the reins in hand. With a couple of clicks and a light shake of the reins, Artimus started on the road back home.

# Chapter 25

Erathal City, Southeast Residential District
22 Frozga, 1087 MT

Artimus pulled back on the rope, making sure it was as tight as possible before tying it off in a knot. Though it took some creativity, they had managed to get everything secured to the carriage. The chest of drawers took up most of the floor in the back of the carriage, but there was space enough to fit the desk in as well, legs up.

One crate was then positioned inside the four legs of the desk. The rest were laid out on the seats in the back. With the limited space, they had removed all their clothes from the drawers and instead packed most of Savannah's gardening supplies in there. The clothes were secured in a large sack at the rear of it all. Finally, everything was tied down with various ropes and straps. Of course, the wardrobe and bed had to be left behind, but they had already considered that as a likelihood.

It was a bit unsightly, but considering the imminent threat to their freedom, it would do just fine. Glancing back, he spotted Savannah with her Yggdril tree in hand. Transferred to one of her largest pots, she had draped a large burlap sack over it, which meant her face was blocked from the view. She clutched it tight, her arms wrapped around the large pot.

Clothed in a long sleeve, flowing green dress, and covered with her fur coat, Savannah looked enchanting. Her baby bump appeared to help her support the weight of the pot, her gardening boots covered in dirt and snow as she stood waiting.

"Are you sure we can't stow that somewhere in the back?" Artimus asked.

"This may be the only Yggdril tree left in Erathal. There's no way I'm letting go of it." Her tone was as resolute as expected.

"Of course," Artimus replied, stepping around the pot and placing his hand on the small of Savannah's back.

"Allow me to help you up to your seat then."

"Allow you too?" Savannah joked, her voice rising in pitch. "You know you *have* to!"

Artimus chuckled, guiding his wife to the carriage, and keeping his hand on her back. As they reached the step up to the seat, he gave her a slight push, holding out his left hand to help guide her and keep her balance. One step, and then onto the bench. Savannah sat down, shifting around in her seat and groaning.

"I'm sorry it's not more comfortable," Artimus offered with a toothy smile.

Savannah glared down at him and shook her head.

"Let's just hope my carrier pigeon reaches the courier and he picks up the pace. The less time I spend in this bench, the better."

"I hope so," Artimus replied, walking around the front of the carriage, and giving both Thoron and Boron a pat on the head.

"So, you told him we'd take the main road heading north?" Artimus asked coming around to his side and stepping into the carriage.

"Yes. Since that was the plan originally, I didn't want to complicate things. I just let him know that we'd meet him somewhere along the road. I told him to make haste, so hopefully he heeds the message."

Clicking for the horses to start and offering a slight shake of the reins, Artimus braced himself and the horses started at a slow trot. Leading them down the path towards the main road headed north, he glanced over to Savannah.

"You are truly an amazing elf. I'm sorry we had to rush out like this."

Savannah smiled, matching his gaze.

"You don't have to be sorry. I know you wanted to wait until after the baby was born to move. But I think this response from Ulagret proves that I made the right choice. I don't want our child born in place like this."

Glancing back at the road ahead, Artimus clicked a couple more times, urging the horses to pick up the pace. While they complied, he glanced back at Savannah for just a moment more.

"I agree. As usual, you made the right choice."

"Well, you didn't just marry me for my good looks!" Savannah joked.

"Ehh…" Artimus smiled. "That was a part of it though!"

Savannah shook her head, gently slapping his arm with the back of her left hand. Replacing her hand on the side of the pot, she nodded ahead.

"Let's just keep our eyes on the road. Do you think Ulagret has already sent guards to our home?"

Artimus glanced back, getting one last glimpse at their home as it faded out of sight.

"It's possible. But if we make it to the main road before they get to the intersection, we should be in the clear. Coming from the castle, they'll be heading east to the road. So, if we make it past that intersection and get enough distance on the northern road, we may just make it without incident."

"I hope it works out that way," Savannah replied.

Smiling, Artimus focused on the road.

"One way or another, I'm making sure the three of us all make it safely to Marftaport."

"I know we will," Savannah replied softly.

The two continued in silence for the next few minutes, the air thick with anticipation.

They were only a couple kilometers away from the main road, so each minute that passed, Artimus knew they were that much closer to safety. Despite his words, however, Artimus was concerned. Clutching the reins tight, he kept focused ahead, continuing to urge the horses to pick up speed as they went.

As the minutes passed and they arrived at the intersection to the main road, he breathed a sigh of relief. There were a couple elves on horseback passing, and a mother and her two children walking west, but otherwise it seemed the road was empty. No sign of soldiers.

Proceeding onto the main road, Artimus steered the horses north. After about a minute heading in that direction, he urged them again to pick up speed. A couple clicks and a stern shake of the reins, and they took up a brisk pace.

"You think this is a good speed?" He asked, glancing at Savannah.

"I won't be comfortable either way," she replied. "But the horses seem to be comfortable at this speed. I wouldn't push them much harder unless we must."

"Urgo." Artimus replied.

This main road was wider and smoother than what they started on, but that came with a cost. As they continued north, they were moving into the eastern commercial district, which was sure to be busy this time of day. Yes, this was the slower time of year, but as they passed by the Silktree Tavern, Artimus could already hear the buzz of people up ahead.

Making it to the top of the slope, he looked out along the road. Merchants of all variety were setup within the zone. Mostly elves, but also felite and lizock vendors had set out tables and tents. Clothing, jewelry, art supplies, crafting materials, and all manner of merchants were ready to peddle their goods.

Dozens of elves were spread about, talking to the various merchants. The larger, established shop in the back had some visitors entering and leaving as well. And while most of the traffic was off the main road, there were a few people passing by on horse and on foot.

Keeping a tight hold on the reins, Artimus kept his eyes trained ahead. His mind was focused on getting through this area without having to stop.

Continuing north, Artimus sniffed at the smell of smoke in the air. Looking ahead to his right, he heard the clang of the blacksmith's hammer. The beating of steel added to the clamor of the district, customers and merchants alike having to raise their voice to be heard over the constant noise.

Of course, the blacksmith had set up a small booth as well, displaying a variety of steel weapons. Under Erathal law, citizens could have personal weapons of any variety. But of course, private blacksmiths were not allowed to work with any 'exotic' metals like mythril or adamantium.

It was one of the many ways to make the people feel like they had some control.

Shaking his head at the thought, Artimus kept tracking the pedestrians as they crossed the road. There were a couple rangers ahead, armed with standard mythril swords and wearing the Republic of Erathal crest. They were a standard patrol, assigned to 'maintain order' in the commercial district. Smiling and nodding towards them as they walked past, Artimus was happy to see neither of them recognized him.

Looking to Savannah, Artimus noticed she had a stern look on her face, her eyes locked ahead. Hoping to ease her trepidation, he spoke.

298

"Once we reach the northeast residential district, we should be in the clear. At least until we hit the northern border. How are you holding up?"

Keeping a blank expression, Savannah shifted her gaze towards Artimus.

"As good as you might expect. I'm hoping our friend from Marftaport has a more comfortable carriage. This one was not designed with pregnancy in mind."

Artimus frowned.

"I'm sorry," he replied. "I hope you don't have to bear it much longer. When we do make the transition, I'll hold the Yggdril tree for you too if that will help."

Turning her head, Savannah offered a smile.

"Thank you. I'm not sure if I trust it in anyone else's hands though." She gave a half-hearted chuckle.

"Well, the option is there is you want to take it."

Focusing back on the road, Artimus coaxed the horses to move to the right side. A carriage was approaching on the other side of the road. Drawn by a single white horse, the smaller carriage has a single coachman in front and a small, enclosed cabin in the back. Judging by the leather finishing and iron details, it was likely an elf of some status riding in the rear.

Of course, Artimus didn't need to draw any attention, so he merely smiled at the other coachman as he passed, exchanging a slight nod of acknowledgment. The coachman offered a tip of his hat, returning the smile before continuing past.

Coming to the edge of the commercial district, Artimus felt tension release from his shoulders. The road started to curve north northwest, which would take them through another residential district before leading to the northern border of the city.

The next stretch was uneventful, only a few others passing by on the road. While the snowfall might have been done for the season, the cold weather meant many were still hunkering down indoors. So even as they passed through some of the more populated parts of town, there were few people outside to take notice of them.

After nearly an hour of uneventful silence, the pair found themselves approaching the northern border.

Since the formation of the Republic, there had been a variety of defensive efforts started around Erathal. Among those efforts, there was a heavy focus on building more substantial city walls around the entire city. Artimus couldn't help but think back to a decade ago, when only the major entry points had walls of any kind.

Aside from the castle, external defenses consisted of a few gatehouses along these major roads. By now, all those gatehouses had seen significant improvements and additions. And while there were still some unwalled ways to enter the city borders, all the roads and the immediately surrounding areas had been effectively walled.

The norther border was one of the most well-developed. With stone walls measuring almost five meters in height and at least a meter thick, the gatehouse was not something one could easily subvert. Fortunately, at this time of day without high alert, it appeared the portcullis was raised, and the gate left open.

However, as they approached the gatehouse, Artimus regarded the towers on either side and paid close attention to the soldiers stationed around it. There was an unusual concentration of troops here.

On a day such as this, having a couple guards on foot was standard. The others would be stationed within the towers and could offer support if needed. As they approached the dozen foot soldiers positioned on the interior of the gate, Artimus prayed they were here for some reason other than he and his wife.

As they neared the gate, he glanced over at Savannah, who was wearing a pleasant smile.

"I see you're ready," he whispered. "I'll get us through the gates one way or the other. If you can help ensure we stay alive in that effort, it would be great."

"We're going to be fine," she replied, an unexpected confidence in her voice.

Fueled by that confidence, Artimus pulled the reins to slow the horses. Approaching the concentration of guards, he derived some hope when he recognized their commander.

"Junior Lieutenant Sylvan!" Artimus exclaimed as they approached. "I hope this day finds you well!"

Looked up at Artimus, Sylvan offered a faint smile. Peering past the smile, Artimus could see the strain in the younger officer's eyes, and the tension on his face. There was a slight twitch of his nose as he stepped back and held up his right hand.

"Lieutenant Atyrmirid! I bid you good day. But I must ask you to halt your carriage."

Keeping his face forward, Artimus glanced at Savannah, making sure they were on the same page. With an almost imperceptible nod, he pulled on the reins more, and gave a verbal "slow" command to the horses.

Coming to a stop, Artimus surveyed the other soldiers around them. No one had adopted an aggressive stance, but there was a definite tension in the air. If they were going to get out of town without a conflict, he had to think fast.

"Let's not mince words Sylvan. You've been ordered to arrest my wife and I, have you not?"

"I have," Sylvan replied, his stance still relaxed, but his voice revealing his nerves.

Glancing around at all the soldiers gathered, Artimus took the opportunity to make eye contact with as many as he could. He recognized a few of them, but most were newer recruits, something he no longer played a part in. Looking back to Sylvan and holding his gaze, Artimus let out a sigh.

"Sylvan, do you remember what I told you when you solved your first case as lead investigator?" Artimus asked, his eyes wide to keep on eye on every potential adversary.

"Yes, sir. I do."

"Do you feel you did the right thing in that instance, letting the widow go?" Artimus continued.

"The evidence didn't implicate her. I was convinced then that the butcher acted alone and that she was just another, unsuspecting victim. I still believe that was the correct choice."

"Seeing my pregnant wife and I on this carriage, all our possessions on hand, do we appear to have violated any law? We are simply exercising our right as children of Evorath to live where we please."

"It does look that way," Sylvan replied, staring directly at Artimus.

"And what is your first duty as an inspector?" Artimus asked.

"To examine the evidence."

"Then I submit," Artimus replied, "that you reexamine the evidence. Before you act on any alleged communication calling for our arrest, an arrest for a crime without any evidence, I recommend you gather some evidence. Do you, in your judgement, see a reason to detain our carriage?"

A couple of the soldiers to the right of the carriage were moving around back, their hands drifting down to their side.

"Stand down," Sylvan ordered.

Artimus glanced side to side before turning his attention back to Sylvan. The younger elf glared at him with narrow eyes, mouth shut tight.

"I see no signs of aggression or any indication you wish harm to the Republic. You may pass," Sylvan offered, motioning ahead.

With a click, a whip of the reins, and a smile, Artimus looked back at Sylvan as they passed.

"Thank you."

## Chapter 26

Marftaport, Vistoro's Estate
23 Frozga, 1087 MT

Tel' Shira winced, closing her eyes, and releasing her breath as the carriage came to a halt.

"OK, are you?" Luna Freya asked.

Looking down, Tel' Shira saw the young felite kneading at her leg. Wondering whether the feeling would ever return to her legs, the former warrior forced a smile.

"OK, I am," Tel' Shira replied before looking across the carriage at Morn and Neman.

They were in an enclosed carriage, the carved wood of the siding providing a beautiful, if not claustrophobic means of travel. The red upholstered chairs appeared comfortable, but in her current state Tel' Shira couldn't confirm that assumption. What was most peculiar was the persistent smell, a fragrant scent of jasmine, lavender, and neroli permeating the cabin.

She couldn't figure out where the scent was coming from, but the smell reminded her of a summer meadow. It helped to relax her during the long ride from Dumner to Marftaport. But now that they had finally arrived at their destination, she regarded the doors on either side of the carriage, recalling how difficult it had been to get inside.

Morn was the first to acknowledge her look, standing up from his seat and eyeing the right door.

"I'll get out first. Neman can help you from in here and I'll help you get down outside."

Tel' Shira offered a subtle nod, a movement that triggered pain to shoot up her neck. It was a little less severe than the last time she tried nodding.

The carriage door creaked open, Vistoro peeking his head in before Morn had a chance to move further.

"We've arrived," he announced, looking at each of the passengers in the carriage.

"Little Luna Freya, why don't you hop on out and meet my good friend Tor Noga. I know he's thrilled to meet you!"

The young felite looked at Tel' Shira, her eyes wide, a look of uncertainty causing them to waver. Tel' Shira smiled down at her, offering a slow and deliberate blink.

"Safe, you are here." Tel' Shira reassured her. "Friend, Tor Noga is."

With a nod and a nervous smile, Luna Freya hoped from her seat and walked on all fours to Vistoro. She glanced back at Tel' Shira for a moment before hopping out of the carriage.

"You must be Luna Freya," a soft, deep-toned felite voice exclaimed from outside the carriage. Tel' Shira couldn't make out a clear response from Luna Freya, but she heard a hushed mumble, followed by a deep chuckle.

"Alright, why don't we head inside. There's a hot kettle of tea waiting for us and some snacks we can enjoy while we wait for your other friends."

Another hushed reply from Luna Freya came, followed by soft footsteps.

"Morn, Neman." Vistoro said. "Why don't both of you step down? I'll get in there and help Tel' Shira out."

The two barghest acknowledged one another with a nod before stepping out of the carriage in turn. As they cleared the threshold, Vistoro hopped up, stepping into the cabin. He looked out and nodded.

"Yes, just move the chair right up to the carriage. Morn, you keep it stable. Neman, when I lower Tel' Shira down, you help ensure we set her in it gently."

"Urgo!"

"Of course!"

The brothers replied in unison. They were good at following orders, but Tel' Shira was still not comfortable with the idea of having them help her get about. Her discomfort must have shown through her face.

"Everyone in Evorath owes you a debt of gratitude," Vistoro offered, his words smooth and even toned. "I can't imagine the pain you are still in, but know you are a blessing to Marftaport."

She almost held her tongue, but something inside her told her to speak truthfully.

"More like a curse, it feels," she said plainly. "Appreciate your words though, I do."

Vistoro closed his eyes and nodded. Opening them up and locking her gaze, he reached out and clasped her hands with his own.

"You still can't feel anything?" he asked.

"No," she replied, unable to feel his touch.

"Well," he started in a hushed tone, "I can never repay the sacrifice you've made or even properly compensate you for the guidance you will provide for me and all people who call Marftaport home. But while you're here, I do promise you will have all you could need."

"A burden, I do not wish to be." Tel' Shira replied, her gaze drifting to the floor.

"And you never will be," Vistoro responded. "You'll understand in time. For now, I'm going to help you get out of this carriage. Are you ready for me to lift you?"

There was a pit in her stomach, a feeling that she was going to have to adapt to. Every bone in her body ached for her to move. She hated how helpless her injuries made her feel.

The pain was one thing. But being bound to a wheeled chair the rest of her days was not a fate she could grapple with. And even just being asked whether she was ready to be helped caused her eyes to water at the thought of living the rest of her life this way.

"I can wait as long as you need," Vistoro said, his voice soft and gentle.

"No. Ready, I am," Tel' Shira replied.

"Alright, then please pardon my hands."

Vistoro reached around Tel' Shira's lower back, reaching under both her armpits and sliding his hands under her buttocks. Not being able to feel the touch was surreal, and instinctually she expected herself to respond in some way. But that wasn't what happened.

Instead, she watched as he lifted her from the seat, her tail dangling down behind her as Vistoro stepped back. Vistoro's tail extended straight back, providing a counterbalance as he stood up and pulled Tel' Shira in close. She had little choice but to rest her head on his left shoulder, keeping her eyes wide as he pivoted toward the door. It reminded her of her vision, like she was floating in place.

As Vistoro reached the door to the carriage, he paused for a moment and took a deep breath.

"Alright Neman. As I lower her, make sure to support her upper back and neck. I'll step down and lower her in the chair myself."

"Urgo," Neman replied.

"Good. Tel' Shira, just hang in there."

Vistoro stepped forward, descending the carriage step. He moved at a snail's pace, slowly lowering Tel' Shira towards the wheelchair. As he approached ground level, he called out to Neman.

"Alright Neman. Just support her back and help me set her down gently."

Though he made no audible response, Tel' Shira assumed he complied. And with the blink of her eyes, she was in the chair, watching as Vistoro took a step back.

"I hope that wasn't too painful," Vistoro offered as he straightened his cloak.

"Feel a thing, I did not," Tel' Shira replied.

She hoped her face didn't convey the pain behind that assertion. For even without feeling physical pain, the thought that she'd have to travel like this again weighed heavy on her mind. How was she going to be of any service to Evorath or anyone else if she was so utterly helpless?

Closing her eyes for a moment and inhaling the fresh winter air, she pushed this concern out of her mind. Or at least she tried to. It remained, scratching away at the back of her thoughts like a pernicious rodent.

"Now, why don't I take you on a tour of the grounds?" Vistoro asked with a smile.

"Lovely, that would be."

"Do you want one of us to help?" Neman asked.

"Yeah, I can push her chair if you'd like," said Morn.

"No, that will not be necessary. You two can head inside and let Tor Noga know we'll be in after I show Tel' Shira around the grounds. It shouldn't take us too long."

"Alright!"

"Will do!"

As the two brothers walked off towards the home, Tel'
Shira shifted her gaze down, taking a closer look at the chair she
would be confined to.

It was well-made from the looks of it. Judging by the
grain, it was made from oak; the entire chair was stained a dark
brown. From the smell of it, they used a tobacco finish to protect
the wood from the elements. The armrests on the chair allowed
her arms to rest, with fashioned contours that helped keep them
stable.

As she continued inspecting the chair, Vistoro knelt and
placed her feet on the footrests. These wooden blocks appeared
well suited for their tasks as well, allowing her feet to rest above
the ground. Next to these footrests, there were two wooden legs,
hanging out in front and offering stability. From what she could
tell, they were installed to ensure the chair would remain stable
when at rest.

Behind these, she noted the large wheels, which would
facilitate her movement. She could only assume there were a
couple handles in the back that would allow Vistoro to push her.
While she had heard of devices like this before, this was her first
time seeing one. She wished it would be her last.

"I can't imagine how difficult this all must be," Vistoro
said as he walked around back. "But if there is any way I can
make your stay more pleasant, please let me know. Are you ready
to go?"

"Yes," Tel' Shira lied. "Ready, I am."

Eyes widening as Vistoro tilted the chair, Tel' Shira took another deep breath. Though she realized the configuration of the chair would require it, she didn't appreciate how jarring it would be to be tilted back like this. And as they began moving, she lowered her chin to try and keep a level perspective.

As Vistoro turned her chair around, she took in first impressions of the estate. The grounds were well landscaped, hedges and flowerbeds strategically placed to create a calm and relaxing courtyard. Covered in the remnants of the last snowfall, the cool winter air created a somewhat eerie feel. With fruit trees laid out symmetrically along the path to the home, this made for a garden of both form and function.

The home itself was grand in design; though smaller than any she had seen, the only word that Tel' Shira knew to do it justice was 'castle'. Stone walls stretching at least six meters high, massive oak double doors, a large central keep (at least eight meters tall), and matching turrets on either end created a grand entryway. It was more ornate than battle-ready, as it lacked both corbels and arrow loops.

Vistoro wasn't going down the path to the castle, however. Instead, he took a path leading off to the left. This path led through additional fruit trees. Looking ahead, Tel' Shira spotted a smaller structure.

It had four marble columns and stood about five meters tall. These columns supported an ornately carved dome roof. Even at this distance, Tel' Shira was able to recognize a shrine. The feminine statue that stood at the center was a dead giveaway, a large stone carving of the goddess Evorath with her arms spread wide.

"I usually find myself starting the day with a stroll in the garden and a visit to Evorath's shrine." Vistoro said as they approached. "I hope at some point you'll join me on those morning strolls, but only if it is your wish."

Tel' Shira said nothing at first, doing her best to take in the grounds. Looking at the snow around the path, she imagined this would be quite a beautiful setting in spring and summer months. As they reached the shrine, Tel' Shira was delighted to look up and see the mural painted on the ceiling.

It depicted one of the stories of creation from the Xyvor, an image of Evorath extending her hand over the world she created. Shades of blue, swirls of black and white, and a green and vibrant world. This artistic rendition of Evorath creating her world gave Tel' Shira pause, struggling to swallow a lump in her throat.

"Beautiful, it is." Tel' Shira said after admiring the painting.

"I thought so too. It's one of Tor Noga's works. In addition to tending the grounds, he has quite the gift for artistic endeavors. I think you'll find he is a great conversationalist as well."

"Quite talented, he certainly is."

Tel' Shira continued looking around the shrine, noting the ornate carvings along the trim of the roof and the pedestal holding the Evoarth statue. Though she never considered herself to be too interested in art, this humble little shrine was indeed breathtaking.

"If we continue around back, you'll find the grounds are still a work in progress. There is a partially cleared field stretching out for some distance. I'm hoping to find a farmer who is interested in joining our community. One with experience raising grapes preferably, so we can start a vineyard here. Around the right side of the manse, you'll find we already have a more structured orchard. But most of these trees don't produce in the winter. With that in mind, we can proceed inside at your convenience."

Tel' Shira held her gaze on the painted ceiling a moment longer. She smiled, perhaps the first real smile she had since her injury.

"Ready to go inside, I am."

"Excellent," Vistoro exclaimed, pivoting Tel' Shira back around and heading back towards the path to the home. They proceeded the rest of the way in silence, Tel' Shira continuing to look around and take in as many details as she could. Getting closer to the door of the castle, she noted the carving along the doorframe matched the carving back at the shrine.

"Carve this also, did Tor Noga?" She asked.

"Yes, if it's anything artistically done, it was Tor Noga. The sculpture of Evorath in the shrine was his work as well. It's one of the few possessions I retained when I left my old life behind in Lizock City. You can imagine how thrilled I was when

I spoke to him about Marftaport and convinced him to come live here."

Reaching the double doors, Vistoro let the wheelchair rest, forcing Tel' Shira to lift her head and look straight ahead.

"Impressive, his abilities are," she said after a moment of reorienting.

Vistoro stepped around to the right door and offered a nod as he pulled it open. Leaving it open wide, he circled back around the wheelchair.

"When you're ready," he said.

"Please, proceed."

This time, Tel' Shira closed her eyes as she was tilted back and pushed forward, lessening the impact of the movement. After a few moments, she opened her eyes and found herself being pushed through a large foyer. Tilting her head around, Tel' Shira took in her surroundings as best she could, trying to ignore the pain caused by her movement.

The walls were mostly bare, save some sconces with candles to offer illumination. By Tel' Shira's estimates, the foyer must have been at least five meters wide and eight meters long. It ended in a grand, circular staircase at the far end.

"As you can see, there's still some decorating to be done in here. And truth be told, there's still a good deal of construction to complete on the top floor. But hopefully you'll find your stay welcoming. The others are undoubtedly in the sitting room here."

There were two doors on either side. The ones to the left were both closed, but the nearest one on the right was left open. Vistoro was wheeling Tel' Shira towards this open door, where she could smell the unmistakable odor of the barghest brothers.

As they entered the room, she took a moment to take in her surroundings. This sitting area appeared to serve as a passthrough, with doors on the north and east walls. A large sofa was accompanied by an array of upholstered chairs and a large, round table in the center of the room. Aside from this, there was a large painting on the south wall; it appeared to be a depiction of this very estate, the style clearly a work of Tor Noga.

Luna Freya sat to the right of the sofa, looking around the room with eyes wide. The barghest brothers were seated on the sofa, both drinking from small teacups. Tor Noga sat across from them. And as Tel' Shira entered the room, the felite artist reached over and picked up the silver teapot. As Vistoro lowered Tel' Shira into a spot just before the table, Tor Noga motioned her way.

"Welcome Tel' Shira. Would you like a cup of tea? It's my own winter blend."

Tel' Shira took a deep breath through her nose, forcing a smile as she did. This was all so much more opulent than she was accustomed to. And still struggling to accept her lack of mobility made it feel overwhelming.

"No, thank you." She replied after a pause, doing her best to hold her smile.

316

"If you change your mind, please let me know." He replied with a nod, placing the teapot down and picking up his own cup. "I'd be happy to serve you in any way I can."

"I think that applies to all of us!" Vistoro exclaimed, stepping around and taking a seat next to Tor Noga; the artist offered him the teapot and an empty cup as he sat.

"Thank you," said Vistoro grabbing the teapot and pouring some into his cup. After pouring his tea, he lifted the cup to his mouth and sniffed it before taking a sip.

"Now, please allow me to make more proper introductions for everyone. Tor Noga, you've had the chance to meet the brothers Morn and Neman. They have spent the last few months as students of the Avatar. He saw it fit that they should have a change of pace. So, they've come to help Tel' Shira and are ready to offer their strong backs in building up Marftaport. Morn, Neman, anything you'd care to add?"

Morn and Neman looked at one another and nodded.

"I'd just say we look forward to the opportunity to serve and learn everything we can from you all here," said Morn.

"And that goes for me too!" Added Neman. "If you ever need anything, day or night, I'll be there to help Miss Tel' Shira."

It was a heartwarming sentiment. The looks in their eyes, the timbre of their voices; they were sincere in their desire to serve.

But Tel' Shira didn't want to be taken care of. She wanted to take care of herself. Feeling a tear forming in her left eye, she closed her eyes for a moment and focused on her breathing.

"Your enthusiasm is surely appreciated," Vistoro said after a moment.

"Now, I think Tel' Shira's reputation proceeds her. Is there anything you'd like to say Tel' Shira?"

"At the moment, no." Tel' Shira shook her head, the sharp pain from this movement another reminder of how fragile and helpless she felt.

"Very good," Vistoro replied with a nod. "Which just leaves our youngest addition: little Luna Freya. Tomorrow, we'll show you around town and introduce you to a few other felite members who have come to call this town home. I hope in time you'll find your new family to be there for you whenever you might need us."

Luna Freya avoided his gaze, looking away as he looked at her. She scratched behind her ears, face downcast and posture defensive.

"Now, there is one other person living here that you'll get to meet this evening. Our chef and housekeeper, Sissera. I believe she is out procuring some supplies, but she'll be thrilled to meet you all tonight at dinner. Tor Noga, would you care to make your own introductions?"

Tor Noga took another sip of his tea. With a smile, he lowered it to his lap and spoke.

"It would be my pleasure. And, I'll start by saying it's a true honor to meet you all. I must also admit that I envy you all. Being able to learn from the Avatar directly, or to fight alongside him; I look forward to learning more about each of you."

He paused, taking another sip of his tea before placing the cup back on the table.

"As for me, I'm sure Lord Vistoro has already told you that I am an artist. I enjoy painting, sculpting, and fancy myself a bit of a gardener as well. I like to think Evorath is the original artist, forming this world and all of us living on it. So, I take a lot of my inspiration from her creation, which is why I enjoy working in it.

"If I'm not wrapped up in my latest artistic endeavor, you'll likely find me tending to the grounds here. Vistoro has been kind enough to provide me with room and board here in exchange for some help in maintaining the grounds. I get the better end of that deal And I know I'm safe to speak for Vistoro when I say you all are welcome to remain here for as long as you desire. But I've said quite enough for now. Again, it's a pleasure to meet you all."

Tel' Shira had never met a felite who spoke in the common tongue so fluently. But as she listened to Tor Noga and looked at the enthusiasm on his face, there was a small tingle in the middle of her back. And for some inexplicable reason, she felt like her time here might not be so bad after all.

"Thank you, Tor Noga. And I want to affirm what he said about you all staying at my estate. I'll speak to you each in turn about your compensation for services rendered around the estate. But please know, you will always be welcome in my home. If you do desire to build a more private home of your own, however, I'd be happy to help you on that journey as well."

Taking another sip of his tea, Vistoro looked around at those gathered and smiled.

"Now, if you'd like, I'll show each of you to your rooms. Morn, Neman, if you would follow me upstairs. I'll return for you Tel' Shira and Luna Freya."

As Vistoro led the barghest brothers from the sitting room, Tel' Shira considered her situation once more. Her physical handicap aside, this was a place she could see herself living.

# Chapter 27

Erathal News Article 101:349
Order Will Prevail
By, High Wizard Guildpac

More than 20 years ago, the Kingdom of Erathal suffered a horrible tragedy. Our great King, Ulagret Jr., was mercilessly killed by lawless lizock criminals. In the aftermath of that incident, I met an elf that I thought would become a valued member of our great Kingdom.

Today, I have the unpleasant duty of admitting I was terribly wrong. That elf, Artimus Atyrmirid, and his wife Savannah have shown their true colors. And those colors are not aligned with our great Republic of Erathal.

Showing themselves to be agents of chaos and disorder, these two have abandoned their positions here in Erathal to align themselves with a group of rogue extremists outposted to the northwest. At present, Chancellor Ulagret has decided not to pursue them, but if anyone encounters either of these two around Erathal City, they are asked to immediately contact the authorities.

After fleeing the city, it seems the pair of former rangers have aligned themselves with a rogue lizock settlement. Full of violent outlaws and anarchists, we do not believe this settlement poses any immediate danger to the sovereignty of Erathal. However, we caution all citizens to avoid traveling west of the western river.

While your leaders discuss how to best handle the situation, I urge you to be on guard. If you believe any of your neighbors may be aligned or otherwise supportive of this rebellious activity, we urge you to contact your local constabulary. Remember, we worked hard to make this Republic a place where all elves can live in safety, knowing they are secure from outside danger.

Knowing this, it is also my duty to comment on the law passed just this morning, which addresses safety concerns in commerce. Additionally, it includes measures to help handle those who might look to disturb the peace we have established here.

In case you missed the decree, here is a short summary of the new law, Erathal Standard Commerce Code 142:

No citizens of Erathal City are to engage in trade of any kind without the formal, written authorization of the Chancellor. If you believe a neighbor or other acquaintance may be involved in illegal commerce activities, you should report it to your local constabulary. The Republic guarantees legal protection for those who report such activity, and in some cases, you may even qualify for a reward for turning in violators.

While the law doesn't change the day-to-day operations of those in the Merchant Guild, keep in mind that restrictions still apply. Specifically, an addendum has been added that all Merchant Guild members must report where and how they are sourcing their goods for sale. Only goods obtained from entities holding a legal treaty with the Republic of Erathal will be accepted. Any exceptions will require signed authorization from the Senator of Trade.

In addition to this trade addendum, I feel it is a good time to remind citizens of Erathal General Code 13, which outlines how citizens are required to report any rebellious activity to their local constabulary.

I have faith in the people of Erathal and I know most of us are loyal, upstanding citizens. Rather than let this news dampen your day, I encourage everyone to consider the benefits that these new laws will have. Safer trade is good for everyone.

For those who have questions or concerns about the new laws, please feel free to visit the Senator of Trade's office at the castle. I'm also pleased to share that the Executive Magistrates have scheduled two town halls in the coming weeks to ensure everyone has a forum to get clarifications and find answers to any questions.

The disorder and chaos of the world can sometimes seem overwhelming but know The Republic of Erathal is on your side. Together, we can make Evorath a safer place for all elves.

.=.=.=.=.=.=.=.=.

Forest Camp, Central Erathal
23 Frozga, 1087 MT

Zelag sat on a log, eyes glued to his feet. Stuck playing back the events of last week, he hadn't even bothered going to the service this morning.

Every time he closed his eyes, he saw the blood-covered snow and the look on Casandra's lifeless face. When he managed to dream, he was haunted by the battle, once again having to witness that monster cut through his only friend. Sleep deprived and filled with grief, he didn't have the willpower to transform into another form, even though he knew it would help alleviate the pain.

Maybe he wanted to feel the pain. Perhaps that was why he maintained this human form, full of its deep emotions and terrible need for food and sleep. Yes, food. That was another thing he had been neglecting as of late.

Normally, the different flavors in this human form provided him with a great sense of enjoyment. But they held no taste anymore. He lived in a black and white world.

No taste, no flavor, and no happiness.

Stuck in this deep pit of despair, the young shapeshifter felt like he was back in his home village, surrounded by his dead loved ones. Without Casandra's voice, her smile, and her ever-present support, how could he even begin to move forward?

He felt numb, drifting through the dark depths of his thoughts, and finding nothing but pain.

"Zelag!"

Like a turtle looking out from its shell, Zelag raised his head, taking his time to behold the speaker. It was Silkhair, her light brown fur and soft features interrupting his haze of despair. She wore a wide smile, her sky-blue eyes much too bright for

Zelag's somber mood. With a blank expression, he looked at her unblinking.

"Hello Zelag. I don't know if you remember me. It's Silkhair. I just arrived this morning from Dumner, and the Avatar suggested I have you show me around."

Zelag blinked, staring past Silkhair.

"You should ask someone else. I'm busy."

Silkhair glanced around, looking to her left and right. Her smile wavered, but only for a moment.

"I hate to call you a liar, but to me it appears you are just sitting on a log. In either case, the Avatar was quite clear. You're supposed to show me around. Apparently, he had you prepare a tent for me as well?"

What nerve? How could she understand what Zelag was feeling?

Zelag stood up with a huff, frowning as he turned around.

"Fine, follow me."

He wanted to collapse. To simply lay out on the floor and fade away into the soil. Perhaps if he changed form to match the dirt, he could force himself to fade out of existence. Then he could join Casandra, his progenitor, and the rest of his kind who had left this world for the next.

That would make things easier. And with each footfall, he felt like he might give into the temptation to try.

"You gave a really touching testimony," Silkhair spoke from behind, her soft voice snapping him out of his head.

"I didn't know Casandra well, but I wish I had," Silkhair continued. "She sounded like a wonderful friend."

Zelag stopped in his tracks, biting his bottom lip, and fighting to hold back tears.

"She was," he muttered, his voice raspy.

He didn't know what else to say. He didn't care to talk about it.

"I'm sorry." Silkhair laid her hand on his shoulder. "If you ever want to talk about anything, know I'm always happy to lend an ear."

Zelag shook his head and sniffed. Rubbing his eyes, he shrugged off her touch and started walking forward.

"No, I'm fine," he lied. "Let's just get you to your tent."

At a brisk pace, Zelag continued southeast. There was a small clearing here and a less direct path heading south, but there was no sense in wasting time. Instead, he continued through the brush, brushing aside some vines and stomping through the uneven forest floor.

"I guess there's still some paths that have to be carved out, huh?" Silkhair asked, slapping aside some overgrown branches.

"You can keep on the path and head south and then east, or we can cut through here. The brush isn't too dense," Zelag declared, pressing forward.

Casandra never complained going off the designated paths.

After a few minutes driving through the bush, Zelag stepped into the clearing. Since everyone else was at the morning sermon, the main camp area was still empty, no one around to slow things down.

Despite the lack of other people, the clearing was still abuzz with noise. The chirping of birds and scurrying of small rodents, along with the light winter breeze created a cacophony of sound.

"This is where most of the Avatar's students live," Zelag said, holding up his hands and motioning around.

Motioning to the longhouse in the center, Zelag continued forward.

"This longhouse has a stove and kitchen, so it's used mostly for group meals. But there are beds in the back as well, which are used for those who might be visiting temporarily. The rest of us live in whatever shelters we care to fashion."

Motioning around at the other structures, he gazed past the shack Morn and Neman had built while they were here, pointed to the small tent where Negla was living, and walked around to the cabin an elf had built.

"How many people live here?" Silkhair asked.

"I'm not sure," Zelag replied. "It seems like new people show up every week. But who stays is another matter. There are at least a dozen students here all the time."

"Wow, I would not have guessed there were so many here. Does the Avatar always choose his students like he did with me, or do some of them just come here seeking his counsel?"

Zelag shrugged. "I think most just come here."

"So which one of these will I be staying in?" Silkhair asked.

"Over here," Zelag replied, walking further to the east.

They reached a large Erath. Standing at least 50 meters tall, Zelag had used this Erath as the anchor point for Silkhair's tent. The large tarp was fixed between the Erath and a neighboring oak, allowing for a footprint big enough to accommodate a full-grown centaur.

Holding both his hands out towards the tent, Zelag looked at Silkhair.

"Here you are," he said. "Why don't you get settled in? Put your bag down inside."

"Thank you Zelag," Silkhair replied with a smile.

Zelag closed his eyes and frowned. "You're welcome."

His voice must have revealed his lack of sincerity, but he really didn't care. And as Silkhair pulled the tent open and went inside, Zelag decided it was his chance to get away.

Without a word, he took off, running west, away from the tent.

He didn't know what he planned at first, but as he got to the edge of the clearing, he continued. Pushing back through the same brush he led Silkhair through, he ran as quickly as he could manage. And when he came out on the other end, he didn't stop.

Snow melting on the ground, trees still mostly barren, he needed to get out of this place.

Yes, that was exactly it.

There was nothing left for him here. Without Casandra, he was once again alone in the world. And waiting here would do nothing but remind him of what he lost. He needed to get away.

Letting out a primal yell, he charged forward. He tore through foliage, not paying any attention to where he was going.

It didn't matter.

A surge of adrenaline fueled his exodus. But as he broke through another clearing, he recognized a familiar creek.

He ran longer than he realized. This little creek was one he and Casandra had visited on many occasions. It was just northwest of the camp and the tranquil setting always brought him a sense of calm. Still iced over for the winter, it didn't have the same impact now.

"Zelag," came an unexpected, but familiar voice.

Turning to the south, he watched the Avatar push aside a branch and step into the clearing.

"I thought you were showing Silkhair around. What are you doing here?" the Avatar asked.

"I'm leaving," Zelag answered without a second thought.

The Avatar glanced around the clearing, taking slow, deliberate steps towards Zelag.

"You are in pain, my child. But you do not have to face that pain alone. Stay, and continue your training with me."

"No," Zelag replied automatically.

"I can't stay here anymore."

Stepping forward, the Avatar kept his hands at his side. He locked eyes with Zelag.

"*Is there really nothing I can do to convince you to stay?*" The Avatar asked, his voice ringing out in Zelag's head.

"*No,*" Zelag thought, holding his teacher's stare.

"*When we first met, you opened my eyes to a new world of possibility. But I was empty, my people gone. Casandra was all I had and having her here helped me move forward. She gave meaning to my life when there was none. How can I ever find that here?*"

The Avatar nodded and closed his eyes.

"*I see. You must find a way to live on your own. You understand that as a Preajin you will outlive everyone you meet. If you keep relying on them to give your life meaning, you will never be free to live as Evorath would want you to.*"

"Yes," Zelag broke the silence. The Avatar opened his eyes, again locking in on the shapeshifter's gaze.

"You will always be welcome here Zelag. And I hope you remember that you still have friends left in Erathal. Not just me,

330

but Artimus, Savannah, Irontail, Tel' Shira, Oogmut. We all cared for Casandra, and we all care for you. Don't forget that."

Sniffing and fighting back tears, Zelag shook his head.

"I won't."

"Then go with Evorath. And when you are ready to resume your training, simply pray to her. I will always be ready to answer."

"Thank you, teacher." Zelag squeezed his eyes tight and rubbed them. Taking a deep breath, he exhaled slowly and looked back at his teacher.

With no intention of returning to this form again, Zelag concentrated on the reliable form of the dingo.

Gritting his teeth through the painful transformation, he felt his body make the shift. As his four legs took form and fur covered his entire body, he thought only of running free. Finishing the transformation, he released a howl.

And without another thought, he ran.

## Chapter 28

Marftaport, Free City
1 Pertga, 1088 MT

Irontail laughed, a deep and hearty sound reverberating throughout the banquet hall.

Oogmut chuckled and shook his head.

The lizock couple, Zachiro and Viviar wore wide grins.

"It's not *that* funny," Mojo interjected, shaking his head.

"Maybe that's because we're laughing at you," Oogmut replied.

Mojo growled.

"Oh, it's all in good fun," Irontail said, his voice still laced with humor.

"Sure, it starts out that way." Said Mojo. "But then suddenly everyone around town is asking me about the 'dye incident' and I'll never live that down."

"With all the new people coming here, I don't think you'll have to worry." Said Oogmut. "But we'll always remember."

While the others laughed, Irontail took a swig from his mug. The sweet honey flavor, hint of crisp apple, and botanical notes made for the perfect beverage to celebrate a new year. As he placed the mug back on the round table, he looked around the room.

His table was only half filled, Oogmut, Mojo, Irontail, and Zachiro and Viviar being its only occupants. While this was

Oogmut and Mojo's first time meeting the lizock couple, Irontail had been acquainted with them for some time. They were two of the lizock who followed Vistoro in forming the original outpost here.

Sitting at the center of Marftaport, they had constructed this longhouse to serve as a community meeting house for celebrations such as this. And looking out at the many unfamiliar faces, Irontail felt encouraged about their mission. The room was buzzing with conversations from people who moved here from every corner of Erathal.

Surveying the room, he looked at the many round tables. While some groups were homogenous, most followed the example of this very table. Of the nearest two tables, one was made up entirely of lizock. But the other had a dwarf, a couple of elves, a lizock, and a felite all gathered in fellowship.

The entire longhouse had this diverse makeup, even a couple of lamias having recently joined the city from an unknown village. They were seated at a table towards the other end of the room. Tel' Shira was seated at that table as well, along with Morn, Neman, and the little orphan Luna Freya. Finally, the table was rounded out by an unfamiliar elf and a couple lizock.

Continuing to look around the room, Irontail spotted Artimus and Savannah next. They were a few tables away, sitting with a few other elves, a couple lizock, and a dwarf.

The sound of clanging metal pulled Irontail back into the moment, shifting his attention towards the table in the center of the room. Vistoro stood on his chair at this table, banging a large spoon against an empty platter.

"If I may have everyone's attention for just a moment, I want to make an announcement," Vistoro exclaimed, his voice a bit hoarse.

"Thank you. Yes, thank you all," he yelled over the other voices. Within a few moments, the side conversations died down, leaving the room in relative silence.

"When I first received a vision from Evorath about this place, I was scared. Leaving behind my position and the lion's share of my wealth was difficult enough. But finding people who listened to the message and understood the cause -that was the real challenge!

"I lost everyone from my previous life. But I gained friendships that are more valuable than any treasure here in this world. I know most of you would prefer to remain unnamed, so I won't call you out now. But for those of you who were there in those early stages, who helped build this longhouse, those who assisted in the construction of my estate, who built the original tower, and the always-welcoming tavern, I offer a profound thank you.

"Of course, all of you who have joined in this past year, I'd like to also extend my gratitude. Without the many faithful and hard-working people who have helped build up this town, we would not be where we are today. It led to our trade relations with Dumner, and it's turned this community from a simple outpost into a full-fledged town.

"And now we consider where we are today. In this past week, we've had forty-seven new members join us -and that could be forty-eight at any time! As our humble little town nears two hundred souls, I want to say from the bottom of my heart: thank you. Every one of you is an important part of this community.

"A year from now when we look back and celebrate the new year, I'd like to make a request. Let us consider this day the official birth of our humble town, Marftaport. In the wake of victory over Death and considering our growing numbers, it's time to declare loud and clear for all Evorath to hear; we are free."

Vistoro reached down, taking a hold of his mug, and raising it overhead.

"So, toast with me now, my new family and dear friends. To freedom!"

"To freedom!" more than one hundred voices rang out, including Irontail's.

Taking a gulp of his mead, Irontail wore a wide smile. Everyone in the room seemed overjoyed, various other cheers flying around.

"Well, that was motivating," Oogmut commented, rocking in his chair, and looking around the room.

"It was indeed," Zachiro said with a nod, his deep monotone always a bit disarming.

"You know, Irontail," Viviar began, her high-pitched voice a sharp contrast to her husband's. "I've been meaning to point out one of our new residents that you might look forward to meeting."

Raising his eyebrows, Irontail put down his mug and leaned in. "Oh, please share the details!"

Smiling, Viviar pointed over to the table with Artimus and Savannah.

"It's that bearded fellow over there. He's a blacksmith named Keldor Stalwart. He's quite the sociable fellow, chatting up a storm at the tavern every night since he arrived. But what you might find interesting is that he is building the town's first forge. In fact, he's not even 130 years old yet, but he brings quite a reputation with him. Apparently, many dwarves already consider him the greatest living blacksmith."

Irontail looked more closely at the dwarf seated so many tables away. He looked to be about average height for a dwarf, just under a meter and a half tall. His auburn and copper hair flowed right into a fiery red beard, which hung down below his chest. With speckles of food lining that beard, he didn't look all that impressive. But Irontail had learned in these past few years just how easily looks could deceive.

"Is he the first dwarf to come here?" Irontail asked. "I see a few others throughout the hall."

"The others came with him," Zachiro interjected.

"Yes," Viviar continued. "He brought along a young apprentice. And it seems a few others followed him as well. All

337

of them are involved in either ore mining or construction, so they've been quite a welcome addition. Once Keldor's forge is up and running, who knows how many others might follow?"

"And does he have all the materials he needs to get the forge up and running?" Irontail asked.

"You'd have to ask him yourself," replied Zachiro.

Viviar glared at her husband, tongue darting between her teeth. "Yes, but I suspect you'll want to introduce yourself for other reasons. Once he is forging again, Dumner might benefit from his skills."

"Yes, I suppose I'll introduce myself then," Irontail replied.

Taking one last gulp of his mead, he regarded Mojo and Oogmut.

"Maybe the two of you should actually look at contributing to the town and see if you can help him with the construction."

Oogmut took a drink and shook his head.

"I don't know about Mojo, but I'm leaving tomorrow. I'll be traveling around Erathal forest and letting all the trolls I can find know that there is safety in Marftaport."

"Do you think many of them will listen?" Zachiro asked.

"I have faith Evorath will touch the hearts of those who need to hear," Oogmut replied confidently.

"While you discuss this," Irontail interjected, "I'll take my leave. I'm curious to meet this Keldor fellow."

Trotting away from the table, Irontail looked around the room. Most of those gathered seemed well entrenched in their seats, but there were still a few wandering about the room. It really was a sight to behold.

The last time Irontail had witnessed such a diverse gathering was the Xyrloom ritual. It had much fewer people and ended much less amicably. But everyone here seemed genuinely interested in peaceful relations with one another. It was amazing to see all Evorath's children, regardless of race, getting along and working towards a common goal.

Approaching the table with Artimus, Savannah, and Keldor, the centaur chieftain smiled.

"Pardon the interruption," he said stepping up beside the table. "I'm wondering if I might join you for a bit."

Artimus and Savannah returned his smile, but it was Keldor who spoke up first.

"Of course! But only if you're ready to toast with the finest dwarven whiskey!"

His boisterous energy was matched with a gruff yet youthful tone. At this distance, Irontail noticed his cheeks were a bit rosy, suggesting he'd likely already consumed a good deal of that whiskey himself.

"Who would I be to refuse such an offer?" Irontail asked, glancing sideways at Artimus. The elf looked like he was holding back a chuckle, averting his eyes from Irontail's gaze.

"Excellent!" Keldor shouted, slapping the table. "You look like a centaur who knows how to have a good time."

Reaching under the table, Keldor pulled out a bottle, about a liter in size. It was brown and had a mountain symbol carved in the side. Bringing it to his mouth, Keldor bit down on the cork and pulled it out with his teeth. In a fluid motion, he spit the cork onto the ground and offered the bottle to Irontail.

"Take the first swig my friend!"

"Oh, I hadn't realized you were opening a new bottle. I hope that wasn't for my behalf," Irontail said nervously.

"Nonsense," Keldor replied, giving the bottle a shake and spilling some in the process.

Grabbing the bottle, Irontail held it out for just a moment, reconsidering whether this was a good idea.

"To Marftaport, and to your forge!"

With that, Irontail tilted his head back and poured some whiskey into his mouth. Gulping down the liquid, he tried to ignore the foul taste. It was like the dwarves had taken pure alcohol and mixed it with pond scum and a dash of swamp water. Even worse, as he swallowed, he felt the burn travel all the way down his esophagus.

Warmth in his stomach, Irontail lowered the bottle and winced, trying to maintain his composure.

"That is," he paused, clearing his throat. "That has to be one of the strongest whiskeys I've ever had."

Releasing a hearty chuckle, Keldor reached out and grabbed the bottle. He threw his head back and chugged down a few mouthfuls before taking it away and letting out a loud belch.

"Such a fine vintage!" he exclaimed.

"And you, my centaur friend. Please, park yourself at our table, and share with me. How might I address such a fearless warrior as thee?"

Again, Irontail glanced at Artimus, who offered a shrug this time.

"You heard the dwarf," Artimus said, nodding towards the two empty chairs.

Shaking his head, Irontail stepped over to the empty spot at the table and pulled both the chairs away. He stepped up and lowered to his knees, putting him at the right height to converse with the others.

As he took this position, Keldor slid the bottle across the table.

"You have to have more than one!" he proclaimed with a laugh.

Not wanting to offend the dwarf, Irontail paused and thought about his options. He wasn't going to admit how awful he thought it tasted. But he also didn't want to have any more. Perhaps there was another option.

"I think I'd be doing you a disservice if I accepted more," Irontail said. "I'm sure you could only bring so many bottles with you, so I'd hate to drink so much of it. I was rather enjoying the honey mead anyways, so I'd prefer to stick with that for now."

Gritting his teeth, he looked intently at Keldor. The dwarf wore a blank expression, but after a few moments he leaned over and grabbed the bottle back with a smile. Letting out a chuckle, he took another swig from the bottle before placing it down.

"Alright then, but don't be afraid to ask if you change your mind!" Keldor said. "Now, tell me about yourself."

"Of course," Irontail replied with a nervous smile.

"I am Irontail, the current chieftain of Dumner."

"You're Irontail?" Keldor interrupted, leaning forward, and slapping his hand on the table. The entire table shook.

"Well, it is a true honor to meet you Irontail. What is a person of your position doing in a free place like Marftaport though?"

Irontail grinned, closing his eyes and nodding.

"Yes, my title does sound a bit out of place. I hope it's one that I'm able to shed sooner than later. But that's another conversation entirely. As for what I'm doing here, Marftaport can count Dumner as an ally. Lord Vistoro and I have been maintaining trade relations for many months now. I hope one day Dumner, and all centaur, will follow the example of Marftaport."

"Now that's a hope that you have to drink to!" Keldor said with a smile. He took a swig of the whiskey before sliding it across the table to Irontail.

"I suppose you're right," Irontail replied, taking the bottle, and preparing his nerves. With just a momentary pause, he held the bottle at his lips and then took the plunge. Closing his eyes as the burn went down his throat to his stomach, he slid the bottle back across to Keldor.

"Dumner could be considered what some have coined a minarchy," Savannah interjected.

"A minarchy?" Keldor asked, tilting his head, and running his thumb and forefinger across his mustache.

"I think what she means," Irontail replied, "is that the function of the government is minimal. There are few laws. And my goal is to eventually eliminate all centralized authority."

"Why not just come join us here?" Keldor asked before taking another drink from his bottle.

"I feel I can make a difference in Dumner," Irontail replied instinctually. "Us centaur are a stubborn people. And I think it's a gradual road to convincing them they can make decisions without the need to rely on a ruler. If I left now, I know there are a few elders who would step into an authoritative role. I owe it to my people to ensure they can experience the freedom Evorath intended."

With a nod, Keldor finished drinking and let out a loud belch. Hitting his fist against his chest a couple of times, he groaned.

"I don't envy your position then," the dwarf coughed after a few more seconds' pause. "But I applaud your dedication to your people."

Savannah pushed away from the table, her chair dragging on the floor. Looking up at her, Irontail noticed the color draining from her face. Artimus leapt from his chair, turning towards his wife.

"I think it's time," Savannah said, her voice strained.

"Right now?" Artimus asked, his voice rising in pitch.

"Yes, now."

Artimus reached out, supporting Savannah and helping her rise from the chair. She clutched her side as she rose, her cheeks tense and eyes wide. Letting out a long exhale, she nodded.

"Definitely now."

"Now it's a real party!" Keldor interrupted, jumping to his feet. "Don't worry, Keldor Stalwart will help this baby find its way out!"

"I think we're better off just the two of us," Artimus replied swiftly, his head darting back and forth across the room.

As Keldor opened his mouth to respond, Irontail stood up and trotted over.

"Keldor, why don't you come with me and meet a couple of my friends who will be moving here sooner or later. How many trolls have you had the privilege of meeting?"

Artimus caught Irontail's gaze, mouthing a 'thank you' before turning and walking off with Savannah. As the two walked away, Keldor shook his head and smiled.

"A troll? Well, let me bring another one of these bottles with me then!"

Keldor reached under the table and pulled out a fresh bottle of whiskey.

How many had he put under there?

Rubbing the back of his neck, Irontail watched as Artimus and Savannah exited the hall. Part of him wished he could follow.

And yet, he couldn't help but remember the words of the Avatar when they had discussed Marftaport back at Dumner.

With this child, Artimus and Savannah were truly preserving the Legacy of Evorath.

## Epilogue

Paxvilla, Old Greg's Tavern
12 Faetre, 1148 MT

Slouching in his seat, eyes trained on the tavern entrance, Zelag watched for any sign of his mark.

The crowd was boisterous tonight; laughter, song, and dance creating quite the clamor. Over the past hour, he had already had to shoo away several parties intruding on his space. But this small, four-seat table in the northeast corner of the bar was the perfect spot. It provided a clear line of sight on the door and gave him free access to the stairs.

He brushed back his shoulder-length blonde hair, hand running over his pointed ear and thinking about his best escape route. Though Paxvilla was exclusively a human settlement, an elvish visitor was not an uncommon sight in these parts. And this form provided him with better vision and hearing than any human shape he might take.

"Excuse me sir," a human interrupted his thoughts. He was a portly fellow, fair-skinned with amber hair and brown eyes. With weathered skin and calloused hands, he was no stranger to hand work. And while he wore a simple brown tunic and pants, the quality of his leather belt and boots suggested he was a man of some means.

A shorter woman stood next to him, her long brown hair and blue dress solidifying Zelag's assumption about the man's station in life. She stared at the ground, shifting nervously with both hands behind her back.

"How might I help?" Zelag asked with a forced smile.

"I couldn't help but notice you sitting here by yourself. Are you from the Erathal Republic? I might have a trade proposition that would interest you if so."

The man spoke with confidence, no hesitation in his deep voice. But there was a hint of desperation in his eyes, which seemed to waver as he spoke.

"I'm sorry," Zelag replied. "I'm afraid I'm not from Erathal and I'm not looking to make any business deals. I'm just here to meet an old friend."

Looking past the couple, Zelag kept his eyes trained on the tavern door.

"Oh, I see," the annoying man replied, stepping to the left and obscuring his view of the door. "Would you be intere-"

"No, thank you." Zelag interrupted with a raised voice. He stood up to keep an eye on the door. "Please leave me in peace while I wait."

The woman frowned, scrunching her face, and glaring at Zelag. Her husband wrapped his arm around her and nodded.

"I'm sorry to have disturbed you sir."

Whispering to one another as they walked away, the couple pushed through the crowd towards the bar. Good riddance.

Sitting back in his seat, Zelag took hold of his tankard, swirling the contents within. He had ordered a single beer to help blend in, and he knew if his mark didn't arrive soon, he'd have to order another. But these elvish tastebuds did not appreciate the strong hoppy flavor of this beer, which made him anxious for his target to arrive.

As if answering his thoughts, the door to the tavern flew open. And a group of young men walked in.

"Damn." Zelag mumbled under his breath. Without a thought, he kicked back and swallowed the rest of his beer. He did his best to get it down quickly, but the overpowering taste of hops and sour warmth still caused him to recoil as he swallowed.

The tavern door opened again. Why hadn't he waited another moment?

It was his mark. Nearly two meters tall, the man wore a mauve, flowing cloak with hood pulled overhead. Though Zelag couldn't get a glimpse of his face, the man's boots were unmistakable. Made from gator skin and dyed a bright blue, these boots were expertly fashioned, shaped into the head of a gator at the toes.

His posture as he strutted into the bar was even more telling. Shoulders pulled back and chest puffed out, the flamboyant figure had to be the collector he was after.

Rising from his seat, Zelag stayed at his table and watched as the man approached the bar. If the reports were accurate, this collector would not spend time at the bar. When he got his room key, Zelag would follow him upstairs and plan his next move from there.

Watching like a hawk, Zelag kept his hands on the table, clasping the tankard with his right. Patience was still a skill he was working to develop, but as he sat and waited, the young shapeshifter reminded himself that it wouldn't take much longer.

The collector slipped through the crowd, arriving at the bar. The barkeep approached, a smile on his face. As they shook hands, Zelag noted a certain familiarity between them. They appeared to be talking about something, but Zelag wasn't going to risk getting closer to try and overhear. Until he had eyes on the prize, it was best to maintain a distance.

After exchanging a laugh, the barkeep held up his hand and stepped back to the key holder on the back wall. He grabbed one of the keys and handed it over to the collector, along with an envelope. The two exchanged a few more words before the collector turned to his right and started towards the stairs.

As crowded as the tavern was, the collector had to weave through quite a few patrons. Men and women from all over Paxvilla stumbled about the floor. But it was peculiar how fluid this man's movements were. It was like he was dancing through the crowd, each step carefully planned and planted.

In fact, Zelag realized as he got closer that the man was moving to the rhythm of the bard. He had gotten so accustomed to tuning noise like that out, that he almost missed it. But sure enough, as the bard sang and strummed on his lute, the collector moved to the rhythm.

Rising from his seat, Zelag did his best to avoid looking directly at the mark. But he kept watch from his peripherals, catching a glimpse of the man's face. The stories weren't an exaggeration.

This man had pale white skin, almost as ghostly as a hájje. His eyes were bright red, and his short hair was white as snow. So far, everything about this albino collector appeared to match the intelligence Zelag had gathered.

And then he saw the prize.

Hanging from a chain, the collector wore a large medallion. Made from white gold, the medallion had the shape of a dragon carved onto its surface. Its eyes were two of the largest rubies Zelag had ever seen. And nestled beneath the dragon head, an even more impressive diamond was inset in the medallion.

This one-of-a-kind piece had been reported lost more than fifty years ago. But like many lost treasures in the continent of Erathal, the albino collector had made it part of his collection. At least that was the rumor Zelag heard.

Hopping to the base of the steps, the collector stopped and shook out his cloak. He rotated his head side to side and started up the stairs.

Not wasting a moment, Zelag followed, carefully watching the man's feet. Timing each footfall to match up with the collector's, he proceeded up the steps like a shadow. And as the noise from downstairs died down, he even adjusted his steps to keep them as quiet as possible. This technique had never failed him before.

The collector stopped at the top of the steps, his right hand still resting on the railing.

"Are you following me, or would you have me believe your steps fell so coincidentally?"

The collector's voice was but a whisper, but his words penetrated Zelag's ears like knives. A smooth and mellow tone, there was something unsettling about the man's voice.

It was disappointing. Zelag had hoped he could use a slight of hand to pilfer the pendant. But now he'd have to show his face, which meant this would be the last time he'd use this particular elvish form.

"You're more impressive than even your reputation suggests," Zelag replied. "And you should take that as a compliment."

"A compliment from a cut-rate thief or assassin. Excuse me if I don't dance for joy."

The collector turned with these words, looking down the steps at Zelag. The two locked eyes, both staring intently and waiting for the other to move.

"So, which is it?" the collector asked after about fifteen seconds. "A thief?" he started, lowering his chin, and tilting his head a few degrees. "Or an assassin?" he finished, narrowing his eyes.

"I'm a survivor," Zelag replied after another few seconds of silence.

With hands hovering at his sides, Zelag prepared himself to draw a blade. So far, the albino collector stories all appeared true. If his fighting prowess matched the tales, this might get a bit dicey.

"A survivor!" the collector clapped his hands, holding them together and waving them overhead in an exaggerated fashion. He stepped back from the stairs, his stance remaining constant.

Two, three, four steps.

As the collector continued his slow retreat, Zelag ascended the stairs. He took great care to match his opponent's pace, making slow and deliberate moves up each step. Upon reaching the landing, he stopped his progress.

The collector seemed content to stop as well, freezing in place just a few meters from Zelag. And then he did something unexpected.

Pursing his lips, the collector began whistling. He started with a prolonged, steady note. Then he added deviations, spinning together a simple melody with his lips. As the tone rose and fell, he started moving his feet.

It looked like some sort of ritual dance. A couple steps forward, a couple back, a rhythmic movement of the hips. Each move perfectly matched the melody of his whistle. With a few seconds, he brought hand movements in as well, letting them move back and forth as if illustrating the movement of a river. All the while, he held Zelag's gaze, peering deep into the shapeshifter's eyes.

Then he stopped.

"Now, follow along," he instructed, immediately resuming the song and dance.

This was a new one. But then it occurred to Zelag what was happening.

Living among these mono-forms as he had, Zelag had learned over the decades to ignore their auras. They could be quite overwhelming, the constant changing with each mood and movement with magic. But at times like this, he was grateful for his unique insight.

And that's what this was, some strange form of magic. He saw it now, a blue-green aura engulfing the collector and flowing outward. The song and dance were all part of the spell. Opening his eyes to the unseen aura, Zelag could see it clearly.

As the blue-green energy flowed from the collector to engulf him, Zelag drew a steel dagger.

"Why would I follow along?" Zelag asked with a smirk.

It took the collector a moment to realize his spell was failing. He tripped over his left foot, stumbling back and catching himself. Now silent, he stood with mouth agape and continued staring at Zelag.

"You really are no common thief," the collector said after a few moments of silence. He fluffed out his cloak, collecting himself and adopting a stern expression.

"I'm more uncommon than you realize," Zelag replied. "But, for what it's worth, you're more impressive than I expected as well."

"Why thank you," the collector said with an exaggerated bow.

His aura turned red as he did, leading Zelag to squint and ready himself to move.

As the collector rose, he flung his left arm forward. Releasing a knife from his grip, Zelag was only just able to respond. Swinging his own dagger in a semi-circle and taking a step to the left, he just narrowly parried the throwing knife. The blade bounced harmlessly off the tavern wall, landing a few centimeters away.

Thank Evorath he was monitoring his foe's aura.

"I appreciate your persistence," Zelag said taking a step forward. "But it's time you realize you're outmatched. Hand over that pendant around your neck and I'll let you go unharmed."

"This pendant?" the collector asked, lifting it up and holding it out a few centimeters from his chest.

"Yes." Zelag took another step forward, ready to respond to anything the collector might try.

"Oh, but why would you want this? It's just an old family heirloom. It's not worth anything."

"Family heirloom? Yes, but not your family." Zelag replied. "And I know exactly what it's worth to the family that's been missing it."

"Alright," the collector replied. He relaxed his stance, standing upright and holding his hands up, palms forward. "I'll just," he began lowering his hands.

"No!" Zelag objected. The collector froze.

"Don't move," Zelag instructed, stepping forward and reaching for the pendant.

"I wouldn't even dream of it," the collector replied.

But just as Zelag was about to grab the pendant, the collector jerked forward. Thrusting his head right into Zelag's nose, the devious opponent dazed the young shapeshifter. Wincing as his vision blurred, Zelag turned and shook his head.

The collector dashed down the steps, making a hasty retreat.

"Son of a gorgon," Zelag spat as he sheathed his dagger and made chase. He leapt down the first few steps, barely catching his balance before bounding down the rest of the steps.

The collector was fast. He was weaving his way through the crowd. Like before, he demonstrated an impeccable sense of timing. And as Zelag started pushing through the members of the crowd, he found he couldn't manage the same haste.

He brushed against a short woman, bumped into a tall man, almost knocked over the portly fellow who engaged him earlier. This was not going to plan. But he managed to keep his eyes on the prize, at least until the collector reached the tavern exit.

Still fumbling his way through the crowd, Zelag cursed as the albino brat slipped out the front door. Every moment counted now. Abandoning any care, Zelag pushed through the crowd, shoving people aside as he ran straight for the door.

Arriving at the other end of the crowd, he stumbled out of the tavern and looked around. The cool autumn breeze of the quiet night caused him to shiver as he looked about and listened for any signs of the collector.

A few pedestrians were passing by, presumably a small family. The little boy and girl both looked at Zelag as they passed, but their mother directed them to move forward. Their father offered a slight nod towards Zelag, which he ignored.

There was no place close enough where the collector could have hidden, so where had he escaped to?

Hearing the neigh of a horse, Zelag looked to the north towards the stables. Travelers from out of town would use those stables to store their horses. Perhaps the collector had found refuge there.

Walking to the stables, Zelag kept listening for any unusual sound. As he approached the open entrance, he could hear some hushed voices from inside. Rounding the corner, he spotted his mark -and some unwelcome guests; two town guards.

"There he is!" the collected exclaimed pointing at Zelag. "He's the man who was threatening to kill me and take my belongings!"

With hands resting on their bastard swords, the two guards stepped forward. Both guards had the Paxvilla symbol brazened on their chest, a white, eight-point star over a blue shield. The one on the left was a few centimeters taller than the other, but both were clean-shaven and well-muscled.

This had really gotten out of hand. But since this form was no longer viable, at least he could have some fun.

"To set the record straight," said Zelag stepping into the stables, "I wasn't trying to kill anyone. The pendant around that albino's neck was stolen. I am simply reclaiming it to return to its rightful owner."

"We care not," the left guard barked, his voice deep and humorless.

"I didn't think you would," Zelag spat back. "But remember you had a choice."

Without allowing them time to react, Zelag charged the taller guard. As the guard was removing his sword from its sheath, Zelag slapped down with his right, forcing the guard to re-sheath the blade. The guard yelped, shaking his hand out. This allowed an opening for Zelag, who reached around and pulled out the man's sword just in time.

The other guard had drawn his blade, swinging for Zelag's side. Using the taller man's sword, Zelag blocked this initial attack. He allowed himself to be pushed back, bumping into the taller man and causing him to lose balance.

While the armed guard recoiled and prepared for another swing, Zelag used his left and stomped the tall guard's right foot. Spinning around, he used the flat of the blade to sweep out this guard's legs. The man fell with a yelp.

One down, one to go.

Again, Zelag pivoted just in time, holding his sword horizontally to block the incoming strike from the other guard. The guard grunted and stepped back. While he regained his footing, Zelag noticed the collector was fleeing further into the stables.

This had to end.

Withdrawing a small knife from his left, Zelag discarded his sword. With a wide opening, he moved in on the second guard and planted the knife in that man's left leg. The man squealed in pain, dropping his own sword, and clutching his injured leg.

Turning back to the taller guard, who was pushing himself up from the ground, Zelag followed up with a swift kick to the stomach. With a yelp, the man doubled over and fell flat. For good measure, Zelag kicked him one more time before turning back to the guard he had stabbed.

This one was still cradling his leg, cursing in pain as he stumbled around. Zelag stepped past him, shoving him, and sending him reeling to his fallen ally. As the shorter guard tripped and fell on top of the taller one, Zelag redirected his full attention to the collector.

But where had he gone?

Surveying the stables, Zelag kept a close eye for anything out of place. The horses in the various stalls all appeared undisturbed, standing about, and minding their own business. As he walked down to the far end of the stables, he checked each stall in turn.

Getting to the second to last stall on the right, he noticed the horse inside was a bit more vocal than the others. Beyond his neighing and nickering, it appeared his aura was a bit agitated.

"Give it up," Zelag said as he peeked over the stall door. The collector was crouched just inside the stall to the left of the door, smiling at Zelag.

"Alright," he replied, holding up his hands. "I'll give you the medallion."

Rising to his feet, the collector patted down his robe, dusting off the hay.

"Are you sure I can't interest you in some gold? Or perhaps something more exotic?"

"I'm only interested in the medallion," Zelag replied with a scowl.

Unlatching the door, Zelag reached over to open the stall.

The collector whistled a single, shrill note. And before Zelag figured out his ruse, the horse kicked the door open with its front legs. Hitting him in the torso, Zelag struggled to stay on his feet, the wind knocked out of him as he stumbled back.

Before he could collect himself, the collector was on the back of the horse. Still clutching his ribs in pain, Zelag was too slow to respond. And as he reached to grab the horse, it was already gone, galloping towards the stable entrance.

"Good luck next time," mocked the collector with a laugh. As he turned and galloped off into the night, Zelag had no choice but to admit.

He had been bested. And it did not feel good.

*But this was not the end of his story.*

-=-=-=-=-=-=-=-=-

The Legacy of Evorath continues to grow. Stay tuned for news on the release of *Legends of Evorath: The Shadows of Erathal*. Coming late 2024.

*The Battle for Erathal* is the third and final book in the Evorath trilogy. Visit us online for free access to additional stories, and to sign up for notifications about future releases. Prepare to revisit the world of Evorath in late 2024 with the Legends of Evorath Series.

If you enjoyed this book, please help other readers find that same enjoyment by returning to where you purchased it and leaving a positive review. Your voice matters.

## www.evorath.com

**Appendices I** - Map of Evorath, continent of Erathal

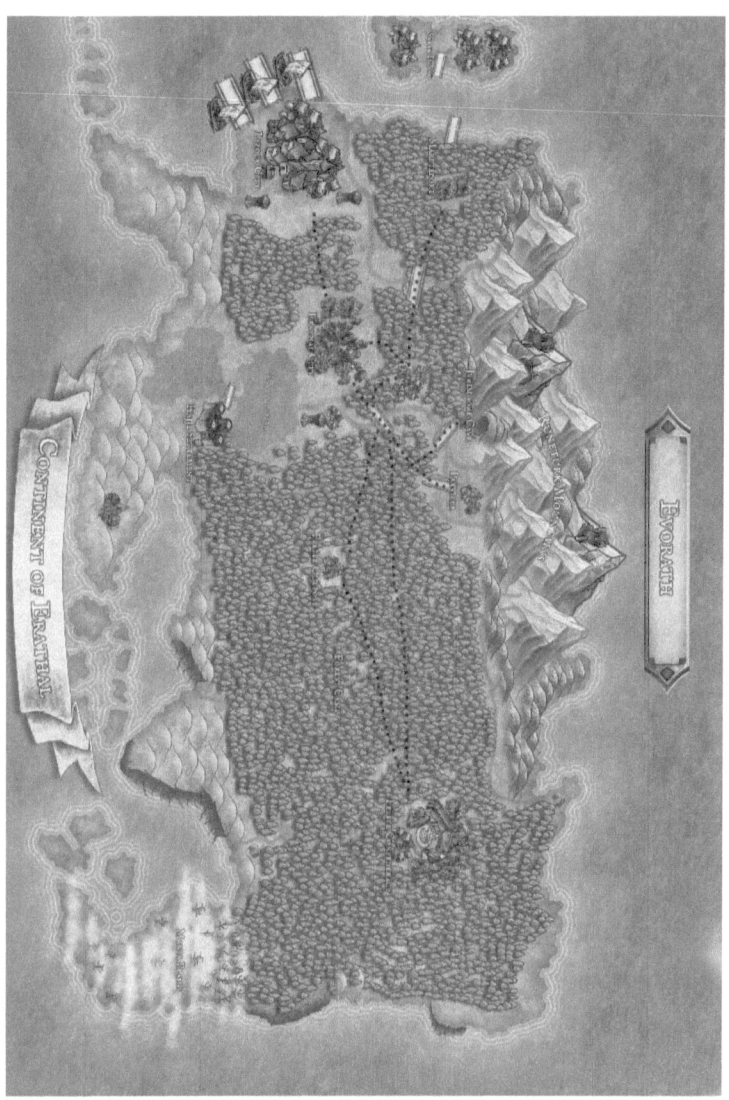

**Appendices II** - Glossary of Select Terms

- Barghest - A broad-shouldered and wide-chested species of bipedal canines. They make up some of the strongest warriors in Evorath but are nearing extinction due to their violent nature.

- Bulwark - A rare creature native to the Runeturk Mountains. Believed to have developed in volcanic activity and is known to have skin as hard as diamonds. They have two pairs of arms, one large and muscular, the other smaller.

- Centaur - Half-horse and half-man, this sentient species has many tribes scattered throughout the continent of Erathal.

- Dryad - Guardians of the forest, there is one dryad for each type of tree on Evorath. They have untold powers over the forest and work to maintain balance in the forest.

- Elf - Similar in stature to the humans of Earth, Elves are the most abundant sentient species in Evorath. They have pointy ears and almost exclusively have light features.

- Erathal - Name of the continent this adventure takes place in. Also, the name of the major Elvish City.

- Ether - The space between different worlds. Reaching through the ether requires great magical abilities and allows a mage to summon creatures from one of these other worlds.

- Felite - One of the most populous species on the continent of Erathal, felite are a bipedal feline species that resemble their four-legged cousins.

- Hájje - Elvish word for a dark elf. It comes from the elvish word Haijja, which means 'dark', or 'evil'.

- Lamia - A sentient race that still maintains a tribal nature. Their lower half resembles a snake and their upper half is that of an elf. Females greatly outnumber the males of the species, which is why their population is diminishing.

- Lizock - One of the most populous sentient species on the continent of Erathal, lizock are a bipedal reptilian race that resembles the common lizard. Though they can vary in size, shape, and color, the race is most well-known for its warriors and merchants.

- Marftaport - A free society without any formal rulers or authorities. Established by Vistoro and a group of Lizock who grew disgruntled with their government and recently opened to all species of Erathal.

- Pertga - The first month of the year and first month of spring. In the original elvish, it means 'birth' or 'new life'.

- Roc - A large, eagle-like bird with light brown feathers. Though wild roc can have wingspans over 15 meters, some species use these tamed birds as mounts for their aerial units. These tamed variety typically have a wingspan under 10 meters.

- Runeturk Mountains - Major mountain range bordering Erathal to the north. This range is populated by thousands of dwarves, some gnomes, and less civilized creatures like ogres, orcs, goblins, and wild animals.

- Satyr - A sentient species of Evorath once known for great works of art and music, they are now known more for their proclivity towards alcoholism. These bipedal creatures are half-elf, half-goat, with their upper half being the former and their lower half resembling the latter.

- Troll - A sentient species of Evorath. Nomadic in nature, trolls are both tall and menacing in their physical features.

- Urgo - An elvish word of affirmation. Essentially equivalent to saying "yes, sir" or "understood."

- Xyvor - A compilation of stories written by the ancient prophets of Evorath. Details stories of the world's creation, it's early history, commands from Evorath herself.